“Finkle is that rare writer who achieves great effe

to try.” – Roger Ebert, film critic, *Chic*

“Lovely writing, smart and insightful. Da

wonderful sense of how media types talk

unintended consequences of how they behave.” – Avery Corman, author of *Kramer vs. Kramer*

“In David Finkle’s exhilarating first-person stories, you hear the bittersweet hubbub of Manhattan: the clash of hilarity and envy, ambition and confusion, energy and terror, grandiosity and exhaustion, gay and straight, chatter and solitude. In his deft hands, ‘the isle of joy’ becomes the isle of irony. Finkle’s droll and knowing prose snaps, crackles, and pops with the high and low brow.” – John Lahr, senior drama critic, *The New Yorker*

“What a great pleasure it is to read Finkle’s candid stories. In a period when cynicism seems to have literature in a stranglehold, Finkle’s modest and pure voice soars.” – Daniel Klein, co-author of *Plato and a Platypus Walk Into a Bar... Understanding Philosophy Through Jokes*

David Finkle has covered the arts for *The New York Times, The New York Post, The Village Voice, The San Francisco Chronicle, The Nation, The New Yorker, New York, Time Out New York, Vogue, Harper’s Bazaar* and *The Huffington Post*. David is represented by Julia Lord Literary Management.

People Tell Me Things

David Finkle

Published by nthposition press, 38 Allcroft Road, London NW5 4NE.

First published 2011

British Library Cataloguing-in-Publication Data
A catalogue record for this book is available from the British Library

Library of Congress Subject Headings
Short stories; Short stories, American; American fiction – 21st century; Gay men – Fiction; New York (N.Y.) – Fiction

BIC Subject Category
FYB

ISBN 9780954626839 (paperback)
ISBN 9780954626846 (ebook)

Frontispiece by Peter Stern
Cover design by Colin Taylor

Contents

Find out what other people thought of *People Tell Me Things* and tell what you think. Visit https://www.facebook.com/nthpositionpress

Hey, that's me up there on the printed page!

i.

Some time ago *The New Yorker* arrived with a lead-off "Talk of the Town" piece identifying the real person behind Swede Levov in Philip Roth's *American Pastoral*. The account began: "The canon of parental cautions – look both ways, don't take candy from strangers, never see a buddy movie starring Chris Farley and David Spade – is silent on the perennial problem of how to avoid being written about as a fictional character."

I can tell you that neither does this vaunted canon indicate a whole helluva lot about the equally pressing problem of positioning oneself to be written about as a fictional character. I know from first-hand experience. I've spent years doing my damnedest to worm my way into fiction with what you would have thought were, if not the best, then very good prospects.

That is, I number among my friends – and have for some time – novelists, short story writers, playwrights, scenarists, poets, stand-up comics, sitcom purveyors. The whole nine yards, the entire palimpsest. I can't say I've befriended them solely in order to turn up in their works, but I'll openly admit that's been part of it.

Why, you might ask, with so much to be sought after and accomplished in our tapioca life, have I made this such a priority? I can only say it wasn't always so. It crept up on me slowly. A driven reader from my earliest days in Trenton, New Jersey, I became aware when relatively young that certain characters in fiction are based on people who actually existed.

As I recall, this struck me as interesting information, but it also struck me as cheating: Fiction was supposed to be made up, I childishly believed, not appropriated. Wasn't that what fiction meant? Of course, that's what it meant. I'd read a lot of fiction and so was in a position to know. I remained this laughably naïve for years and only began to see the light when I understood that Nick Adams was Ernest Hemingway's version of his younger self and Pat Hobby was Scott Fitzgerald's version of his baser self and Willy Stark was Robert Penn Warren's version of Huey Long's demagogic self.

Who could make it up?

It wasn't until I moved to Manhattan, however, and began building a circle of friends that I noticed the writers among them were often memorializing people with whom I was actually acquainted, with whom we all, all my friends, were acquainted. Cheating was clearly the order of the day. Acquaintance after acquaintance was becoming a *cléf* in some *roman* or other. That's when I cheerfully figured the chances were very good that sooner or later I'd join their auspicious number. As the years passed, however, none of my scribbler pals was getting around to me.

So it turned into a matter of pride. Why wouldn't it? Being transformed from life to the printed page is getting a toehold on immortality. It's being remembered. It's an indication that you're worth remembering. It's a corroboration that what you do, who you are, how you behave – for good or ill – is noticeable, notable. Enough so that some writer in the act of holding the mirror up to life – in whatever manner and for whatever mode – sees you reflected in it.

It started to bother me as I remained passed over that perhaps I have no reflection. But why don't I, why haven't I, when so many people I knew/know were/are popping up all over the literary landscape – and have been for a while? Some of them in more than one book; some of them in the output of more than one author. Smile as I might when I was with these successful "based on" figures, I found the situation galling.

Take my friend Alice Fishler, for instance, memorialized when she was nineteen – nineteen! – as the girl wearing white boots in Brad Gersten's *Fast Times, Bad Times*. You've read the book, which was Brad's first and put his name on lips as well as him on Easy Street at the age of twenty-one – $1.1 million hardback sale, $2.5 million paperback sale, $1.5 million movie sale. You remember the girl wearing white boots. She appears in the blockbuster's first sentence: "She was wearing white boots. She was reading Salinger. She looked bored. In less than an hour I got her to put the book down and take the boots off. I was unable to change her expression. In those days I considered two out of three the bare minimum. Today I'd settle for one. Or none."

Alice denies she was reading Salinger when she met Brad – "I was bored out of my gourd with Jerome David [Salinger, for you Philistines] by the time I was sixteen." (Brad was down from Middlebury – where else if you're publishing a first novel while still an undergraduate?; Alice was down from Smith; they were both being stood up at MOMA. It's all in the book.) But she cops to the rest, admits the sex was as uninteresting as reported and that the two weeks they spent together was "Okay, I guess. I'll have to reread the book and find out."

The Alice who shows up in the second act of Armin Wertheimer's *A Touch of Harry in the Night* is an entirely different character, of course, but indisputably Alice, since Armin was living in her Murray Hill apartment when he wrote the play, and she'd just decided to drop out of publishing to take up law, as Celia (notice the anagram) Beller does in the play. Armin told Alice on opening night (she hadn't seen or read the script before then) that, yes, he'd "drawn on her" but only for some of the particulars. Others of the particulars – the blowzy drunkenness, the foul mouth ("You fuck! You Harvard fuck!") – were traits heisted from another of Armin's acquaintances, "whom" – he told her – "you don't know." Alice wasn't so sure, and neither was I, since I'd heard her say more than once, "Every time I meet a truly unsalvageable shitheel, he turns out to be Harvard. Often the same year, Harvard '72. What was in the Cambridge water supply then?"

Alice has less to complain about, though, than Carole Karlen, who is the model for Karin Carroll in Sally Ottinger's *Clever Girl* (the 1991 National Book Award nominee). Sally and Carole were roommates at Wellesley and continued to split space their first few years in Manhattan, which is when and where I met them. Sally was more my chum than Carole, but I sided with Carole on the issue of the book, which, perhaps needless to say, put paid to their friendship.

Sally hadn't been anywhere near honest about what she'd done, maintaining that when she was writing, she was "totally unconscious" of the similarity between the names Carole Karlen and Karin Carroll. But even if she had been up-front, the friendship undoubtedly wouldn't have lasted longer than a pepperoni pizza at a beer party.

It was apparent to anyone who knew her that Carole and her slick ambition had inspired a genuinely first-rate character study in a genuinely first-rate book. I know that in my wistful, wishful frame of mind I wouldn't have indulged in the balking Carole did at having been the impetus behind:

Stealth is such an underrated talent, Karin quite coolly observed to herself. Maybe it's because true talent of any sort has been debased in a time when genius is considered to be opening a chain of moderately-priced boutiques or designing a computer game every teenage boy has to own. Karin immediately decided stealth would be her specialty. No one of her crowd, no one in the industry, would be the wiser, she reasoned. They all lacked the acumen that would have predisposed them to notice.

Good prose, bad prose? I don't know. It's enough that it's prose – a whole book of it, when I, who lunch on the average once a month with Sally, haven't prompted a paragraph of the abundant stuff, not a sentence, not a phrase, not, near as I can ascertain, a vowel or consonant.

And what about Bobby Norwood? You've seen him as the character Willie Myrick if you know Larry Prideaux's *How It All Fell Apart* from either stage or screen. Bobby, Larry and I were at Andover and Yale together and started out in New York at the same time. Both Bobby and I were in Larry's wedding. So why is it just Bobby who gets the fiction makeover? Is it because his quirks are more stage-worthy, more photogenic than mine? Must be, because there Bobby is throughout the action. The play, written in three acts (Thanksgiving 1978, Christmas 1985, Valentine's Day 1992) is Larry's idea of how he and Gayle (Norman and Jen in the scripts) stopped loving one another.

Bobby is the comic relief. He's the guy who sees everything and notices nothing. The irony is that Bobby knew exactly what was happening to Larry and Gayle. I was the one who insisted there was no trouble in paradise. But it's not me Larry's immortalized. It's Bobby's physical description slugged into the character break-down – "Willie is short and energetic. He never sits still and he never shuts up, despite his pronounced speech impediment." Yessir, that's Bobby's drone, his stammer built into the dialogue. I know, because I was there for these verbatim exchanges:

Willie/Bobby: What ma-akes you say I'm se-e-elf-absorbed?

Norman/Larry: I'll make it short but blunt. Whenever I ask you to do me the least favor, you find a way to wriggle out of it. There's always a legitimate reason, but the bottom line is, you're always around but never available. Everyone notices. Jen [Gayle] pointed it out the night I introduced you to her. Come on, try to deny it.

Bobby/Willie (ignoring the question): Didn't you used to ha-ave a m-mirror over the sofa?

Ba-da-boom. And does Bobby resent being the butt of belly laughs? Not at all. He loves it. When *How It All Fell Apart* played 763 performances at the Brooks Atkinson, he went at least once a month, dragging friends, co-workers, new girlfriends, always laughing loudest at how he was portrayed. (I almost wrote "betrayed"). Then, when the curtain fell, he got to trump the author by proclaiming to everyone in a fifteen-foot radius that he'd tried to warn Larry about what was obvious to him all along. So he establishes himself as both good sport and insightful friend. I'd have done the same, of course. Only I was never given the opportunity.

Have I complained to Larry? Nuh-uh. Airing assorted grudges to keep a friendship afloat is fair game, but one you sure as shit can't bring up is being overlooked in a pal's autobiographical fiction. What are you going to say?: "I'm more than a little pissed off you haven't made me a character in any of your novels. And after all I've done for you, you ingrate!" It doesn't wash.

Come to that, though, I am annoyed at the total wipe-out. I felt I was owed at least a cameo in a Larry Prideaux opus, because if it hadn't been for me, he'd have never met John Toynbee, and if he'd never met John Toynbee, it's for sure he wouldn't have created *At Your Service*, and if he hadn't created *At Your Service*, he wouldn't have the top-rated sitcom in the country. For which – even now that he no longer writes any of the segments and has handed the executive story editor slot over to some Hollywood *wunderkind* – he still collects thousands weekly simply by having concocted the whole *megillah*.

John Toynbee, by the way, I've known since Miss Rank's third grade, which is to say ever since he and I were suspended from school for the rock-throwing incident. His mother blamed me, and my mother blamed him, and for a while we had to keep away from each other. But we got past that and resumed the friendship by sixth grade.

When we grew up, moved to the City and he turned his ingenuity and enthusiasm into a business doing odd jobs for rich people, I wasn't surprised. When he really hit paydirt in the Eighties as yuppies inherited the earth, I was even less surprised. I certainly wasn't surprised either that Larry, the beneficiary of my intro, turned John's business into *At Your Service*, the linchpin of NBC's Thursday night powerpack of comedies. And since money makes money, I'm also not surprised that as a serendipitous result of Larry's show, John has landed his own two-book contract.

I am pleased to report that not abso-fucking-lutely everything has worked out smoothly for Larry who's never had much compunction about mining his life – or anyone else's – for material. A few years back, a bunch of us were invited to the New Dramatists to hear a reading of a two-character play Larry had run up over a weekend, as was his habit. Hannah Weiss – yes, that Hannah Weiss – was one of us. Why Larry invited her, I can't say. Some outbreak of conscious or unconscious guilt, I suppose. Or maybe not. Maybe he thought Hannah would take it as a compliment to have her relationship with her dying mother – about which she'd carelessly confided much to him – carpentered into a play by the prolific Larry Prideaux.

If that's what he thought, he had another think coming. Hannah didn't even wait until the room cleared before announcing with a shake of her tight red curls, "Nice play, Larry, but I want you to understand I have first refusal on the rights to my life." So Larry was shamed into putting his (extremely so-so) play in a drawer, and Hannah was able to publish *Notes on My Mother's Death* to a clear field. It did cross my mind to tell Larry he could do anything he wanted with my mother's death, but since the event didn't seem imminent, I kept my mouth shut.

On it goes. If there are two novels I'm almost – but not quite – happy at being left out of, they're Howard Anglim's *Social Lies* and Peter Worley's *Left to His Own Devices*. Since I'd known both of them for at least twenty years, I'd also assumed they had to know each other. They were both Random House authors, and therefore, it seemed to me, they had more reason to be acquainted with one another than I – who lack that credential – had to be friendly with either of them. I was startled, then – when was it?, three, four springs ago – at bumping into Howard on Third Avenue and 50th Street and beginning a conversation about not much of anything only to have Peter belly up, say a big hello and ask to be introduced to his RH colleague.

I obliged, and after an innocuous trialogue, they went off to talk shop and get their ultimately short-lived buddyhood underway. I suppose you could say that without me they might never have come to know one another, but there was me. So they did. Therefore, as handy catalyst, I'm at least partially responsible for the ensuing damaged lives. I also suppose I can, at least tangentially, be credited with the resultant dueling novels – without, is it necessary to add?, my appearing in either of them. Howard, of course, was married to Anna Parsons at the time, but he wasn't two years later when Anna divorced him and married Peter and – she being a leading book designer – became known within the gossipy book biz as "the designing woman." The sobriquet becoming that much more apt six months later when she left Peter and went back to Howard.

It was about then that both men gracefully arranged to leave Random House so as to spare the editors embarrassment over simultaneously having to send out two similar, retaliatory novels. (And they say publishing is no longer a gentleman's trade.) Since columnists from *The New York Post* to *Publishers Weekly* to *Entertainment Tonight* have had field days over the happenstance, I'm not giving away anything by reporting that in *Social Lies*, Howard, Peter and Anna are, respectively, Nathaniel, Ezra and Sarah (very Old Testament), and in *Left to His Own Devices* Howard, Peter and Anna are, again respectively, Matt, Thomas, and Mary (very New Testament).

Also – this is what gets me exercised – in *Social Lies*, Nathaniel and Ezra meet at a Knicks game, seated glamorously behind Woody and Soon-Yi; in *Left to His Own Devices* Matt and Thomas meet at a joint Barnes & Noble book signing.

What am I – chopped liver?

Maybe that's why I'm not above reprinting two of the many amusingly similar passages in their vengeful tomes. Maybe that's why I get such a secret kick out of the two books looking as if each was a plagiarism of the other, which, many reporters on the publishing beat have pointed out, couldn't be the case:

From *Social Lies*:

Nathaniel realized he wasn't going to stare Sarah down. She was far too steady, far too steely. Interestingly, that was the trait, or one of them, he'd most admired in her. Now he hated it.

He knew he ought to walk out of the room, leaving her to her mun-

dane betrayal, but the wise thing was exactly what he couldn't do. He continued to stare at her on the other side of the bed. "You're still fucking him, aren't you? Aren't you?"

"No. I'm not." Another woman, lying as blatantly as Sarah was, would have turned away or at least have lowered her eyes. Not Sarah. "Yes, I am. I'm fucking the daylights out of him."

"And presumably he's fucking the daylights out of you, even with that 'little dick'" – he put the last two words in aural quotes – "of his."

"He may have a 'little dick,' but he's a better lover."

From *Left to His Own Devices*:

Thomas wondered if he hadn't unconsciously chosen to meet at Granita, known to be noisy, for just that reason. In order to be heard, he'd have to yell at Mary. Of course, he didn't expect to be eavesdropped on in the cacophony, but he didn't care if he were. "You still love him. I know it. You're still fucking him. You fucked him before you came here. I can see it on your face. I can smell it on you."

"I'm not still fucking him," Mary said and fixed him with a stare he hated now but loved when she turned it on during intercourse. "All right, yes. I'm fucking him, but I'm not going back to him."

"Why? Because my cock is bigger?" He shouted this at such a level that a few diners stopped what they were doing and looked at him. Some of them laughed. He gave them the finger. They laughed harder.

"Nice," Mary commented. "Why do men always think it comes down to penis size?"

"Maybe because you told me it did."

"I lied. Women, Thomas, don't give a flying fuck about the size of a man's member. They want a good lover. Matthew may have a small cock, but didn't you ever notice? He has a long tongue."

Let me call your attention to the fact – if we can credit these exchanges with being taken from real life, and I think we can – that at least one of the concerned parties here has to be lying. I'd also like to stress that the above-mentioned illustrations are only a small sampling from a wide array of fictional works I might have appeared in but don't.

(Both excerpts – I hasten to remind lawyers on the sniff – are covered by "fair use" copyright stipulations.)

Sometimes it seems to me I'm just about the only one of my friends and acquaintances who hasn't made the transition from real life to word-processed life, many of them in the most unexpected places. If, for example, you pick up Gideon Platt's newest volume of poems – newest as of this writing – you'll find a prefatory ode dedicated to 'EL':

You asked me softly, simply, too,
Just what exactly do I do.
I thought for minutes, then for days
How I could put it in a phrase,
And finally the phrase occurred:
I am a man who keeps his word.

EL, I'm in a position to tell you, is Emily Little. How do I know? It was at a party of mine where I heard Emily asking Gideon what he did for a living. She asked him because, in addition to being soft and simple, as Gideon so accurately observed, Emily is dizzy and surprisingly dim. Asking people what they do for a living is about the extent of her small talk. But Gideon, being the prone-to-pretense poet he is, had to hike the inquiry to the metaphysical. I could just as easily have asked him the same thing and been rewarded with 'To DF,' but – dammit – I already knew what Gideon did for a living.

Considering the monumental oversight to which I've been subjected, a fair query is whether I've really tried to ingratiate myself into contemporary literature as forcibly as I'm claiming. The answer is yes. Short of declaring to any and all of my writer friends, “I want very much to be in your next ____ (fill in the blank)” and ponying up a persuasive sum of money, I’ve done everything within my control only to learn that control – as every twelve-step promotional brochure explains – doesn’t mean a thing, is, on the contrary, illusory.

First, I’ve been very open about my life – and that includes my secret life, what there is of it. Which is to say I’ve been open about my sexual preferences and practices. Not that any of the particulars are out of the ordinary. But then again, they shouldn’t have to be, should they, since some of our greatest literature has been written about ordinary Bovarys and Babbitts. Not to press a point, but my life – son, brother, uncle, nephew, friend, Andover and Yale grad, trade magazine editor, political liberal, fitness club member, tennis and scrabble player, HIV-negative gay man, jazz and country music lover – seems as ripe for picking as the next fellow’s.

Additionally, I’ve made a habit, when I’m around my fiction-writing friends and acquaintances, to drop anecdotes into the conversation that seem to me to have some appreciable bearing on the human condition. In doing so, I’m not being exclusively self-serving either. All writers need material. I’m supplying it *gratis*. If anything, I’m being more generous about myself than most people are about themselves, and I refuse to apologize for not having to be pumped or primed.

Why should I be stingy about me and my experiences?

I shouldn’t be.

Actually my magnanimity once did look as if it were going to pay off. A few winters ago Ralph Clymer decided to set the novel following *Random Thoughts* in my hometown – i.e., in Trenton, New Jersey. He’d often been through Trenton on the train and figured what he’d seen out of the window could be just right for the city weathering post-industrial growing pains he needed as a location. Would I mind if he came over on a Saturday with a tape recorder and picked my brain? I said I wouldn't mind at all. In fact, I said, why not let's drive down to Trenton so I can show you around the old environs?

You can see where this seemed like a foolproof way to inveigle my story into his. I'd simply show him my Trenton – where I grew up, where I went to school, where my father practiced law and so on. Ralph would have to use at least some of it, since I would have stacked everything in my favor. So off we went for a day in which I zapped Ralph from all angles, guiding him through East Trenton and the 'Burg and along River Road, pointed out where the East–West highway had replaced the old canal in the Fifties and irreversibly changed the tenor of the city, took him around the Battle Monument for a lesson on Trenton's pivotal part in the American Revolution. Facts and figures came back to me I hadn't thought about in years, and I peppered my *spiel* with them. Through it all, Ralph kept his palm-sized tape-recorder whirring.

It's crossing your mind, isn't it, which of the lauded Ralph Clymer novels should you pick up for at least a glimpse of the thinly-veiled me? None of them. Ralph, so he claims, wrote a first draft and wasn't happy. He moved it to a back burner, possibly for resuming at a later date. And although I asked if I could have a gander, he refused.

"Maybe you're too close to it," I added in as off-handed a manner as I could muster. Nothing doing. He said his policy was never to show unfinished work, especially when he wasn't satisfied with it. So possibly I'm in a drawer of his somewhere. But what good is that? I'm not about to ransack his home. Although I've considered it.

It was after the Ralph Clymer debacle that I figured I might as well throw in the towel. I told myself I have a good life, a good job, good – if not always co-operative – friends. All right, so I'm not going to be a factor

– an actor – between hard or soft covers. There are worse things. That's what I kidded myself into believing.

Really.

ii.

There's an actress I know who insists the only time she gets work is when she's about to leave for vacation. Vacations get her assignments – it never fails. She's named the phenomenon Cora Walton's Law. The catch, however, is you can't fake it. You really have to be going; you have to have the hotel reservations, the plane tickets, receipts for the purchase of resort clothes.

Well, Cora Walton's Law has other applications. Just when I decided it was time to leave my incursion-into-fiction days behind and go about my business, CWL went into effect. It all began, as so many things do nowadays, online. One slow night I was surfing along, dropping into chat rooms, when I happened on an area where men in New York "seeking similar" congregate cyberly. One fellow whose windy handle was Amanuensis (you max out at 10 letters) was posting a series of amusing comments. So amusing that I checked for the biographical data he'd provided in his easily-accessible profile. No name, but, along with a nondescript summing up ("five ten, brown hair/brown eyes, nice-looking"), were – next to "Profession" – the words "pen for hire." Oh, yes, and another piece of skinny. Alongside marital status, he'd typed "loosely hitched."

Given the famous unreliability of facts launched into c-space, none of this had to be true, of course, but I figured it was worth a shot and typed in a private message to him: "Readerman here. Written any good books lately?" The reply: "A few critics think so." There began a volley, at the end of which we'd agreed we had much in common (favorite authors: Bellow, Cheever, McGuane; favorite movies: *Casablanca, Jules et Jim, Snow*

White and the Seven Dwarfs) and that we also shared the conviction a lunch together mightn't be an altogether nutty idea. What he also learned was my actual first name. What I thought I learned was his – Wally. What we both knew was that we were hooking up the following afternoon at a the bar in a restaurant near me.

He was wearing what he said he'd be wearing – a corduroy jacket, khaki trousers and rimless glasses. He was checking stocks in the business section of the *Times*. I said, "Wally?" He looked at me blankly and then spurted, "Oh. Yes. Glad to know you." We shook hands. He rose as I sat down, and we both laughed the laugh you laugh when you're trying to cover an awkward moment. Then we swung unrhythmically into a negotiation about whether we should stay at the bar or take a table. The table won, and within a minute a waiter who walked as if he were blading – he was blading – had positioned us at a window.

So: Wally. A pleasant guy who was, as advertised, about five ten, medium build. His brown hair was parted in the middle, a high brow. His "nice-looking" translated into close-set brown eyes, a pug nose I incorrectly read as WASP. Body language? Even when seated, he seemed to be shuffling. Strong hands – thick, spatular fingers – that he put through jerky motions when he wanted to make a point. The clothes were writer-shabby – the khaki trousers frayed at the cuffs, which, of course, didn't necessarily mean hard-up but, more likely, affectation.

In sum, he was what he'd indicated, but there was also something familiar about him: I knew the face. Or maybe not. I was checking all this out as we made initial small talk (my Q: "Did you have trouble finding the place?"; his A: "I've been here before.") and ordered a couple of salads and a bottle of mineral water. Wally smiled a good deal. It was an easy smile, and, taking it in, I saw that one of his two front teeth overlapped the other.

"You're married," I said when the salads were in place and we'd tucked into them with nervous gusto.

He stole a look at his wedding band. "I thought you knew that."

"I did. I just wondered."

"Twelve years."

"Kids?"

"Two." He decided to butter a bread stick. "I love my wife."

"But oh you kid!"

"What? Oh. Yes. Cute. I suppose you hear the I-love-my-wife line all the time..."

I had no quick response to that one, so I chuckled and said, "Well."

"Whoa, that was presumptuous of me, wasn't it?"

"Look, why are you here?"

"I probably shouldn't be. But you look like a nice guy..."

"I am a nice guy."

"...and I feel like staying."

The text of the get-acquainted gab that followed was standard. Wally was married, happily he insisted, but there were certain things he couldn't get from his marriage that he'd come to think he had the right to pursue. Not that he wasn't "conflicted still." His intentions, he proclaimed while chewing and swallowing, were not to harm anyone, certainly not his wife and children, all of whom he "loved to death." The words "trust" and "discreet" and "discretion" and "dishonesty" and "indiscretion" were tossed into the verbal salad as we made our way through the actual ones.

My recollection is that I did a good deal of reassurance nodding and, when it seemed to be my turn, made free with the autobiographical data – having, I swear, no ulterior motive. But if the text was routine – perhaps no more than a version of the lunchtime chitchat being carried on at half a dozen other tables – the subtext was titillating.

Although I'm often not a good judge of these things, allowing what I'd like to happen to obscure what's actually happening, I began to get the impression there was connection here to which E.M. Forster would have affixed his seal of approval. The evidence? There were the smiles that rode on the tail-ends of his sentences, that lingered after the words faded into momentary silences. When I met each smile, he'd smile again and thus the ante was upped. There were the opportunities he took to reach over and tap me on the hand and forearm when he was driving home a point. There was his eventually relaxing against the back of the chair and, alternatively, his jolting forward to the edge of his seat so he could lean over the table closer to me. There was the shift in his laughter from a high chortle to a low, masculine rumble.

And I suppose – according to the rules of the mirror game we all play with people in whom we're interested – I was doing my share of the same. Eventually, though – but long after you might have predicted, with my history – I got around to his writing. There was a pause, then a flicker in his brown eyes. We were on to coffees now. "Would you mind if we went into it all next time?" he asked.

That certainly gave me a great opening. "Providing there is a next time."

"Oh, there'll be a next time." A couple more of those shared smiles.

We finished lunch, and he walked me the two blocks back to my corner where we had a brief exchange about the advisability of my inviting him up and the advisability of his accepting the invite. Not advisable yet, we concurred. "It isn't because I think you're might be indiscreet," he said. "I'm sure you aren't, but I need to think this over. We can be that kind of indiscreet at a later date."

So we parted. But not before he put his hand to my cheek for a moment, a gesture I found warm, intimate and thoughtful.

And romantic, no? And a little reckless for someone who adamantly believed he could be putting so much in jeopardy. But who was I to question his impulse? I decided to enjoy it as I sauntered the half-block to my squatting but never squalid Federal brownstone and up to my apartment where I dispatched an e-note to him in which I mentioned the hand-on-cheek gesture. He replied about an hour later, "When I see you again, I'll put my lips where my hand was."

I spent the afternoon with the budding romance set aside so I could finish off some office work I'd brought home. After a couple hours of this, an odd thing happened. Something clicked. It's funny how the memory works. I always think of mine as non-state-of-the-art library stacks where one ageing drudge has the job of taking slips out of pneumatic tubes and retrieving requests. He can only handle so many at a time and with great effort, which means it may take him a long while to get around to all of them. It took him three or four hours to get around to this one.

But now the wage-slave within arrived hefting the book, and it had Wally's picture on the dust jacket. So that's why he looked familiar! I went over to my real library and ran a finger along the tightly packed volumes. It took me a few shelves to locate what I was after, but there it was – *Guess Who I Ran Into on the Grand Concourse* by Warren Nemitz. A short story collection some friend – who had it been? – insisted I read at least a decade back. I'd acquiesced and liked what I'd found, even remembered a couple of the pieces clearly – the one about the *bar mitzvah* where the wacky uncle drew graffiti on the Torah portion, the one about the boy whose mother found his girlfriend's bra in his night-table drawer and baked it into the Passover *kugel*. Not ground-breaking work – maybe a little too second-generation Bruce Jay Friedman – but deft and funny.

I pulled the book free and turned it over. It was Wally, alright, a younger Wally, whose brown hair covered his ears and whose tie was wide enough to double as a napkin. But the smile with the overlapping front tooth was the same. Oh, yes, this was the guy who'd sat through lunch not four hours before encouraging me to think his name was Wally.

Interested to discover what all that talk about honesty and integrity added up to, I emailed Wally – uh, Warren – with my discovery. And since he had my phone number, whereas I didn't have his, he rang me back soonest. "I just went online and found your letter."

"Should I call you Wally? Or Warren? Or what?"

"I'm sorry," he said. "I was planning to tell you when we talked again. You can understand why I wasn't ready to tell you before we met."

"And after?"

"You're right. I should have said something. It was lousy of me not to."

"Maybe you could have worked it in during one of your disquisitions on honesty as a *sine qua non* of any relationship."

Laying it on a little thick I was, no?

"I understand why you're angry. I would be, too. But I have a lot at risk here."

"So you said. Maybe the best thing for you – for both of us – is we chalk this one up to a swell lunch and forget about taking it any farther."

There was silence at the other end of the line. "Look," he said and started to talk. That's when it came out that as much as he felt he could be risking, it didn't outweigh what he thought he'd gain by satisfying his emotional and libidinal needs. Could I forgive his misguided caution and, since he had thought things over, meet him again? Could I make lunch the day after tomorrow?

I couldn't, but – since I heard the apologetic tone in his voice and the unnecessarily harsh one in mine – I told him I could rearrange my schedule for the day after that to make myself free for lunch and perhaps the rest of the afternoon. How would it suit him? It would suit him fine.

Before I get to that, however, let me confirm what I think may have already occurred to you. Warren Nemitz is one of the Writing Nemitzes. That's what I ruminated about when I put down the phone. As all – or much – of the world knows, there are six Nemitzes, each of them smart as a whip, each of them well-connected, each of them prolific. In addition to the five brothers and the one sister, three are also married to novelists (Warren rather famously to Audrey Bliss), one to a playwright, one to a poet and one to a screenwriter. And that's when they don't invade each other's territory. And that's not to mention Audrey Bliss's sister is the mystery writer Madeleine Coffin.

What pot of jam, I asked myself, had I just landed in? Or what strip of flypaper had I just landed on? Who knew what would or could develop from this incipient liaison? If anything of interest did occur, there was potential for nearly a dozen works, or a baker's dozen. And that was only the immediate family.

But, of course, it was me we were talking about, and what were the odds? With me involved, it was likely nothing would show up in print – nothing people could point to and say with conviction, "You know who that is, don't you?" I brought this up when we met for our second lunch. Him – same or similar khaki slacks, different corduroy jacket, loose tie and checkered Gap shirt; me – flannel trousers, white shirt, Charvet bow tie purchased for a buck at Goodwill Industries around the corner.

I brought it up, yes, but not in so many words. I figured it would be politic to be oblique. Indeed, I was so oblique I never mentioned what sitting ducks we could be in regard to future manuscripts. Instead:

"You're discreet, Warren, and I'm discreet," I said blithely over his grilled tuna with wasabi and my poached salmon without. "But discretion doesn't amount to a hill of beans in this crazy burg. Okay, you don't talk about it and I don't talk about it and we don't go anyplace where we give other people the opportunity to talk about it. You think that's enough?"

"I..."

"No, no. Let me finish. People notice things. You're married to a writer." I wanted to downplay how much thought I'd given this. "Near as I can figure out."

"Audrey."

"Audrey. Writers are trained to notice things. I don't have to tell you this. You start spending time with someone else, you don't think Audrey is going to pick something up? You're bound to be different, act differently. There'll be unaccounted-for time. Or you'll use an expression of mine without realizing it and without ever having used it to Audrey before. Or to your kids. Or you'll know something you didn't used to know. Or you'll refer to a book or movie, and Audrey will ask when you read it or saw it, because, funny, you never mentioned it. And you'll say, oh, well, you have read it or seen it, and then you'll be vague about just when. Or because sex is good or bad with me, it'll have a subtle but detectable effect on the sex you're having or not having with her. It's the little things, Warren, that something as grandiose as 'discretion' doesn't cover."

"Of course, you're right. In the abstract. But you don't know Audrey."

"No, I don't know her, but I've read a couple of her books..."

"Oh, yes?" He leaned into me at this, and I could swear there was the slightest whiff of professional competitiveness. "Which ones?"

"*Ellen Stark* and *Rotten Apples*." I didn't mention I'd read *Rotten Apples* only the day before. Just to sort of catch up. "This isn't a woman who misses the nuances."

"No, that's true enough. What else did you think?"

"About the books?"

"Yes."

"I agree with all the blurbs on the dust jackets. I think Audrey Bliss is 'an excellent writer.' That she has 'X-rays where the rest of us have retinas.'"

He knew I was quoting, of course. Without acknowledging it, he said, "But?"

"But nothing. I like the books."

"Oh." He leaned back, clearly disappointed, and started biting the skin around his left forefinger.

"Shouldn't I? Like them?"

"No, no, no. Of course, you should. I just wondered whether you thought there were any problems with them. You know, any at all."

I gave it some thought. "I wish the endings weren't so bright and upbeat."

He took his forefinger out of his mouth. "Go on."

"With both books that wasn't where they seemed to be going."

He pointed at me with the bitten and spatular forefinger. "Bingo! That's what I can never tell Audrey. I tried once, and she wouldn't hear it. She thought it was my 'male bias' – whatever the hell that's supposed to mean. Next time I kept quiet. But that's it. Audrey is a good writer with the potential to be very good. But she won't be until she stops trying to make everything come out all right in the end."

I noted that he said "very good" and not "great." I asked, "You mean you don't like the way your wife writes?"

"I didn't say that. I didn't say that at all. I think she's a wonderful writer. Funny, insightful. I love the way she fools around with form."

One nice thing about me is I know when it's a good idea to drop a subject; so I did. "I agree. How's your tuna?"

"But don't you know," Warren continued, "it's just what Audrey doesn't see or doesn't want to see or doesn't want to acknowledge she sees that'll work in our favor. If you see what I mean."

"Yeah, I think I do see. You want to exploit one of your wife's vulnerable areas in order to pursue an extramarital affair with a guy."

A shadow crossed Warren's face. Then he let go a low, delightful laugh. "That sounds a little judgmental. But you're right." He rearranged a few items on his platter. "Are you interested in me? Romantically?"

"No reason to beat around the bush. Yes."

"And I think you're kind of swell, too. So why don't we put my actions in another light? I'm prepared to take advantage of a predisposition of my wife's in order to provide myself with something that won't hurt her. As long as she doesn't know about it or admit to herself it might be happening."

"But..."

"No. This time you let me finish. You could say what I choose to do with my time and my heart – other than how it affects you directly – is none of your business, couldn't you?"

"Yeah, you could say that. I could say that."

"What goes on between me and my wife isn't your concern." He had me there. I confess I was in the mood to be had. "We needn't talk about it any longer." He reached across the table and took my hand in a way I realized could be interpreted by onlookers as merely a reassuring, masculine grip. "Do we?"

We didn't. We didn't discuss it for the rest of the afternoon, which included a stop at my place and a hop into my bed. We didn't discuss it whenever we got together – usually at my place, usually very low-profile – over the next three months. What did we discuss? Aside from discussing sexual practices we wanted to explore – you know, the old does-it-feel-good-if-I-whatever chat – we talked about our work. We talked about politics and sports. We talked about what we were reading. We talked about the music we liked. The more we talked, the more intimate the talking seemed.

I'm not going to say we fell in love, because, aside from my not truly knowing what love is, we both intuited that it behooved us to avoid falling in love if we could. So instead of "falling in love" – the phrase, of course, implying a vertiginous condition – we merely began to love each other in a manner that precluded vertigo. We loved each other as... as – I don't know. Not as brothers. As friends, I suppose – as friends whose sexual activity was just another, if not quite everyday, element of friendship.

How close did we become? How entangled in each other's lives? Let me see. Though Warren was at my place as often as he could manage, I never gave him a set of keys. It crossed my mind to, but I reckoned he'd say no, and I didn't want to think too hard about the implications of that. The implications were that he couldn't be caught carrying keys unfamiliar to Audrey and for which he'd have no plausible explanation. He didn't keep a toothbrush at my place either, because no matter how frequent his visits, there were going to be no overnight stays, so no need to brush and floss at bedtime or on awakening.

I'm not going to say it was all smooth sailing. There were days where one or the other of us was irritable. Or both of us. Although different reasons – or no reasons – were given for why we were suddenly stepping rather clumsily on each other's exposed feelings, my hunch is that it all stemmed from the same source: No matter how you sliced it, we were running around behind his wife's back, and it was uncomfortable.

There were also the annoying little things people get to noticing about each other when the bloom fades from the early rose. Or maybe, put another way, there were the annoying little things that people notice almost immediately but dismiss as merely little things, not worth paying attention to. And it's just these annoying little things, isn't it, that threat-en to become annoying big things when dwelled on at times when the emotional climate turns momentarily foul? They're the things you wait to see occur yet again – hoping they won't, knowing they will. When they do, you feel the skin tighten on some part of your body.

I'll just mention two of Warren's unappealing habits. I've already made reference to one: biting the skin around his nails. Sometimes when he'd be silent for a few minutes, I'd look over at him, and there he'd be, absent-mindedly going at it as if he were trying to chomp through to the bone. It seemed such a childish way to pass time, about one remove from thumb-sucking. (Both require putting digits in one's mouth.) The other thing that pissed me off is that he never did anything around the house. He didn't so much as take an empty glass into the kitchen. Granted, it was my house and not his, but since we never were at his – where the policy you-do-the-dishes-here-I'll-do-the-dishes-there would make sense – I began to get resentful. I'd give him long, hard looks at the ends of meals as I stood up to bus. He'd just look at me and smile.

What bothered him about me, I can't say, but there must have been something or somethings. There always is, or are. Maybe it was that I didn't say what I was thinking when I was thinking it. Maybe when I was giving him those long, hard looks at the ends of meals, he knew exactly what I meant by them but had decided he wasn't going to oblige me until I came out with it. It wouldn't have been the first time my passive-aggressive inclinations had gotten someone's goat.

On the other hand, Warren and I did like each other, we "got" each other. There was something gratifying about sitting around just talking with our shoes off, sitting around in various states of undress or entirely naked – dicks sometimes erect, usually not. There was something relaxing about the time we spent together, something I came to think of as sharing the comforts of a mid-life idyll. Who would want to quarrel with that kind of rare *mise en scène*?

So I suppose I could say our (illicit?) relationship didn't feel entirely wrong, but, on the other hand, it didn't feel entirely right, but, on the third hand, it didn't feel so un-right that we remained fully circumspect about our activities. Hunkering in my apartment whenever we met began to feel claustrophobic and, moreover, began to impress us as an admission that what we were about was surreptitious. We never quite said it in so many words, but we both clearly concluded that if what we were doing was, oh, on the up-and-up, then we had the right – within reason – to do on-the-up-and-up things.

Which is another way of saying that in our misguided sense of entitlement, we got sloppy.

"I mentioned your name to Audrey," Warren said one day when he'd arrived, had taken that day's corduroy jacket off (it was rust-colored with elbow patches) and had picked up a book to riffle through.

"Oh?" I said. "Yeah?"

"Yes." He put the book down. "I said I was having lunch at EJ's and that I'd gotten into a conversation with a guy at the next table." He was shucking his loafers. "I said he was reading one of my books, and since I'd never actually sat next to someone reading a book of mine, I had to say something."

"Jesus, you didn't?"

"I did. I said I leaned over and asked him – you – how he liked the book."

"Uh-huh. And how did I like the book? Which book was it?"

"It was *The Thing of It Is*, and you didn't especially."

"I didn't?" This was getting interesting. "What didn't I like about it?"

"You found the character of Horace unsympathetic. Which really intrigued Audrey, because I'd already suspected she never liked Horace either. 'Oh, really,' she said, 'Who is this guy – a critic or something?' I said you did turn out to be a writer, but not a critic. A journalist. 'Did you agree with him?' she asked. And I said, 'No, I didn't. Do you?' She said, of course she didn't, but she could see where you might've gotten that impression."

"Sounds like you had quite a discussion about me."

"Actually we did, because then I said that, while we were talking, you turned the book over and realized I was the author."

We were now both in our underwear. Warren always wore T-shirts and boxers. I'm a briefs-and-tank-top man.

"What did I do then?"

"You got embarrassed and said so. But you also said you guessed your comment stood."

"Gee, I sound like quite a stalwart guy. I say what I mean and I mean what I say."

"That's what Audrey said, or something to that effect, and then she said, and I quote, 'We all could use people like that around us.'"

"She didn't."

"She did. And that gave me the opportunity to say, that's what I thought and that I'd continued talking to you, that you seemed like a guy worth knowing. I said I'd taken your name and number and might talk to you again, but probably I wouldn't. Then I changed the subject."

"And that seemed perfectly fine to you."

"I'd say it went down like a yogurt smoothie."

"If you say so," I said, but wondered.

And was right to wonder, because Warren had misjudged Audrey. We didn't find out immediately, of course. It took a while. It took a couple of months during which Warren became convinced he'd covered himself with her enough so that he and I could stop in at restaurants, go to a movie or two. The plan was that if we ran into anyone he knew – and who knew Audrey or some, or all, of the other writing Nemitzes – he'd simply introduce me by name and trust people to assume we were friends. If word got back to Audrey, she'd recognize the name and think nothing of it.

If we ran into anyone I knew, he was Warren Nemitz, and let the chips fall where they may. Certainly, there was nothing to worry about from my friends, none of whom knew him – or her. Or did they? As a matter of fact, one of them did, since, of course, we were living in New York, where the degrees of separation are many fewer than six.

You see, we never did bump into any of Warren acquaintances. (Or we didn't think we did, although you can never be sure who sees you and chooses to remain silent for whatever reason.) But one day at a Starbucks on Upper Broadway we did run into, of all people, the ubiquitous and predatory Larry Prideaux.

I don't think I've mentioned that Larry wears very thick lenses, which give unwary onlookers the impression he's thick through and through. He isn't. He picks up on everything.

Larry had never met Warren before and, so far as I can tell, also had never met Audrey, but it turned out that one of the actresses on *At Your Service* had acted in a television adaptation of one of Audrey's books and had become palsy-walsy with her and still talked to Audrey occasionally when she was in Manhattan or Audrey was in Hollywood.

At least that's how I think the news traveled: Larry, who knew my story, mentioned to his actress friend that he'd met Audrey's husband at Starbucks having a double latte with gay old me, and the actress must have said something to Audrey that got Audrey thinking. When she did, it was exactly as I'd predicted – or near enough – and not what Warren, talking himself into his wife's iron-clad imperviousness, counted on. Or hoped against hope wouldn't transpire.

She was a smart woman and could put two and two together to get the time-honored four. She got that untidy sum, and all I got was a terse piece of email, which went as follows, "D: I won't be in touch in the future. We've been found out. It's all I can do to keep things together at this end. I'll always think of you fondly, and thanks, W."

iii.

Allora, il romanzo é finito, ma non la commedia. Translation: The romance was over but not the high-low comedy.

Which had nothing at all to do with my subsequent actions, because, regarding the end of the affair, I took no actions. What might I have done? Sued his wife for alienation of affection? Not on the cards.

Besides, although I was angry – at myself for letting him kid me into believing this wasn't how it would finish, at him for kidding himself into believing this wasn't how it would finish – and although I was hurt at being cut off so abruptly from someone whom I'm come to like, I wasn't devastated. I'd guarded enough of my feelings that I was able to keep a balance and, with friends to talk to who more or less understood what I was going through (without necessarily being sympathetic about what I'd let myself in for), I even kept my sense of humor.

Something I needed, because what followed over the next twenty-four months or so was certainly funny.

The books started coming out – oh yes, the books about me, the Nemitz and relations books. And the movies and the play. The first book – because easier and faster to write and get on a publisher's list? – was from Madeleine Coffin, a mystery called *Dead to Wrongs*, which, for those of you who haven't read it, begins like this:

No one in the family had ever met him, although they had known about him.

He was the other man, the one who had caused all the trouble in Evelyn's and Graham's marriage.

He hadn't been Evelyn's boyfriend, however. He had been Graham's.

When he was discovered in his kitchen bludgeoned with a meat pulverizer, the NYPD took some time linking him to the Warriners, and only then because they discovered an incriminating email correspondence.

When they showed his picture to Evelyn and Graham, the only thing she said to him was, "You told me he was good-looking."

Next to press was Andrew Nemitz's novel of domestic disarray, *The Interruption*. Late in his *New York Sunday Times Book Review* assessment, Benjamin Carver opined, "Perhaps because the story is told from the points of view of the embattled Flinders, the character of Toby remains shadowy. He's the sort of interloper we all have in our lives, a personage memorable for the effect he has rather than who he is. It might have behooved Nemitz, however, to give us at least a little more of the latter."

Marlene Richter – Andrew's wife – had her tragicomedy *Darby and Joan and Arnold* produced off-Broadway last fall. As you might guess, I'm Arnold, who, the program informs us, is "not what you'd expect a home-wrecker to look like." I went and took notes about this "three-character play in six two-character scenes." In an exchange at the middle of the first act, Darby and Arnold, naked under glaring lights and facing each other in rocking chairs, are discovered:

Darby: I think my wife suspects something.
Arnold: What makes you think that?
Darby: She asked me if I'm having an affair.
Arnold: What did you tell her?
Darby: I said that if I were, would she prefer a man or a woman?

Arnold: What did she answer?

Darby: She said what they all say: she'd rather it were a woman, because she wouldn't know how to compete with a man.

Arnold: What did you say to that?

Darby: I said, Yes, I am having an affair. It is with a man, but he's ugly.

Arnold: What did she say then?

Darby: Nothing. She laughed. Proof once again, as if we need it, that honesty is the best policy.

As you may know, the movie *Who Was That Masked Man?* won Annick Lehner Nemitz the New York Film Critic's award for best screenplay of the year. This quote from *Newsweek* is the one I can get behind and second: "Nemitz's screenplay is notable for its intelligent understanding of a triangle's geometry. She realizes, as so few writers do, that there are three sides and three angles, and she tells each of them well. Not since Penelope Gilliatt examined a similar love story in 1971's *Sunday Bloody Sunday* has the other (gay) man been so appealing and sympathetic. That he also has something to gain and lose and not merely something to destroy is accurate – though rarely-comprehended – reporting. He's someone we all know, and, what's more, he's someone we can all admire."

My counterpart in Bernard Nemitz's *Circle of Fiends* is peripheral, since, if you've read it, you'll recall the 735-page book is an examination of infidelity in nine bicoastal marriages. I didn't think much of the work, and neither did the reviewers. Of course, they haven't liked a Bernard Nemitz tome, since the first one, *Street Kid*, came out in 1964 and caused such a stir. His fans, of course, couldn't have cared less what the reviewers said. So they bought the bestseller – and me in it. I only show up in one paragraph, however. You'll know who I am in the following excerpt from the chapter entitled, "Window Shopping":

Maria knew Sidney had a little something on the side. She'd guessed it weeks before. It was as plain as the bulbous nose on his florid face.

How she hated that face! How she laughed at him when she was riding her afternoon cowboys. As she reached orgasm after orgasm after orgasm, she imagined Sidney's face would only get uglier if he could see her now!

She hated him, too, for thinking he could run around on her. With a man. With a faggot.

It's okay if I have my men, she thought. It's okay if I have my women. I'm beautiful and vital. I need beauty and vitality. But who is he to run around on me?

So the day after she picked up the telephone and heard him planning his sordid little tryst, she followed him to the Chelsea coffee shop. He went in and sat down opposite a thin man with thin lips who was wearing a sports coat no designer she knew would have admitted to. She guessed that if he even knew about cologne, he probably bought it at one of those discount places on West 28th Street.

She'd seen enough. "Sidney, you are such a loser," she mouthed to herself as she turned on her high heel. She plucked an Elizabeth Arden address book from her Louis Vuitton carryall and found Gino Armenti's number. She pulled out her cellular phone and dialed.

"'Baby,' she cooed when Gino answered, "put on your leather jock strap. Mama's coming over to snap it.'"

At the other end of the spectrum, Alexander Nemitz's *As Evening Loudly Falls* includes this line in a poem called "Younger Brother":

Carrying his wounded soul –
Like autumn's wonderful gift –
Up adulterous stairs
To the man with Band-aids for eyes.

No need to trot out every one of the other seven works. That is, seven others so far. Larry Prideaux is putting something together that'll bring the number to eight, and counting. He said to me one night when Bobby Norwood (you know, the proud inspiration for Willie Myrick) had us over for dinner, "I'm using something in a story you might recognize – you and Wally Nemitz the day I ran into the two of you at Starbucks. I hope you don't mind. I realized I'd never used you in any of my things. I couldn't believe it, knowing how I use everybody." None of the three of us said anything about his use of the verb "use," though Bobby and I looked at each other.

So that almost wraps it up, although you may want to know, if you don't already, that the novel Audrey Bliss released, *Her Worst Fears*, contains this rather poignant (at least I think so) passage:

She told herself it couldn't be going on. She rained other clichés down on her thick head as well. The ones about things like this happening to other women but not to her, about things like this only occurring in stories. But finally she had to admit to herself that life is nothing but stories. Some are made up and written down. Others simply unfold around us. She was in the middle of one of those. Her husband was seeing a man. Probably even – since Wakefield had such an aversion to abrasive men – a man who, in any other circumstance, she'd like.

You may also want to know, if you missed it, that Warren's novel, *Unstructured Time*, was called his best in no less than sixteen prestige reviews. (I collected them all.) And, in no small part, because Henry Rifkind – me – is, as *Kirkus* said in a bulleted report, "as real as a copper penny." The book – in which I, among other things, "have a smile that transforms an otherwise plain face" – remains on the bestseller lists after a year.

How do I feel about that? About any of it? About how copiously my prayer has finally been answered. Not precisely how I expected to feel when I wanted – what seems like a long time ago now – this kind of recognition. But maybe we never do feel how we expected to feel when we get what we've always wanted and discover it isn't what it's cracked up to be, when we discover that we'd lost track of why we wanted it in the first place and really want something entirely different – like real meaning in our lives.

It suddenly occurs to me that perhaps, in wanting to make the thrilling leap into fiction, what I really wanted was to have others define me, since I was disinclined or unable to. I wanted others to save me the work of locating the meaning of my own life. And now that they have, if even from their remove, I realize there's no consensus.

Nor could there be. I'm just someone open to interpretation. I suppose we all are and therefore we – each of us – have to do the interpreting that counts.

Oh, well, what the hell? Maybe I will, and maybe I won't – get around to doing what may be clear to everyone but me. If it turns out I don't, there's still some truth to my pointing and saying, Hey, that's me up there on the printed page!

People tell me things

People tell me things. I don't know why. I guess they think I'm a good listener. Or understanding. Or compassionate. Or discreet – though my writing what you're about to read gives the lie to this apprehension.

They may even think I give good advice, although I don't. I make a point of not giving any advice, good or bad. Why? How many times has a friend of yours gotten you alone, leaned forward confidentially, spilled some sticky problem all over your lap and asked, "What should I do?" You answer as thoughtfully as you know how; you hear yourself sounding knowledgeable, *simpatico*; you like what you hear. A couple of weeks later the same friend comes to you, same sticky problem, same canted posture, same question, "What should I do?"

Hoo-boy!

So, no, I don't give advice. I just let them talk. And maybe, in the end, that's what they like – unburdening themselves but not in the service of seeking advice they know they'll eventually feel guilty about not taking.

Let me give you an example of what I mean: my friend, Peter Fleming. Peter and I go, as they say, way back. We know each other since we came to New York in the late Sixties. I was introduced to him by a college roommate, Ted Kirstein, when we all hit the Big Apple to pursue our various careers – what another friend of mine refers to, with a mocking glint in his eye, as "First-Year New York."

The way it goes with Manhattan friendships, I don't see Ted much any more, but Peter and I are in constant touch. You might say there isn't a lot I don't know about him. A girl I was seeing back then (when we still saw girls, not women), Nancy Lang, had a friend, Bonnie Reddick, she wanted to fix up. I greased the wheels: Peter. In short, I introduced him to the woman he married. Which also means that, while I no longer communicate with Nancy – haven't since the early Seventies, and really have no idea where she is – I've remained friendly with Bonnie.

More than that, I serve, and have served for some time, as a confidant to them both, to Peter and Bonnie. It's no surprise to get a call from either of them asking if I'm free for lunch. Truth to tell, it's no surprise to get a call from any of my friends asking if I'm free for lunch. As I say, people tell me things, and lunch is often when they do it.

Oh, the lunches I've had all over Manhattan: in coffee shops where the tomatoes are as chewable as baboon's ears and the rice pudding is pure heaven; in fast-food holes where I don't order anything; and in four-star restaurants where the waiters give themselves brownie points for anticipating your every selfish need. And the trends in food I've been through and the updates on nutritional eating! From the time pasta wasn't good for you to the time it was to the time it wasn't again. Suffice it to say, if I hear the words *tapenade* or *coulis* one more time, I'll... I'll – I don't know what I'll.

But that's to digress. Back to Peter. A couple of weeks back I got a late morning bell from him. Was I free for lunch? I was, since – maybe I should throw in – I'm a writer and my hours tend to be flexible. Unless I'm on deadline, and then all bets are off.

Good, Peter said, he needed to talk; he'd even come to my neighborhood. (If you're taking notes, write this down. There are many ways to gauge how dire a friend's predicament is. The availability to travel is one of them. If they're willing to come to you, things are bad. If they'd rather do it "closer to my office," not only do they have little to grouse about, but there's a good chance they're thinking they're doing you a favor.)

Peter was ready to come to me, and, moreover, we could eat wherever I wanted – he didn't care, probably wouldn't eat much anyway. (The willingness to eat anything, anywhere indicated – it always does – the truly dire.)

I suggested a small Italian restaurant just around the corner from me where the food is unostentatious, where the help leaves you alone and where you're charged a budget-hunter's seven bucks plus tax and tip for a perfectly acceptable dish of pasta and a salad.

When I arrived at the which-shall-remain-nameless-for-fear-of-its-being-overrun spot only minutes later, Peter was already there. A very, very bad sign. He had a glass of white wine in front of him, and it had been heavily drained.

In one fell gesture I sat down and asked him what was up.

"The worst" came back at me like a winter wind.

I should say that Peter is, or was, a very good-looking guy. Square features, solid jaw, a comma of black hair punctuating a high forehead, ice-blue eyes Paul Newman only wished he had. There was a time in my life when I thought it might be nice to look more like Peter, but that was in my naïve days when self-doubt kept me from noticing how much deep shit – you should pardon the profanity – his brand of good looks can get you in. The years waltzed by, however, and I wised up. I learned that the only people who really care whether men are good-looking are homosexuals.

And although I've dipped my toes in that fountain, too, I've tried never to make looks a priority.

For his part, Peter had lost what I think is still called the bloom of youth. Some would say he's become lined; others that time has put character on his face. I'd say both, but he was looking particularly drawn as he gazed from me to his glass of wine and back again.

Incidentally, his declaring that the worst had occurred didn't necessarily mean much to me. I'd heard it before. The worsts Peter and I had parsed over lunch included those of the financial and the career kind (often related), but mostly they'd involved the amorous. Peter was – is – a womanizer. (If understatement were a criminal offense, I'd be facing twenty-five years to life.) He had the womanizing inclination, and those drop-dead looks gave him the wherewithal. The blue eyes – which, by the way, I finally realized were just a little too close together – had been enough to put in motion the seductions of many women over the years. Usually they were one-night stands, occasionally two- or three-week affairs, once a year-long liaison that might have gone on longer had the actress under discussion not left her soap to make a full-court press in Hollywood. Successfully; you'd know her bold-face name, but there's no need for me to include it.

I know about all Peter's dalliances because the details had been supplied me in moods ranging from the boastful to the beaten, from the cocky to the confounded. What should he do about this one? Or that one? Usually there wasn't much debate. He certainly wasn't going to leave Bonnie. We both knew it, knew he was no different from all the other men who tell the girlfriend that they're about to leave the wife right up to the moment when leaving begins to take on the faintest hint of reality. Then it's goodbye, Charlotte, so long, Sheila. (If you're still taking notes, write this down, too. Everyone knows the husband never leaves the wife; far fewer know that's how, *au fond*, the other woman wants it.)

So with Peter, in the past "the worst" had meant that he had to make a decision about leaving Bonnie (which we both knew he'd already made); or that he'd picked up some venereal disease (this was in the long ago days before AIDS) and how was he going to spare Bonnie from it and the fact of it; or that the current girlfriend had taken to calling him at home and hanging up if Bonnie answered; or any one of a broad range of tiresome predicaments.

(You know the old saw about a stiff dick having no conscience. That's only part of it. A stiff dick also gets great satisfaction from threatening its owner with the possibility of drastic consequences.)

From where I sat, Peter had been phenomenally lucky. He'd never been caught with his pants down – and I choose the cliché with care, which you'll see as I go on.

"Bonnie wants a divorce," he said, the bald four words accompanied by a slow side-to-side shaking of his head. (Remember: I talk to Bonnie, too, but I hadn't heard anything like this.)

As he reported this piece of domestic and social news, I noticed a look on Peter's face I'd never seen before. It was something far deeper than concern, something only slightly less than fear. It was an expression that told me in no uncertain terms he was very worried. To demonstrate the extent of my understanding I put down the hunk of bread I was nibbling. "No kidding," I said.

"I wouldn't kid about something like this."

"No, you wouldn't. That was just me batting the conversational ball back in your court. When did she get this idea? Why?"

"She got it last night."

"And she still had it this morning?"

"This morning she was packing her bags. Then she said, the hell with this, and she was packing my bags."

I resumed eating bread – more nerves than hunger, because this didn't sound good.

The waiter arrived, Giorgio, the owner's fifteen-year-old son, who had that pizza-dough complexion many waiters in Italian restaurants get for reasons I suppose make a kind of sense. I ordered what I always order (*pasta pomodoro* – simple and reliably fresh). Peter, having no time to waste on inessentials, said he'd have what I was having. When Giorgio brought the food, Paul didn't touch his.

"What's going on?" I asked.

"When I tell you, you won't believe it. No one would."

"Try me."

"You know Alice Feld."

"For a hundred years."

"Uhm." Alice is known to many. She's bright, she's funny, she's attractive in a brassy way – lots of big, highlighted hair, lots of make-up, so much costume jewelry that when she crosses the room she sounds like the Sousa band tuning up. She's always shopping for clothes and "whatevah"; she's married and divorced five times; she's flirtatious. When Alice is at a cocktail party, even the most secure wives find it inadvisable to concentrate fully on their conversations.

"I ran into her yesterday."

"Cause for caution but not necessarily alarm."

"Let me finish?"

"Sorry." I resumed wrapping *pasta pomodoro* around my fork.

"I was having lunch at that new place on East 50th. You know the one. Lescene – all one word, very smart."

"How'd you like it?"

"It doesn't matter how I liked it."

"Right."

"I was with this guy from Pittsburgh who's interested in giving me some of the capitalization for my magazine. Alice Feld was there, too, with a woman friend at a table across the room. And of course she had to come over."

"Of course."

"I'm getting very close to tying the guy down to a couple-hundred-thousand-dollar commitment when I hear this commotion at my side. It's Alice on her way out with her shopping bags—from Bloomingdale's and that place on Madison Avenue where they only sell cashmere. She sees me and rushes over, leaves her friend standing there with the silly grin people get on their face when they're trying to look agreeable. Anyway, I've never disliked Alice. She's kind of fun. She always acts as if we share some secret. As if we got it on sometime in the past." He stops, thinks. "It's possible we did, but I can't for the life of me remember when it could have been. She makes me laugh, though. Or did. And you have to admit there's something sexy about her."

"Admitted."

"Her timing couldn't have been worse. It was precisely at that moment – you can always feel it – when the guy you're hustling is thinking over the pros and cons and is about to throw business caution to the wind. You have to know just how to negotiate that crucial shoal. I do. But right in the middle of it, here's Alice, and there's nothing for me to do but get up and give her the big hug she's waiting for. I wrap my arms about her. I'm aware of her breasts under her coat – those monster boobs of hers."

"Uh-huh."

"I introduce her to Goodrich, and as I do, I see a look in his eyes that spells hesitation. I'm ready to brain Alice, when I hear her shriek something like 'My earring.' I turn around and see her rubbing an ear lobe. 'I think I've just lost an earring,' she says. The evidence is she has, since she's got this gold-and-silver hub cap on one ear and nothing on the other. Now she's looking around to see if it dropped on the floor. And I start to look, and so does Goodrich. Before you know it, people at the tables around us are looking around at their feet. They don't know what they're looking for, but I guess they figure that if they locate some foreign object, it must be what we're missing.

"'Herb gave me these for our anniversary,' she says. 'They cost a fortune.' She's addressing this to everyone around us to explain her frenzy. 'He'll kill me if I lose them. I'll kill myself.' With that she drops her bags and falls to her knees and starts crawling under the table. By now the waiters and the maitre d' have come over, and they're all asking what's the matter. *'Qu'y a-t-il, monsieur, madame? Qu'est-ce qui se passe?'* Alice decides to tell them and straightens up. But she bangs her head on the underside of the table, which is enough to make Goodrich's wine glass topple. So here's my two-hundred-thousand-dollar-man with Merlot all over his trousers. He's trying to act as if it's no problem.

"The *maître d'* and the waiters are making a big show of concern, and patrons are pushing their chairs back as a demonstration of heartfelt co-operation – Charlie Rose over here and Georgette Mosbacher over there. And nobody's finding anything. Then somebody finds something, but it's not the earring. It's the doo-hickey, whatever they call it, that fits over the stem of the earring and locks it in place. So now we know there's every reason to believe the earring has fallen off and must be somewhere nearby. Meanwhile Alice is demanding to go into the kitchen and search any plates that've been bussed. She's threatening to go through the garbage. Still no earring.

"After ten minutes of this, with the restaurant taking on the look of an exploded carnival ride, the *maître d'* quiets Alice down long enough to assure her that the earring must be some place. When it turns up, he'll contact her. The woman Alice is with, who's never introduced and whom I don't recognize and who now has affected a look of profound concern, helps Alice out the door. Alice has the stooped shoulders and uncertain gait of someone who's lost a child. The *maître d'* looks greatly relieved, and everyone goes back to his lunch. I try to regroup. To no avail. Goodrich, who's still dabbing his napkin at his pants, says he wants to think it over and get back to me. I leave the restaurant convinced his money is just about as likely to happen as me winning the Cy Young award."

Peter falls silent for a second. His face hanging over the cold pasta is as forlorn as I've seen. But since there's no explanation of Bonnie's cataclysmic decision in what's – let's face it – a very funny story if you don't happen to be its leading player, I figure there's more to come. I know enough not to ask. Peter needs time, and I'm giving it to him. He distractedly drinks some water and looks off at a wall where hangs a truly hideous rendition of the Tour Eiffel.

"You're probably wondering what this has to do with Bonnie."

"I am. Yes."

"I'm about to tell you. I put Goodrich in a taxi and go home to see if I can try some alternate money sources, people I've tried before who've said no whom I hope I can get to change their minds. I get on my computer and draft a letter to Goodrich that sounds so obsequious when I reread it that I push delete. Bonnie comes home and we have a quiet evening. I never tell her about lunch, because I've taken to not saying very much about the magazine. I've suspected for a long time she's not completely sold on it. Whenever it comes up, she assumes a serious posture and asks backhanded questions like, Do you really think the time is right for a cigarette smokers' magazine? Everybody's so anti-smoking these days, she says. As if maybe I haven't heard. As if I don't read the papers and see how out for blood the government is, tobacco lobby be damned. As if there's not an indoor space in all of Manhattan where you can't have yourself a relaxing smoke. I tell her that's just the time to go after a hardcore segment of smokers who want somewhere to turn for reassurance and revenge. Think of the advertising potential, I say, if I can get around those obstacles. Phillip Morris and R.J. Reynolds alone could keep me afloat. Look at the success of *Cigar Aficionado*, blah-blah-blah. She says, Well, yes. But I can tell she's not buying.

"When it comes time to go to bed, we're in the bedroom. Bonnie's already under the sheets, and I'm taking my pants off. 'What's that?' she asks. 'What's what?' I say. 'That,' she says and points in the general direction of my groin. I look down at my boxers. Right by the fly there's this metal object. For a second I'm as baffled as she is. I don't know what to make of it. I grab at it, and stab myself with what feels like a needle. I hold it up, this fucking gold-and-silver thing. My forefinger is bleeding."

Peter pokes his forefinger my way. I look at it but see no damage.

"Now I know what it is," he says. "'It's an earring,' Bonnie yells. 'How did it..? You didn't...' she says. I know what she's thinking. She was thinking what I'd be thinking. What anybody would be thinking. Especially in these post-Oval Office days. Cheap blow-job. 'Of course, I didn't,' I say. But the evidence is incriminating."

This is too much for me. "Well, how did it get there?" I beg. "Was it Alice's?"

"Of course, it was Alice's. Who else's? All I can think is that when Alice hugged me, the earring somehow slid down between my jacket and my shirt, caught at my belt or something and then somehow managed to work its way down inside my trousers."

"And you didn't feel anything? Didn't the stem thing prick you?"

"You mean, didn't it prick my prick? No, you frigging fool. If it had, I would have noticed and pulled it out."

"Didn't you have to take a piss at some point?"

"Don't think I didn't think of that. Of course, I had to piss. A couple of times. I just never felt it. I kept asking myself how I could have missed it. Eventually I started thinking that at some time late in the afternoon I unconsciously became aware of an unusual weight dragging at my boxers, a presence I just didn't register. But maybe I'm making that up."

"And you didn't try to explain?"

"Yes, I tried to explain. I even told Bonnie to call Alice Feld. And she said, 'The hell I will.' And I said, 'Okay, I'll call her.' And she said, 'The hell you will. Alice Feld's been after you for years. Even if that is her earring, you don't think I'm going to believe it just happened to fall into your pants. "Oh, hell-o!" How dumb do you think I am? I guess I know the answer to that question: very dumb. You don't think I know about all the women over all the years? I do. I chose to look the other way. But even I'm too proud to look the other way when you parade the evidence in front of me. I can't. And don't insult me by trying to deny it. Any of it.'"

Peter brushed some imaginary lint off his lapels. He said, "I realized I could take another stab at denying this one incident. But what about the rest, since they did take place? Think of it, Dan. All my infidelities over the years, and a freak occurrence turns me into a condemned man." He gave me a long look and cracked a rueful grin. In that one expression I saw the shrinking man he'd become.

But as I say, I don't give advice. I just listen. There wasn't much more to listen to that day. I finished what little was left of my pasta, and Peter continued ignoring his. We made some small talk. But it was very small, and I knew whatever I was saying did nothing to alleviate his glaring woe. His past had caught up with him. I saw in those ice-blue eyes he was beginning to accept what he'd gambled he'd never have to accept.

He'd bet wrong, and his loss had been slapped on him as farce.

We finished lunch, and Peter went back uptown. I talked to him over the next weeks, conferred about the changes he was making – finding an affordable apartment, furnishing it. He was subdued, absent-minded, downhearted, what you'd expect. He was also too busy to get together.

But, of course, that wasn't all there was to it, because, as I say, I'm friendly with Bonnie as well. I decided, though, that I wasn't going to call her. That could possibly be interpreted as my setting myself up as go-between, and I certainly wasn't prepared for that. I figured I'd let Bonnie call me.

She didn't at first, and then she did. Peter had been out of their apartment at least a month when she phoned to ask me over for "a drink and something light to eat."

When I arrived, the first thing I noticed was that little had changed. It seemed to me one or two paintings in their – her – living-room were missing, but I wasn't even sure about that. Most of the furniture, and heavy it was, had come from Bonnie's mother's house, and it remained where it had always been. At least what of it I could look around and see while Bonnie was at the wet sink arranging lime wedges around our designer waters. It was as if Peter hadn't left or, more disturbingly, as if he'd never lived there.

I didn't get a good look at Bonnie until she sat down on an ottoman at an angle to me. She looked, as she always had, fashionable and pretty. I know that if I had been holding a photograph of her taken around the time we met, I would have been able to compare it with how she appeared now and would see a difference. But I had no photograph, and my impression was that, aside from wearing her unretouched auburn hair shorter, she looked very much as she always had.

Nothing had happened to change the deep green of her eyes or the line of her strong, jaunty nose or her languid mouth. More to the point, wearing a silk blouse loosely over fawn trousers and not much in the way of make-up, she looked remarkably at ease – as good, I'd venture to say, as I'd seen her in a long time.

Bonnie, I realized then, was one of those women who, even smiling, always seems tense – as if there's something she can't quite get off her mind. Now it appeared as if she had gotten it – had gotten him, the worst of him – off her mind.

"Have you talked to him?" she asked, all but nonchalantly.

"Not in a few days. Have you?"

"No. I asked him not to call until he feels up to calling. It seemed a good idea."

"Sounds like it."

"How did he seem when you talked to him last?"

"Not good."

"No, I guess not." Bonnie was wearing carpet slippers with clever insignias on the toe. Not the sort of thing I normally notice, but I did now because she was taking time to look at them. Then she said, "I don't know how much he told you."

"Not a hell of a lot. And I didn't ask too much."

"No. You don't, Dan. I think that's why of all our friends you may be the only one we'll both be able to continue seeing. Sad, huh, but true. When I think of all of this, the friends choosing up sides is what I hate most. Maybe if we had children, that would have been worse to deal with." She was still contemplating her slippers. "I suppose he told you about the earring incident."

"Yes." I noticed – who wouldn't have? – that Bonnie pointedly kept using pronouns – he, him – instead of saying "Peter." I picked up not so much hostility or stridence in the usage but rather dismay and a letting-go that was the onset of forgetting.

"All about Alice Feld *et cetera*?" she said.

"Yes."

"And you believed him?"

"I believed him. And you didn't."

"Is that what he told you? That I didn't believe him about Alice and the traveling earring?"

"Yes. Why? Was he lying? Why would he lie about something as crucial as that?"

"No, he wasn't lying. I told him I didn't believe him."

"But you did believe him?" I was confused. "I'm confused."

"How long have you known me, Dan?"

"You know how long."

"And in all that time, have I ever asked you anything about Peter and his women?"

"Never. I thought it was classy of you. Or stupid. I could never decide which. But you did find ways to let me know you knew."

"Of course I knew. What woman with an IQ above forty doesn't? I just chose to deal with it in my way. I felt making scenes – or even just bringing it up not to make scenes – was lowering myself to his schoolboy level. Acting as if it wasn't going on was how I protected myself."

"Then why did you make such a final issue out of it this time?" I asked, somewhat puzzled. "When you had no cause?"

Bonnie was sitting on the ottoman with her legs in front of her. Now she shifted position and, resting her elbows on her thighs, arched towards me. She looked me straight in the eye, and I thought, She never looks me in the eye, or hasn't for years. It was as if a long-standing but unspoken embarrassment had thawed and evaporated.

"I'm going to tell you something, Dan. I knew the earring story was true, because Alice Feld herself told me. If I've got the chronology right, she tracked me down at my office only minutes after it happened. She described the entire episode and said she was calling me because she didn't want to phone Peter at the restaurant. She was so mortified she didn't want to speak to anyone at the restaurant. What she wanted was to ask me to ask Peter, whenever I saw him, whether he had by any chance found the earring after she left. She told me how Herb had given them to her for their fifteenth anniversary. I knew the earrings she meant. I'd seen her wearing them enough. You could see them from the next county. She was devastated. She said the earring had to be somewhere. I assured her it had to be. I calmed her down by telling her if Peter said anything to me, I'd let her know. Then I forgot about the whole thing until Peter took his pants off that night. I recognized the earring at once."

She still hadn't broken her eye contact with me. I opened my mouth to speak. She put a slim forefinger to my lips. "Now you're going to ask why I would believe Alice had lost it in the way she said and not in the way the world would assume. The answer is, I've known Alice Feld for a long time. She may be showy. She may be silly. But one thing she isn't is a liar. She tells social lies. We all do. But unlike many of us, she can't make them stick. If she'd been manufacturing the story, if she'd really lost the earring while keeping busy between Peter's legs and was trying to cover up the sordid truth, I'd have seen through her in a second. I'd have heard it in her voice."

Bonnie leaned in closer to me and rested her hand on my knee. "But here's what you have to understand, Dan. Peter didn't expect me to believe the story."

"Did he say that?"

"Of course not. He wanted me to believe it, but he didn't expect me to. Nobody could be expected to believe a story like that. And you have to remember, Peter's lied to me all these years. I knew if I said I believed him, if I said Alice had called me and told me everything, he still wouldn't have expected me to believe it. He'd have been relieved, of course. I knew that. But somewhere in the back of his mind he'd have thought I'd fallen for another lie. An impossible, blatant, ludicrous lie. A quantum leap forward in lies. Then there'd be no telling what he thought he could get away with in the future. I know him. My presumed gullibility would have been too irresistible not to act on further. Because I've loved him for so long now – because I love him still – I've allowed myself to be a laughing-stock. Pretended I didn't hear the 'poor Bonnie' gossip. But I couldn't allow the stakes to be raised."

I had a thought. "But what if someday Alice tells Peter she spoke to you? Or asks him about the earring again?"

Bonnie looked away from me then. "Oh, she won't ask about the earring. I returned it to her on condition that she never mention it again."

"But what if she does? You know Alice. She opens her mouth and anything can come out."

"It won't matter. Peter knows and I know and you know that just as there are lies like truth, there are truths that sound like lies."

Bonnie let that thought work its way into the white noise the air-conditioned air was making. Then she gave me a dry look that slowly became a smile of such relief I joined her in it. We finished our drinks and talked about what she was going to do next. "Get on with my life," she said and convinced me as much as I was likely to be convinced that she meant it.

So, as I say, people tell me things. That doesn't mean I pass them on. There's no reason or need. Possibly to change those things, someone might suggest. But things of this nature rarely change anything just because a pious bystander decides to pass them on as moral lessons.

People tell me things, and – save for just this once – I've learned to keep them to myself.

Rembrandt paints again

When Cleve Morris called to ask how soon I could drop over to scope out his new Rembrandt, I chuckled. I'm not sure why, since the remark struck me as a joke that hadn't landed squarely.

"You've bought a new painting?" I said.

"Not bought," Cleve said. "I guess you could call it a gift."

"Who's the artist? Another Fischl?" Some years before, Cleve had purchased an early Eric Fischl on a tip from a gallery owner pal, and I knew it had appreciated considerably. Maybe he'd decided he was going to concentrate on collecting Fischl. You know who Fischl is, of course: the Edgar Degas-influenced realist with a big Hamptons following.

Considering some of Cleve's other, um, affectations, accumulating Fischls would make sense.

"I told you," Cleve said. "Rembrandt van Rijn. The Rembrandt you've heard so much about."

Yes, but I waited to hear more. I figured an explanation was coming for what I took to be some form of prank. Although when I thought about it for another second or two, I realized I never knew Cleve to be a prankster.

Quite the opposite. The Cleve I knew and had known since childhood abhorred pranks and pranksters. He'd once had a severe falling out with Dave Radin over rattling cans outside Molly Eckstein's windows to tick off her sour mother. "What's the point?" Cleve asked Dave. "No point," Dave said in his typical no-beating-around-the-bush manner. "Does everything have to have a point? Fun. That's the point." "Where's the fun in rattling cans outside a nasty woman's windows?" Cleve demanded. And it went on like that until Dave threw Cleve out of his rusty Ford and they didn't speak for a few months.

Until they did speak. They were seventeen going on severely-immature at the time, but Cleve has never changed in that aspect. He's still the same. I don't know about Dave. I haven't seen him or heard from him – or about him – in more than fifteen years. But I'll bet he hasn't changed either. He's probably somewhere playing dirty tricks on his golf buddies, loosening the wires on their carts or bribing their caddies (if they have caddies) to substitute exploding golf balls for the real thing.

But Cleve I was still in touch with and now he resumed. "I don't expect you to believe me," he said, "but it's a Rembrandt, all right. You know I wouldn't kid you. I'm not a kidder."

As I said, I knew he wasn't, but nevertheless something was fishy. "Someone gave you a Rembrandt," I said. "Just like that. I know you have a few rich relatives, but I didn't know any of them owned a Rembrandt."

"Not a relative – no rich aunts," Cleve said. "No studio of Rembrandt. Rembrandt himself!" Cleve affixed an exclamation point at the end of "Rembrandt himself!" It was particularly noticeable to me, because he never was much of one for aural exclamation points. I don't want to say that ever since childhood – and perhaps the cradle – Cleve had been a glum one, but despite (or because of) his intelligence (a reputed 173 IQ), he would never have been described by anyone acquainted with him as effusive. Certainly Dave Radin wouldn't have summed him up that way.

Short and dark and with eyes so deep-set they look like a train approaching in a subway tunnel, Cleve gave the impression of someone who'd had a major disappointment at an early age. (Could it be from glimpsing this ageing world for the first time as he left the womb?) From then on, it was as if he'd determined never to put too much faith in the likelihood of only good things happening. He had the air of a man always listening for the other size fifteen shoe to drop – and expecting to be directly under it when it did.

"I don't count on you to believe me," he continued. "Who would? I barely believe it myself, but if you come over, I'll explain everything." He stopped, waiting for me to say something. Which I didn't. He appended, "As well as I can explain it. How soon will you get here?"

"Look, Cleve," I said, "are you all right? If you don't mind my saying so, you don't sound like yourself."

"I suppose I don't," Cleve said, with an uncharacteristic note of cheer in his voice, "but what I'm telling you is God's honest truth. I've got a brand-new Rembrandt done by the man himself."

"I'm coming right over," I said, making a snap decision. I figured I'd better. I'd known Cleve for so long. We'd never been best friends, but our parents were chummy and wished we would be, too – though we weren't for the above-mentioned cloud under which he labored.

Nevertheless, I felt I owed his parents and mine consideration for doing the best they knew how for us boys, especially if Cleve were in some kind of emotional upheaval – hallucinating, losing a tenuous grasp on reality, whatever.

Cleve lives well. To begin with, the Morrises have money, and Cleve's mother, Irene Benjamin Morris, has taste that she damn well made sure Cleve absorbed. And don't you know he did – and then raised Irene Benjamin Morris one? He developed the strain of good taste – certainly in his home – that doesn't hit you over the head with just how good the taste is.

He favors clean design, simple woods, plain fabrics, unobtrusive lighting, nothing showy, nothing that screams, "My dreckorator is better than your dreckorator." Actually, I'd been led to believe Cleve selected everything himself after finessing his mother's suggestions, and I had no reason not to believe it.

There were show pieces on view at his place, however, though not in excess. They were the paintings and the photographs. There was the early Fischl, of course, and there were a few other contemporary artists, but nothing, I'd been advised, that had ever carried an exorbitant price tag – other early works from Brice Marden and Elizabeth Murray, a few choice drawings (a Christo sketch for the Pont Neuf project). There was a Robert Frank photograph and something of extreme quality by Bruce Cratsley. Everything was classy and all secured out of Cleve's pocket – or I should say, on the salary he drew as head of his own public relations firm, The Cleve Morris Agency, which specialized in sports.

(Cleve had always liked sports, although he was physically ill-equipped to play them well. He might have been a coxswain or wrestled in the lightweight range, but he didn't choose those teen paths. Instead, he did things like serve as water-boy for varsity teams.)

I would never have predicted that the Cleve with whom I grew up would become a successful flack. I would have envisioned a more contemplative life for him.

(Then again, I have often been wrong about foreseeing where people would end up, or if not end up, pass through on the way to the inevitable end I would or wouldn't know about.)

But it turns out that Cleve's ruminative air is just what attracts clients to him. They're the sort of sportsmen who claim to disdain publicity but concede it's a necessary evil. If they must endure it, they choose to do so with someone like Cleve, who at least gives the impression of gravity and who – getting down to the nuts and bolts of his appeal – eschews any use of the press-release exclamation point (see above).

I've occasionally witnessed Cleve with this player or that owner or manager whose clenched faces or eye-rolls reveal their aversion to publicity when they think Cleve has momentarily divided his attention. It's their way of indicating that they though they hate the ballyhoo game, they'll play it and oh-well-that's-life-isn't-it.

The fact is, Cleve is on to them but doesn't care. Rather, he expects the behavior. He's come to consider it as confirmation of his world view. Or *weltanschauung*, as just about none of his burlier clients would put it.

It's possible to say that Cleve was skeptical enough about the nature of business to do very well at it and consequently to live well from it.

That's on top of the family swag.

When Cleve had buzzed me in and I arrived at his eleventh-floor Fifth Avenue apartment overlooking Central Park, the tan door was open and he was waiting in it. I've said he's not tall – about five feet six or seven and built like the bantamweight wrestler he never was.

(Funny how some men who look naturally athletic aren't.)

Cleve was leaning against the doorframe wearing various shades of brown and tan (to match his furnishings, I imagine) and looking mighty pleased with his well-put-together self. His expression mixed expectation with a kind of pleasure at being who he is. It's an affect that makes you want to say something caustic just to clear the air.

Anyway, it made me consider saying something sharpish, but I elected to suppress the impulse.

Not that I had the opportunity to slip in a *mal mot*, because I hadn't even reached the door when Cleve said, "When you come inside, I'm going to ask you to close your eyes. Then I'm going to lead you in, and I'll tell you when to open them."

"Lord, love a duck, do I have to?" I said, as I approached him.

(I 'd like to make it clear right off that I'm not the type of person who ordinarily says things like "Lord, love a duck." But the occasion seemed to call for something along those lines. On the other hand, maybe I said it because I knew it would bother Cleve just the slightest bit.)

Cleve didn't acknowledge the comment but merely said that yes, it was imperative I close my eyes. I obliged, because I'm that kind of accommodating friend. As I did, I felt his left hand on my left upper arm and his right hand on my right shoulder, and since I knew the lay-out of his apartment, I knew I was being led through the generous entrance hall – or foyer, if you please – to his living-room.

When we stopped walking and he turned me at a sixty-degree angle, I knew I was facing the sofa over which for some time the Fischl had been holding pride of place. Since I could feel my left leg pressing against his coffee table, I reckoned I was standing at about a six- or seven-foot remove from that cherished art work.

"You can open them now," Cleve said, his low and resonant voice as fraught with mischief as I'd ever known it.

I did as bid, and here's what I saw. There on the wall where the Fischl had been was a portrait of Cleve. I don't mean just any commonplace likeness. I mean a magnificent specimen. Cleve, in a single-breasted brown suit (Tom Ford?), olive-green shirt and green-and-brown patterned tie, sat against a black backdrop looking simultaneously intelligent, affluent and ineffably sad.

The likeness was remarkable. Not because it was flattering, which in a way it was, but because it depicted him as someone wise enough to allow the painter – whoever it was – to paint what he (she?) saw (and saw into) and not what he thought would please the sitter. In particular, the eyes – how deep-set and troubled they can be – had it.

"Not half bad," I said. "It definitely looks as if it was painted by someone for whom Rembrandt is a big influence." I was referring to the technique, the characteristic touches. More than that, I was talking about every nuance that makes a Rembrandt a Rembrandt. In the painting Cleve's eyes were Rembrandt eyes. Not the eyes rendered by a Rembrandt follower – Gerard Dou or Frans Hals, say – who'd eventually evolved a separate but indebted style.

Everything caught the Dutch master's manner. Everything: the pose with the torso turned slightly away from the painter but the head facing directly out, the flesh tones, the bold brush strokes obvious even from ten feet away, the black backdrop palpable yet insubstantial, the impeccable understanding of humanity and the absolute disinclination to flinch from it, the sense that the emotion in the work had been intuited by an injured heart.

I shut up for at least three minutes while I studied Cleve in the portrait and Cleve in the flesh.

Cleve – looking from me to the painting and back to me again and then back to the painting – was more than ready to participate in the silence.

I broke my staring only to look quickly around for the Fischl and located it on the wall behind me. Near it was a large, square glass vase holding an array of yellow and white tulips.

After I spent another minute or more taking the portrait of Cleve in and – I have to admit this – wishing I had one of myself like it, I said, "You're right. It looks like a Rembrandt. Who's the painter? And where did you find him or her?"

"I didn't say it was like a Rembrandt," Cleve replied. "I said it was a Rembrandt." The emphasis in the first of those two sentences was on the "like"; the emphasis in the second of the sentences was on the "was." "Okay, you've seen the painting. Now the back story."

"As they're always quick to say in the public relations arena."

Cleve ignored the quip. "Let's sit on the sofa. We have to look away from the painting. If we look at it, we won't be able to concentrate. If we look away, we look at the Fischl. Which we both know and which looks good where it is now, don't you think?"

The reality was that the Fischl held its own against the portrait, even took on an added weight.

"It looks fine," I said, as I sat down to face it as well as to face whatever else Cleve was going to present me with.

But before I get to that, I ought to say that when I'd stepped around the coffee table and closer to the portrait of Cleve, I saw it was signed. The name said "Rembrandt." Faintly. To my mind, it was the only cheap element on the canvas. It turned a work of art into a sight gag. I wondered how normally impeccable Cleve, who knew the value of small details, had allowed that to happen.

I wondered but I didn't have the opportunity to ask, because once again Cleve got the conversational jump on me. "What I'm about to tell you is going to strain your credulity, but I want you to hold your questions until I finish. At that point, you may find you don't have any questions. Just total wonderment."

As he said this, he fixed me with a look somewhere between imploring and stern.

"No questions?" I said. "This isn't going to be easy."

"For you, I know," Cleve said. "But work with me here."

I nodded assent, all the while thinking I may not stick to the promise. I decided the thing to do for the moment was not to look at the Fischl, which, by the way, is a domestic scene of a boy and an older woman, whom I always took to be the boy's emotionally careless mother. What would serve the situation best, I thought, would be for me to gaze out the window at Cleve's expansive, expensive view across Central Park. I followed my instinct.

"Okay, here goes," Cleve said. "About two months ago, I got on the crosstown bus at Seventy-Ninth Street. This was mid-afternoon. I was at Broadway. I'd left the office and was coming home to change for a meeting starting in the early evening that was going to keep me out until at least midnight. I was on one of those double buses, and I'd walked towards the back. I found a seat facing front and wasn't paying much attention to what was happening around me.

"I was thinking about a few office matters. When the bus reached Amsterdam Avenue, I suppose I was idly watching the line of people getting off and getting on. You know, the way you do. A few people came towards the back and found seats. A few stood, even though there were seats empty.

"Then as the bus pulled away from the stop, I saw a man heading towards me who looked familiar. I'd say he was in his late twenties, maybe early thirties. He was medium height – five eight, five nine, maybe – was wearing loose-fitting trousers, a vest and a loose off-white shirt. More like a blouse than a shirt. He had on a kind of outsized beret. He was carrying a medium-sized portfolio tied with a faded orange string.

"He spotted an empty seat at an angle next to me, sat down, rested the portfolio on his lap, untied the string, opened it and started flipping sheets of paper. I couldn't see them. Nobody paid him any attention, but I couldn't get over the feeling I knew him from somewhere. But I didn't want to stare. So I didn't. As we continued to Columbus and on to Central Park West, I kept giving him sidelong glances to see if anything about him jogged my memory. As we're approaching Central Park West, I got it. He looked exactly like Rembrandt. But I mean exactly. The Rembrandt in one of the earlier self-portraits. There was no missing the resemblance.

"So now I guess I'm staring at him, trying to convince myself I'm making this up. He catches me looking at him. I do one of those things you do when someone catches you looking too long. Small smile and turn away, as if to say, I wasn't really staring at you – I was lost in a thought and happened to be turned in your direction.

"Now we're speeding through Central Park, and the fellow reaches into a leather pouch he has around his waist and fishes something out. It's a card. We're now crossing Fifth Avenue to my stop. He hands the card to me. I rise to go towards the door and read the card on the way. It says 'Rembrandt van Rijn' in – I don't know – Dutch Gothic lettering? The only other thing on it is an email address in all lower case: rembrandt@rembrandtvanrijn.com. But now I'm getting off the bus, and someone is directly behind me. So I can't stop. As the bus pulls away, I look up and there this fellow is in the window making typing gestures at me. He's telling me to look for him online."

This is too much for me. Cemented to Cleve's dictates, I've held my tongue, but I have to make a comment. I have to say something about this being some guy's clever ruse to drum up business for – for who knows what?

But when all I've gotten out is an alarmed "You didn't..." Cleve raises an open palm at me and goes, "Uh-uh-uh." I remember the pledge of silence I made. I also remember childhood when more than once I saw Irene Benjamin Morris raise an open palm to Cleve and say, "Uh-uh-uh."

I couldn't tell whether Cleve was deliberately mimicking his mother because he knew I'd recognize the gesture or whether he had simply become her for a second. And don't forget, I knew he wasn't ordinarily the jokester type. Whichever it was, I knew he really meant business with the "uh-uh-uh." I didn't bother to finish my sentence.

"Of course, I got in touch," Cleve said, knowing that's what I wanted to ask. "For reasons you can figure out. After all, I'm in public relations. I assumed the guy was running some kind of Rembrandt business. Maybe – even though I couldn't figure out how – it was on the square. He might need representation. How about if he could pull down big bucks painting in the style of Rembrandt? I know any number of people ostentatious enough to want something that looks like a Rembrandt on their walls. My mother, for starters. Anyway, that's what I told myself. So what if he isn't in major-league sports? I can bend my mission to include the plastic arts. After all, I like them.

"But I also couldn't get past the incredible physical resemblance to Rembrandt. I mean the shape of the head, the clean-shaven and ruddy cheeks, the chin, the angle of the cap on his curly dark hair, the glint in his slightly melancholy eyes. When I say dead ringer, I mean dead ringer. But more than that. A brilliant plastic surgeon can only go so far in replicating a face. No plastic surgeon can affect an absolute duplicate.

"I went home and before I changed, went online to rembrandt@rembrandtvanrijn.com. What came up was a website with a home page that had on it only a signature – Rembrandt's, and it looked like the full-bodied signature we all know. It looked too irrefutably like the barely discernible signature on the painting behind me. Nothing else on the page. So I clicked on the signature, and up came a drawing and the word 'next.'

"How can I describe the drawing? It was a street scene with people milling about. In the background was a store window with Banana Republic above it. You have to understand it was a contemporary scene, but drawn in Rembrandt's style. Had whoever the guy is put the figure of Jesus in the foreground with followers gathered around, it could have passed for one of Rembrandt's biblical drawings. Okay, the Banana Republic would have been anachronistic. I looked it over and over and then clicked on 'next.' What followed was another drawing and then another – all contemporary scenes but all in uncanny reiteration of Rembrandt."

The urge to speak rose in my gorge like a poised cobra, but again Cleve raised an open palm – leaving out the "uh-uh-uh" this time. "I know what you're thinking. I thought the same thing. Forgery. Whoever the guy is, he's talented, he'd studied Rembrandt. He'd gotten him down pat. What he's doing is a form of visual plagiarism. If so, it's nothing to turn your nose up at. Have you ever looked at any of the work by artists in Rembrandt's studio, the ones who schooled at his elbow? Much of what they did is, in my estimation, inferior to what whoever this person was doing.

"And there was the physical resemblance. I couldn't get it out of my mind. So when the last drawing came up with the word 'contact' underneath, I did. And received a return email within the hour. Signed Rembrandt. Computer typeface, of course, so not in the recognizable penmanship. He invited me to meet him."

At that, Cleve leaned toward me. "At his studio," he said, with an air of both confidentiality and conspiracy. He leaned back. "At his studio in Nolita, where it's all going on these days. Next day I take a cab down to 37 Prince Street and ring 4D. The buzzer goes – the intercom doesn't work – and I walk up the three flights. The door to 4D is slightly ajar. I push it open. The studio is at the back of the building, so there's northern light.

"The guy passing himself off as Rembrandt is standing in the middle of the room with an easel behind him and a blank canvas on it. On the walls are pinned a number of drawings – some of them looking like nothing more than doodles, five-finger exercises. There are a number of drawings of himself. Studies, maybe, for self-portraits in oils, although he tells me later that he doesn't often do studies for paintings.

"Against one wall is a pipe rack with what look like costumes hung on twenty or thirty hangers. I don't need to remind you Rembrandt was fascinated by costumes and painted himself in more than a few. But this Rembrandt is still wearing the same outfit I'd seen him in the day before, and he's still the spitting image of the painter the world knows and loves. Closer to me and facing the easel is an elaborate wooden chair on a small riser.

"On the wall directly behind it – one side of the door I'd just come through – a black muslin curtain is draped from a brass curtain rod with elaborate ram heads at both ends. On the other side of the door and along the wall is a long counter with long, narrow drawers underneath it. A few of them are partially open, and I can see more sheets of paper. I take all of these to be signs of great constant output.

"On the counter are palettes, jars with brushes in them, tubes of oils. There's a plastic bag that says Pearl Paints on it. It's collapsed so that I only see the "P-e" of "Pearl" and the "a-i-n-t-s" of "Paints," but I can figure it out. The guy shops at Pearl Paints. On Canal Street. I'm so astounded by what I see that I've forgotten to speak.

"It doesn't matter. He isn't waiting for me to say anything. Instead, he says to me, 'Welcome, Mr. Morris.' In accented English, but only barely accented. You know how beautifully the Dutch speak English. 'I'm Rembrandt van Rijn,' he says, bold as you please. What do you say to that, huh? What I say is, 'Just like the great Dutch painter.' When I've said it, he just looks at me, and his eyes well up, go soft. You know the look from some of his self-portraits – the later ones. 'I am the great Dutch painter,' he says. 'I don't expect you to believe me. I can hardly believe it myself.

'But I am Rembrandt. I am the man who painted the pictures they exhibit in the Metropolitan Museum of Art. They're some of my best, don't you think? Every time I go visit them, I go with trepidation. I expect they will disappoint me. As yet they have not. Perhaps I am as good as they say I am – and have said for over three and a half centuries now. I am very impressed with "Aristotle Contemplating a Bust of Homer." I thought I had overdone it, but it stands the test of time. And they purchased it at such a great price! I would never had been able to ask that much for it, although I could have used the money to pay off my many creditors.'

"He's telling me this in his only slightly accented English, and I don't know what to say. I'm flabbergasted. I'm flummoxed. I'm tongue-tied, which isn't good for someone in my line of business. But I'm looking at a man who looks like a Rembrandt self-portrait come to life, and he's telling me in no uncertain terms he is Rembrandt. I regain my senses, though, and remember I'm the one in PR. I'm the one supposed to be spinning the facts, not the other guy. 'Look here,' I say, 'I like the approach, but I'm not sure what you hope to gain by it.'"

"'I am Rembrandt,' the man repeats. 'I can not tell you why I am here, only that I am. One moment it was the year 1660, and I was in my home in Amsterdam – a painter in advancing age recovering from financial setbacks. The next moment I am a young man again and in this room, a room furnished something like my Amsterdam studio but not completely like it. I do not know how I arrived here. I only remember vaguely being dissatisfied with how a painting was progressing and saying aloud to myself, "I wish I were somewhere far away from here with the energy I had as a younger man."'"

"'Nice try,' I said, 'I may look gullible, but I'm not. Do you really expect me to believe a man travels a few centuries through time and somehow becomes completely acclimated – to the point where he has an email address? ' 'I am an intelligent man,' he replies. 'Do you think it is so difficult to understand the computer? In my home country I came to understand mercantilism as an outgrowth of the expanding tulip market. Next to that, computers are nothing.'

"'Cute answer,' I said, 'but you have a studio. You're paying rent. You're getting around the City. You don't seem to be experiencing culture shock.' 'What can I tell you?' he said, 'New Yorkers are friendly – as long as you do not interrupt them during rush hour. I have learned much in the three months I have been here. To pay my rent, I have drawn many likenesses in Times Square.' 'And signed them Rembrandt?' I said. 'Yes,' he said, 'if I do enough of them, it keeps a roof over my head.'

"'How many people have come here – to your studio?' I asked. 'Oh,' he said, 'You are the first, Mr Morris.' 'The first?' I said, somewhat taken aback. 'Why me?' 'It is simple,' he said. 'In the time I have been here, you are the only person who has looked at me as if he knew I am Rembrandt. I have needed the – what is your contemporary word? – validation, because for the longest time I thought I was Rembrandt, but I was not sure.' 'On the bus, you mean,' I said. 'I have to tell you I looked at you because I thought you looked like Rembrandt – not because I thought you actually were Rembrandt.'"

Cleve stopped there to catch his breath and to let what he'd just said register with me. I could tell he was revving up to report something crucial. He also looked as if he were waiting for me to say something, but right then I didn't want to tempt the raised palm or the "uh-uh-uh."

He gave me a slight smile of approval and took in a large preparatory breath. "When I said the thing about his only looking like Rembrandt to me, he shook his head and said, 'No, Mr. Morris, you did not look at me because you were merely thinking I looked like the Rembrandt about whom you have heard and whose works you have appreciated. You forget

I am a painter who understands what people are thinking, what they are seeing. That is my forte. That is I how I earned my reputation. And why I held on to it – from what I can tell when I watch people at the Metropolitan and the Frick study my paintings.

"I can discern the difference between you and the people in Times Square who think it is comical when I draw them and then sign my name. They have a genuine Rembrandt, but they will never know it. For you it is different. You looked at me and continued looking at me, because you recognized me. You did think I was Rembrandt. You did not know how it could be true, but you knew somehow it was. It is. You realize the man standing before you now is Rembrandt van Rijn of Amsterdam, formerly of Leiden.'

"Again I was speechless. He said, 'You do not speak, because you can not bring yourself to deny what I say. Then he said, and the hair on my arms rises every time I think of it, 'Of course, there is only one way I can prove to you who I am beyond a doubt. I must paint your portrait. No one but Rembrandt can paint a Rembrandt portrait. The apprentice painters in my studio try to paint like me. They come close, yes, but not one of them paints as I do. Not one of them understands the human psyche as I do. When I apply paint to a canvas, I am not applying paint. I am empathizing with my brush. So,' he said and pointed to the chair in front of the black curtain, 'if you will please sit down, I will paint your portrait.'"

"What could I do?" Cleve said. "I sat down."

At that moment, something strange came over me. I recognized that I better believe everything Cleve was saying. As I allowed myself to buy into his reality – the reality of unreality – I suddenly felt aware of my whole body. It was as if my body were suspended an inch or two above the sofa – not pressing into it.

Cleve was looking at me as if he knew precisely what I was experiencing. Then he turned around to look at the portrait, which I took to be a signal I could examine it again. I did and again was astonished at how much it appeared to have been painted by Rembrandt, the Rembrandt whom any number of art historians designate the greatest Western painter who ever lived – or who is, at the least, irrevocably established among the top five.

"You sat down," I said, "and a man whom you truly believe is the reborn Rembrandt dashed off this portrait of you?"

"No," Cleve said with a certain amount of impatience. "He didn't 'dash off' a portrait. That's not how Rembrandt works."

"Oh, it isn't, is it?"

"No. He takes his time. He requires many sittings."

"You mean to tell me, you made more than one visit to his studio."

"Seventeen."

"Seventeen? Over what period of time?"

"Over nine weeks – pretty much twice a week for nine weeks."

"You're telling me you sat for Rembrandt seventeen times."

"Absolutely. He's not an Impressionist who does some sort of fast daubing – wham-blur-thank-you-sir, and that's it. This is Rembrandt we're talking about. He takes his time. He gets it right. I don't have to tell you. You've seen the evidence. You've seen the paintings."

Well, yes, I had seen Rembrandt paintings – at a number of museums in the states and abroad. Even in Rembrandt's Amsterdam home, now that I think of it. But Cleve's adamant comments made me take stock. Here I was, on his sofa and listening to him tell me how Rembrandt van Rijn went about his work. Not an everyday occurrence by any stretch of the imagination.

Cleve picked up where he'd left off. "For Rembrandt, painting is painstaking. It's very slow. He likes to get everything right the first time.

And there are all those layers."

"You had to sit absolutely still for seventeen sittings?" I asked.

"Oh, no. I could move. I could talk. He likes to get you talking. I know now that's how he gets all the feeling on the canvas. And he talks, too."

"What did you talk about?"

"We talked about him and me. He wanted to find out who I am, and I told him."

"You talked about yourself." I'd never known Cleve to be one for talking about himself.

"Why not? This was Rembrandt. The greatest portraitist in the history of art, and he was painting my portrait. I wasn't going to make it hard for him."

"What did you tell him?"

"Funny you should ask," Cleve said. His good-looking features relaxed. "I told him things I never told anyone."

I leaped at that one. "Like what?"

"Like things I'll tell you next time you paint my portrait."

"*Touché*!"

"You can say that again," Cleve said. "But you've seen the self-portraits. You know how disarming those eyes are and the round cheeks. If you want to know how Rembrandt got his results, I'm telling you. He listens to you when you talk. 'Tell me more about that,' he'll say, and you tell him. Leastways, I did. I told him things about my childhood I thought I'd forgotten. I told him about work. He got me to admit I like what I do. He got me to admit I'm good at it. I've never said that to anyone."

That was true enough. Cleve had never told me he liked running The Cleve Morris Agency. He'd always made it seem as if the agency was something he did because he didn't have the gumption to do something he'd rather be doing. Come to think of it, I'd always imagined a life for him as a writer or producer and suddenly realized that was presumptuous of me.

"And all the while," he went on, "Rembrandt is painting and muttering every once in a while about 'oils' and 'gesso' and 'egg tempera' and then looking at you with those black eyes of his and then looking back at what he's doing. You wonder what he's seeing. He's so empathetic, you begin to drop whatever defenses you've put up consciously or unconsciously."

I couldn't contain my next remark. "Put up defenses? You, Cleve?"

"As if you don't," he countered. "But he has another fail-safe tactic, old Rembrandt does. He tells you about himself. Or maybe it isn't a tactic. Maybe he needs to talk. I suppose I would also need to talk if I were a couple of thousand miles and three and a half centuries away from home. You know, as long as I work with world-class athletes, I remain astonished that for all they do, it doesn't mitigate against unhappiness, depression, despair and steroids. And now I'm having my portrait painted by Rembrandt, and he has more tales of woe than I've ever heard.

"Saskia, his child bride, dies at 30. When he talks about her, she's already been dead for eighteen years – and three hundred and sixty-plus years. But he's not over her death yet. You should see how his eyes well up. The truth is, he didn't need to paint my portrait to convince me he's Rembrandt. He only had to talk about Saskia to me. How much he loved her when they married and she was only sixteen. How he dressed her up as Flora – the portrait is in London's National Gallery, in case you didn't know – because he, quotes, saw her as eternal spring, end quote. She proved not to be eternal, though. He was so moved when he described how she died that I was almost embarrassed to look at him. My heart went out to him."

Something crossed my mind that should have crossed it much sooner, even if I'd come over to his side.

"Cleve, what you're telling me is all well and good, but anyone could look the information up in a good Rembrandt biography."

"I thought the same thing, but you didn't hear the way his voice broke when he talked about Saskia on her death bed. No one is that good an actor. The same when he talked about their son, Titus. He's estranged from him now – I mean, then. And things just get worse. He declares bankruptcy in 1658. Did you know that? I didn't. He thinks that's why he's landed here. He's bankrupt. He feels he's in some kind of disgrace. He doesn't think he's appreciated by the Dutch bourgeoisie who have been his subjects since he left Leiden for Amsterdam in 1631. This is Rembrandt, mind you. Those people scoffing at him never had it so good. No one anywhere ever had it so good as having Rembrandt for your neighborhood portraitist. Hendrickje Stoeffels, the woman in his life, isn't well. He's fifty-four and beginning to feel his age.

"Think of it. You've seen the late portraits – the ones he paints when he's older than he is when he's living on Prince Street. Would you say they're the portraits of a man who's only sixty-three? Never. He looks like a man in his seventies, at least. Yet, he was only sixty-three when he died. The first time."

While Cleve was talking, something occurred to me. I was thinking about how he'd described the Prince Street studio. I was fixing on the costume rack. "May I ask you a question," I said.

"Not yet," Cleve said, "I just wanted to say that with all his travails, it wasn't surprising that Rembrandt wished he were somewhere else. He wanted out, and he got out, didn't he? I'm here to attest to that. Now what did you want to know?"

"You said he has a rack of what looked like costumes."

"That's right," Cleve said. "Sometimes he put on a funny hat to paint in – or a fur-lined cape, which he'd wear until he decided it was hampering his movements."

"But in your portrait you're just wearing street clothes," I said. "Did he ever suggest that you wear one of those Hallowe'en get-ups?"

"I asked about that. He said my street clothes were costume enough for him. Everything everyone wore in the twenty-first century looked odd to him."

"What about painting himself in modern gear?" I asked.

"He wasn't interested," Cleve said. "He did a few self-etchings, though. Did I mention there were tools for etching among his paraphernalia?"

"Were the etchings gloomy?" I wanted to know. "Was he always gloomy?"

"Oh, no," Cleve said, brightening right up. "When he talked about the low country – he called it the low country; I don't think I ever heard him say 'Holland' or 'The Netherlands' – he was very animated. He could even be funny. He told a very funny joke about Peter Minuit buying Manhattan for twenty-four dollars. Apparently, it was an old joke, but I'd never heard it, of course. Peter Minuit buys Manhattan for twenty-four dollars, and the news reaches the royal court. When the monarch hears it, he shouts, 'Twenty-four dollars! Minuit never could drive a hard bargain.'

"A laugh riot," I said.

"I thought it was funny," Cleve said. "He was also amusing the day we went to the Met."

"You went to the Met. With Rembrandt."

"The only time we did anything together outside his studio. He'd already been there a number of times but always to look at his own work. He said he'd like to go at least once to look closely at what other painters had done – painters who came after him, as you might imagine. He already knew Giotto and Duccio and Leonardo da Vinci and Titian. He knew about Velázquez, although he hadn't seen much. He didn't want to look at Rubens and called Anthony van Dyke an upstart, although he allowed as how he had talent. You know what really impressed him?"

"No," I said, "I don't."

"The Impressionists – no pun intended. He liked Manet and Monet. He liked Cézanne, although he thought the landscapes were too cerebral. 'He paints too often with his head and not his heart, this Cézanne,' he said. When he got to the van Goghs, he stood before each one for a long time, saying nothing. When he walked away from the last one, he finally spoke. 'Here is a painter,' he said. Then he said it again. 'Here is a painter. And he's from the low country!'

"By the time we left, he said he had learned a great deal. He wasn't convinced by the changes in how colors were used – he preferred ochre, red – but he liked what he saw painters influenced by him were doing with form. What I find fascinating is, if you look at the work he did after 1660, his colors become much more muted but his brush strokes are broader, looser. Look closely at some of them, and they are practically abstract. You're going to tell me he wasn't applying then what he learned here now? Don't. And I was privy to it all.'"

"All right, all right," I said. "I believe you. Rembrandt and you are not only painter and subject. You're friends. You're pals. You're bosom buddies. Given that, when do you introduce me to him? How soon do I get to meet him?"

When I asked that, a figurative cloud came over Cleve. His dark eyes darkened further. "That's just it," he said. "You don't get to meet him. And before you jump to any conclusions about my not thinking you're good enough to meet him, let me say you are good enough. The problem is, he's not here to meet any longer."

"Not here," I said, sounding more miffed than I'd intended to sound –

sounding as if I'd gone along with the entire tale and was now cut off from what was only my due after lending credence to it.

I said before I could stop myself, "You get me over here to dangle a rendez-vous with the real Rembrandt van Rijn before me only to say he's no longer on the premises?"

"Sorry," Cleve said. "But that's the way things are. He's disappeared. He's gone."

I was crestfallen. My chance to meet Rembrandt, and I'd lost it.

"Where is he?" I asked with more than a twinge of dismay.

"I don't know," Cleve said. "He finished the portrait last Wednesday. Or almost finished it. As I left the final sitting, he said he wanted to look at it, perhaps make a few adjustments, let it dry. I could pick it up the next day. On Thursday I went down to Prince Street to collect it. He showed it to me. Not to get my approval, you understand. It pleased him, and that was all that mattered. He wrapped it in brown paper, handed it to me and showed me to the door.

"It's not as if we said goodbye. We didn't. We even made plans to get together on the weekend. He hadn't had much Dutch cuisine since he'd arrived, but he'd heard of a restaurant he wanted to try in Brooklyn. Breukelen, he called it. I said that sounded like a plan to me and reached in my breast pocket for my check book. When I pulled it out, he took it, placed it back in the pocket and patted my chest. He said he wouldn't accept payment, couldn't accept payment. I'd done him the favor of believing who he was and therefore enabling him to believe in himself. He said that was a gesture on which it's impossible to put a value.

"So I left. But I felt I had to thank him in some way. I thought flowers – tulips. To remind him of home. Maybe they would inspire him to do a still life with tulips. It's not tulip weather, of course, but I know Rennie Reynolds, and I knew if there were any way to get tulips, he could do it.

He could, and Friday I went down to 37 Prince Street with a bouquet of two dozen yellow and white tulips. I went to press the button for 4D, but there was no button for 4D. I looked at the set of buttons and noticed for the first time that none of the floors have a D apartment – only A, B and C.

"While I'm taking this in, a tall blonde woman came up behind me with a key poised. I asked her about apartment 4D. She looked at me askance. She said she keeps a studio in 4A, and as far as she knew, there is no 4D. There never was. I think she thought I was a masher. I asked her if she'd recently seen a medium-sized man with curly hair under a large beret-like cap going in and out of the building. 'He looks like Rembrandt,' I said. I didn't want to say he is Rembrandt. She was suspicious enough already.

"'No,' she said. 'Nobody of that description has lived in the building for as long as I' ve been there, which is twelve years.' What could I say to that? If I insisted I'd been in 4D many times with a man who looked exactly like Rembrandt, she would only have thought I was crazy and might have run screaming from me or pressed an app on her smartphone to summon the cops. So I left – with the two dozen tulips."

He pointed to the large, square glass vase across the room to the left side of the Fischl. "There they are," he said.

There they were, at the moment looking especially triumphant. Cleve said, "I thought I might take them to the Met and place them under one of the Rembrandt self-portraits, but I didn't see them letting me carry a large bouquet up to the Rembrandt room, no matter what story I gave them."

With that, Cleve let go a large sigh and sank back in the sofa. It was as if he'd had a heavy burden lifted from his shoulders. I suppose he had. When he'd collected himself, he did something I'd never seen him do in all the years I'd known him: He smiled at me with as open a smile as you can imagine. There was nothing in it of melancholy momentarily suppressed, nothing in it suggesting a profound awareness of ultimate letdown. Turning from me, he looked at the portrait. His smile widened.

Cleve was happy. I'm not sure Irene Benjamin Morris would be entirely pleased to know she has a happy child. But I thought it was a good sign.

"You've seen the portrait, and you've heard the story," Cleve said. "If you want, you can leave now."

As things were going, there really was nothing for me to do but exit. I rose, and Cleve saw me to the door. Where he did something else I had never known him to do – with me, anyhow. He hugged me. As he did, he said, "You know you're invited to see the portrait whenever you want."

I said I knew I was and headed for the elevator as he started to close the door behind him.

"One more thing," he called after me.

I turned.

He was framed in the door, looking as I'd seen him when I arrived. "They say that every portrait a painter paints is a self-portrait. If that's true, then I not only have a portrait of myself by Rembrandt, I have a Rembrandt self-portrait."

With that he closed the door, and I pushed the elevator call button. While I waited, I thought about what had just occurred. Frankly, I wasn't sure what to make of it. I couldn't imagine who would be sure. I knew I wanted to believe everything Cleve so obviously believed. It would mean believing in a miracle.

What else could you call a portrait by Rembrandt painted in the present day? But was I ready to commit to such a belief? Put another way, was I ready to believe my eyes? Shouldn't we all be less disposed to be cynical about our surroundings?

All right, I thought, maybe I can – and do – believe in miracles, maybe I can lend credence to Cleve's story, given the portrait he's got to show for it. But for those who can't, perhaps I can draw a moral lesson here – perhaps I can draw a few.

Moral lesson one: When people tell you who and what they are, it might be a good idea to believe them. They could be telling the truth, and unexpected results could come of it.

Moral lesson two: When you're riding a New York City bus, you shouldn't ignore the people around you, because you never know whom you could have the good fortune to meet.

Duck! Here comes Diane Arbus!

"Duck! Here comes Diane Arbus!"

Charley Devin was speaking, and I was doing a good job of keeping my promise not to laugh. It so happens that until that line, I hadn't been challenged. The "Duck! Here comes..!" exclamation, however, was too much temptation, and I broke the vow. Shattered it. I tried to hold things to a smile, as a good friend should. Or at worst to a titter. Maybe venture as far as a sotto voce giggle. But no dice. I had to let go with a full-out guffaw that struck me and very possibly him as if it were bouncing off the nearby buildings with all the vibrating echo of a hard rubber ball.

Dismay spliced with anger shanghaied Charley's expression. His fleshy face turned a piquant shade of red. "You think it's funny, but it's not," he said and momentarily fell silent.

Attempting to recover my composure, I said, "I'm laughing but not because it's funny."

Feeble recovery, I know.

The setting: Madison Square Park, where we habitually did a lot of our breeze-shooting. Charley was seated on a weathered bench and in the closest thing to a panic I'd ever seen him. And I'd seen him close to panics on many occasions.

On the phone he'd said he was calling from the street outside the Metropolitan Museum of Art and needed to meet me downtown for a talk. He'd declared as much any number of times but never in that audibly shaky way. I could usually imagine how his face looked from the tenor of his remarks, I knew him that well. But this time, I couldn't, and it wasn't just the cell phone static. So I said I'd drop what I was doing – balancing my checkbook, actually, and relieved to be excused from it – and join him in fifteen.

This, by the way, was late-ish on an early spring afternoon when the trees are still a matte celadon and the tulips are trumpeting.

Charley beat me there. As I approached him from the side, he was looking down with his heavy arms resting on his thighs, thick hands and fingers drooping like melting stalactites. He seemed to be examining the ground – for what I couldn't imagine. When I said hello, he reacted as if I'd threatened to rob him.

"Oh, it's you," he said.

"Whom were you expecting?" I asked.

"No one. You. You just startled me." He certainly looked startled. His onyx eyes were blank, as if mammoth steel doors behind them had slammed shut. His eyebrows, which had always been florid, sagged like tired black-and-white bunting.

Some people would consider Charley good-looking in a rugged, unconventional manner; others would not. I remain on the fence. His wardrobe never helps the image, since he dresses as if the concept of fashion escapes him entirely. Were Charley ever to be confronted with an issue of

GQ, he'd have to have it explained to him. If Charley knew about matching colors, he kept it to himself. He only owned three ties. He'd told me so with a certain amount of pride.

It's been a while, so maybe he's come by a couple more. If so, I haven't seen them. At the moment he was wearing a familiar one, and it, too, was as droopy as Harpo's trousers. His own trousers, which were also familiar, could have been Harpo hand-me-downs.

"Sorry I roused you from your stupor," I said.

"No time for amenities," Charley countered before I even had time to sit down next to him. He resumed scrutinizing the cracked concrete in front of the bench.

"What's up, then?" I asked.

That's when he said, "You have to promise not to laugh," and I said, with the solemnity I realized was required, "I promise. Absolutely."

(Unbeknownst to him, I slotted in an internal query that went, "Why do so many of my friends tell me things I'm not supposed to laugh at?")

"No," he said, turning to look me in the eye(s), "I mean, really."

"I promise," I said.

This was sounding a little high school to me, which was a bit much for two people significantly past high school age. But I went along with it. In my experience, it's a small coterie of men who completely mature beyond late adolescence – or early adolescence – and I wasn't convinced either Charley or I were among them. I remember André Malraux once writing something along the same lines about the men he knew, and I figure, who am I to one-up Malraux, whom I'm not ready to abandon as a culture hero even if the years have not been kind to his memory?

But I digress.

"I promise. I promise," I added, "I won't laugh."

"All right then," Charley said. "I'll tell you why I called." He shifted his ham-like extremities into news-conveying mode. "Do you remember me ever mentioning a guy named Hartley Warner?"

"I can't say I do."

"Hart Warner?"

"I don't know. Maybe." I was stretching for the sake of politeness. I'd never heard the name; if I had, I'd forgotten it.

"Maybe I haven't," Charley said. "I don't think about him much any more. I probably haven't seen him in twenty-five years. He was someone I was chummy with when I first came to Manhattan."

Suddenly, a little light came into Charley's eyes. I could tell it was shining on a memory. "We'd been at school together. Not Princeton. Exeter. And shortly after I moved into Manhattan, I bumped into him again. He suggested we get together, and I said, 'Why not?' The thing about Hart is he had these great connections. Those were the days when I believed connections meant something. Well, they do, but not what I thought they meant then.

"Hart knew everybody. Or if he didn't know somebody personally, he knew someone who did. He certainly knew whatever there was to know about everybody – everybody who was considered anybody. His family was the Warner family. You know."

"Oh, yes," I mumbled. "Sure." I had no idea who the Warner family is or was. Nevertheless, this was the patch of back-story through which I was successfully keeping a straight face.

"It didn't matter what field people were in, Hart knew about them," Charley barreled on. "You sure I never mentioned him? Tall guy, well-built, rowed on the Princeton crew?"

Now I knew I'd never heard about him. The Princeton crew? I'd have remembered. "You knew someone who rowed on the crew," I said to Charley. "I would have thought that was about the last kind of person you'd know."

"He was in my entry all four years. I never saw him row. I just saw him carrying an oar around every once in a while."

"How Ivy," I said.

"Yeah," Charley said, annoyed, I could tell, that we had gotten off the immediate subject. "Anyway," he said, putting much shoulder into the "anyway," "Hart knew scientists, lawyers, entertainment people, corporate moguls, editors and reporters, artists. He knew who was hot and who was not."

"Good friend to have," I said as a way of indicating I was still with him.

"You'd think so, wouldn't you? But in some cases – like what I'm about to tell you – you'd be wrong. We're now talking the mid-Sixties. This was about the time Diane Arbus was making a name for herself. You know who she is, right? Or was? She died in 1971 – took her own life."

"Yes," I said, "I know who she is. Who doesn't?"

"Right. Who doesn't?" Charley said. "Now. Back then I wouldn't have said she was a household name."

"She probably isn't a household name today."

"You know what I'm saying. She's a household name in the households you and I know."

Why argue? "Point taken."

"Back then she wasn't," he went on. "A lot of people didn't know about her and her bizarre photographs of the everyday weird. Ordinary, everyday people photographed in their homes or on their lawns or in the great outdoors who she somehow gets to look like inmates at a lunatic asylum. I, for one, didn't know about her, and that's what I'm getting to."

He put his fists on his thighs, like a football coach about to give his losing team half-time what-for. "I was with Hart Warner in Central Park one spring afternoon in 1966 – sitting around like we are now – talking about nothing in particular. And suddenly he turns a different color. Hart, who was a kind of Ur-WASP, was fair-skinned. But he almost always had a tan. Summers in the Hamptons, winters in Antibes or Majorca, wherever. So he usually was brown as a Bosc pear. But suddenly he went – not white, really, but a paler shade of Bosc. Are you with me so far?"

"Yes," I said, sensing Charley's urgent whatever was about to be revealed.

"I was just going to ask him if something is wrong, when he says – and this is the important part – 'Duck! Here comes Diane Arbus!'"

That's when I lose it, when we have our little exchange about the comment not being funny. That's when Charley regains his verbal footing and throws me a warning glare. "Hart recognizes her, you see, but I don't. He knows her. I'd never even heard her name. Not that I'm aware of. He says, 'Don't look now.' But it's too late. I'd already turned in the direction he'd been facing.

"I see a short, thin, dark-haired woman – short-cropped hair – coming our way wearing a sleeveless white blouse and dark pedal pushers and flats, you know, like ballerina shoes or, you know. She's carrying something in her right hand that could be a camera. It is a camera. I turn back to Hart, who's now facing away from me. And her.

"'Who is Diane Arbus?' I say. Hart doesn't move. 'Is she still heading in this direction?' he says. I look her way, and she is. She's about ten feet off. 'Yes,' I say. 'No time to explain,' he says. Hart still isn't moving. 'Whatever you do, don't look at her,' he says. But that's the wrong thing to say to me, because all it does is make me want to look. I do. She's practically on top of me. Except she isn't looking at me. She's looking at Hart."

Charley stops there to let the whatever-you-do-don't-look-at-her sink in. I let it sink in as far as it was going to sink, which wasn't that far.

"And?" I said.

"That's right. '*And*.'" Charley says. "And..." He puts the spoken ampersand into verbal italics. "...that's when she says to him, 'Hart?' Hart turns towards her, as if he's completely surprised to see her, and says, 'Diane. Hello. Fancy meeting you here.' That's what he says, 'Fancy meeting you here,' blithe as a chorus girl greeting a stage-door Johnny she knows is carrying a diamond choker to give her. She says, 'I haven't seen you since my opening.' Charley says, 'No, that's right. Quite an opening it was, too. *Le tout* New York.'

"That's when he brings me into the conversation. 'Diane, this is my friend, Charley Devin. Charley, Diane Arbus, the photographer.' He says 'the photographer,' not 'a photographer,' as if I'm supposed to know who she is. At that, she shifts the camera from her right hand to her left and puts her right hand out for me to shake. Which I do, and say – as God is my witness – 'Oh, a photographer? You out here photographing?' I'm trying to be courteous, because I'm still wondering what she's done that had Hart so eager to avoid her. And she says, 'Yes, I am. I'm in Central Park often.' Then she says, 'Why don't I take a picture of you two?'"

"She didn't!" I said to Charley.

"She did."

I had the urge to laugh again, but this time I suppressed it."And you had no idea who she was?"

"I didn't know her from Adam."

"Diane Arbus – and you didn't know who she was."

Charley looked at me as if I were the enemy. His eyes were flashing ooga-booga signals. "I hadn't been in the City for a year yet. I wasn't interested in the arts. I hadn't stepped inside a museum. Unless you consider Yankee Stadium a museum. The way they're playing so far this year, you could."

"But in the mid-Sixties Diane Arbus was getting attention," I said. "She was flavor of the month. Her photographs were being reproduced in magazines. *Life, Time*."

I could see my confrontational mode wasn't going down well with Charley. "Maybe I'd seen the photographs," he said, "but I hadn't remembered the name. If I had, it hadn't registered. To me photographs were what my mother took with a Brownie. Who knew they were art?"

Good old Charley. His field was ancient Middle East history; it was really all that interested him. He'd written his dissertation on some aspect of the Dead Sea Scrolls. Since there were no photographs in the Dead Sea Scrolls, he could be forgiven for not knowing in 1966 what the camera had wrought.

I said, "I think I've got the picture. So to speak. Diane Arbus offered to photograph you, and your friend Hart said no, because he knew who she was. He knew the kind of pictures she took and what she did with them."

Charley shifted uncomfortably. "That's right. Hart said no."

"And you agreed with him, because you figured he had his reasons." I said, knowing full well I was as off the track as Wrong-way Corrigan.

"Not exactly," Charley said.

"You agreed to have Diane Arbus take your picture." Charley gave a nod that wasn't as good as a wink. It was a mini-nod, an almost-but-not-quite nod.

I'd always liked Charley. As long as I'd known him – which must have been about 20 years by then – he's been a curmudgeon, but a likeable curmudgeon. He looked menacing but was harmless. Now I knew that the hunch I had while heading to meet him was correct: Charley would have something to tell me worth hearing.

"Why shouldn't I say yes to her offer? I had no idea what Hart was trying to get across, and she looked like a perfectly ordinary person. She liked taking pictures of people in Central Park. It sounded like a nice pastime for her. When she had finished with us, I imagined her heading towards the carousel to take pictures of kids waving for their parents to show off."

"So you said yes."

Charley nodded again, giving it a mite more energy this time.

"And Hart Warner did what? Stood aside while Diane Arbus snapped away at you?"

"She wouldn't let him stand aside. Looking back on it now, I can say she knew exactly why he'd said no. So she coaxed him into joining me. He couldn't continue to refuse, because if she asked why, he'd have to say. He couldn't do that. Manners, you know. Hart had been raised to do the right thing. It was deeply embedded in his DNA. Hurting someone's feelings was *verboten*. So he acquiesced.

"'How about over by that tree?' she said, pointing to a nearby oak. 'Why don't we just sit here?' Hart said. That was as far as he'd go to resist her. 'The light's better over there for my purposes,' she said. Maybe the 'my purposes' should have been some kind of tip-off to me, but it wasn't.

"So we picked ourselves up and stood where she was pointing, but I knew Hart enough to realize something was wrong. His walk gave him away. Normally, he strode around as if he owned the place. A lot of places he did own, by the way. But he was walking as if he was approaching the gallows. For the life of me, I couldn't figure out why. Far as I knew we were just having our picture taken by someone who was evidently getting something of a reputation for taking pictures. She had to be good, right?"

"So you had your picture taken by Diane Arbus," I said. "What was that like?"

"What was it like? It was like nothing. Hart and I stood by the tree. She directed us this way and that. Move a few inches to the right, a few inches to the left. We did as told."

"What did she say?" I asked. "Enquiring minds want to know."

"Not much," Charley said. "Mostly, she was concentrating. She asked Hart about his brother. Brad, his name was. She asked about a few people they knew that I didn't."

"Did she say, 'Say, "cheese"?'"

This rankled. "No, she didn't say, 'Say, "cheese."' She didn't need to. I figured I'd give her a smile. That's what you do when you're having your picture taken in the park, right? But when I did, she said there was no need to do that. I should just be myself. So I did what I thought being myself was, and I think Hart was doing the same, although I could sense he continued not to be thrilled with any of this. I couldn't understand why, because at school he was always sitting for team sport pictures."

"And then what happened? Did she just take the one picture? I'm interested in Arbus's process."

Charley wasn't going to dignify that remark with a lengthy reply. "I don't know. She took a couple pictures, near as I could tell. People were walking by. Dogs were smelling the grass for places to piss. She was snapping photos. It was like any other day in the park. When she was done, she told Hart it was nice to run into him and he should say hello to Brad and to so-and-so and so-and-so, and then she said she needed to move on, and she went."

"Then what?"

"Then Hart told me who Diane Arbus was and why he thought letting her take our picture wasn't the smartest thing in the world. Let's just say, he filled me in."

"So Diane Arbus took your picture. I've heard of worse fates," I said.

"Easy for you to say," Charley said.

"Maybe she never developed it," I said, knowing as I said it that if Diane Arbus had never developed the roll of film, there would be no reason for our sitting together on a sumptuous afternoon that was beginning to feel as if it were there merely to mock Charley.

"I'm getting to that." Charley said. "That's why I called you. She developed it, all right." He let the sentence float in the air.

"I'll bite," I said. "When did she show it to you?"

"She never showed it to me."

"Then what's the problem? Did you ever even see it?" I knew as I said this that I was dealing in quasi-rhetorical questions: There had to be a problem; Charley had to have seen the photograph – or, at the very least, had to have heard about it.

"Yes, I've seen it," Charley said.

I was about to ask when, but Charley beat me to it. "About an hour ago."

"Don't tell me," I said. "You saw it in the Arbus exhibit at the Met."

"You knew about this?" Charley asked.

"Sure," I said, "I know about the exhibit. It's gotten plenty of press."

"I don't follow the arts press," Charley says. "You know me. I'm still not much of a museum-goer."

"But you went today."

"I went today, because I had a call from Carole Restow." I knew about Charley's friend Carole, although I'd never met her. "She called me late this morning to ask whether I was the guy in the photograph, because it looked a lot like me. Like what I might have looked like years ago. She didn't know me then. And I said, 'What photo?' And she said, 'The photo in the Diane Arbus exhibit.'"

"And you said, 'What Diane Arbus exhibit?'"

"That's right, because to tell you the truth, I'd practically forgotten about Diane Arbus. Hart Warner had carried on about her that afternoon

– telling me I should never have agreed to be photographed. He'd even dragged me to a bookstore to look at some of her pictures. I saw what he meant. The pictures of young girls looking deluded – or Qualuuded. Young boys looking demented.

"On the other hand, I knew I wasn't demented. That's what I said to Hart. He said I didn't understand. Arbus could and did make anyone she came into contact with look like a candidate for the loony bin. I remember him saying she could make Grace Kelly look like Lizzie Borden."

"You didn't believe him."

"Not really," Charley said. "I thought, What the hell. Diane Arbus took a picture of me. So what? Hart said, 'Wait until you see the picture. You'll know what I'm talking about.' But I never did see the picture. I forgot about it. I didn't see Hart, either. Not long after that he went to California. One of his Hollywood chums said there was a part for him in a movie. He'd never acted, but that wasn't going to stop him. Or them. Apparently, when he got out there, he took a gander at the movie biz, didn't like it, begged off his screen test and started buying real estate instead. I hear he owns a lot of Orange County now. So that was that. Until today."

Reminiscing about Hart Warner and his escapades, Charley had lightened up. Not that his craggy face ever took on the aspect of a day at the beach. But now the storm clouds rolled back in. "You're always in museums," he said to me, as if he were accusing me of a major crime. "You haven't seen this exhibit? Or you have, and you're just sparing my feelings."

"I don't see everything," I said by way of defending myself. "I mean to see this one, but I haven't gotten around to it yet. I take it your friend Carole was right when she thought she recognized you. You might as well tell me what I'm going to see."

"She recognized me, all right," Charley said and put his heavy head into his heavy hands. I waited. “You got to understand, this exhibit is huge. I can’t tell you how many photographs are in it. It seemed like thousands. Rooms of them.”

“There you go,” I said, intending to be positive. “Too many for everyone to take in.”

“Don’t try to make me feel better,” Charley said.

“I thought that’s why I’m here,” I said. “Something’s upset you, and I’m supposed to talk you through it.”

“I’ll never get over this,” Charley said. With that, he stood up and produced a paper bag he’d been sitting on. It had the Metropolitan Museum of Art logo on it. I could tell there was some sort of book inside. “You’ll see what I’m talking about,” he said as he removed the bag’s contents. “The catalogue.” He held it aloft as a guerrilla might hold up a rifle at a rally. “See this,” he said, sitting down and paging furiously through the book which had on its cover Arbus’s famous photograph of identical twins looking as if they’d been drugged and then abused by unseen parents. “Where is it, where is it? It’s towards the back.” He dragged out the last sentence in his guttural tones. “Ah-hah! Look at this.”

He regarded me expectantly, as if he were waiting for me to do something I didn’t understand I was to do. The penny dropped. He wanted me to uncross my legs, straighten up and make a flat lap. I did as tacitly bid. He set the catalogue down, held the left side with one hand and with the pudgy index finger of his left hand pointed at the lone photograph on the right page. “Now do you see what I mean? Huh? Huh?” Quick as he indicated the picture, he turned away. “You look at it. I can’t.”

I could; I knew I must. It was in large part why I was there. So I applied myself.

What I saw in the black-and-white parallel world Arbus had made her own was two young men standing in front of a tree. An oak tree, as advertised. One of the men was tall and blonde; the other was medium-sized and heavy. They both looked awkward, as if they'd been caught doing something they oughtn't be doing. The taller one, whom I took to be Hartley Warner, was on the left and was looking off to the left. Because of the way he was gazing, he seemed slightly cross-eyed. His sneer made him appear as if he were aiming for nonchalance but failing badly. He was wearing a short-sleeved, striped jersey and had his arms folded over his chest. He also wore pressed khaki trousers, but his left pant leg was caught in his sock. It was hiked up inadvertently, that was clear. The overall effect was upper-class superciliousness. For him, the photograph amounted to a caustic statement on male swagger.

The heavy, medium-sized one – Charley – had a large Jewish afro, sloping shoulders and arms that seemed longer than his legs. If Charley, in a shapeless denim jacket and shapeless denim jeans and patterned scarf knotted around his neck and dangling over his bare chest and belly, had been trying to accommodate Arbus's request to be himself, the result fell short of the intention. He looked as if he had no idea who he was – or where he was. She'd caught him looking directly at the camera as if he were about to ask for a hand-out or directions to the nearest homeless shelter.

An eerie aspect of the dreaded snapshot was that not less than a few minutes before, I had seen an expression on his face not unlike the one Arbus captured for all time – the hanging full lower lip, the eyes like a cornered animal. If Arbus had ventured upon a lost tribe somewhere in a darker continent and gestured for one of its members to pose for her, she would likely have prompted the same apprehensive gaze.

The caption under the photograph read as follows: "Two Men Friends, NYC (1966)."

The caption was misleading, however, because in addition to Hartley

Warner and Charley there was someone else in the photograph. Approximately seven or eight feet behind them to the right was a toddler in a soiled shirt and bib and what looked like a full diaper. The tow-headed boy, who was peering quizzically at the two men, had his thumb in his mouth. Reaching in from the right side of the photograph was a disembodied arm. Perhaps it belonged to a mother running to snatch her toddler away from the action. If so, she hadn't arrived speedily enough to keep her child from serving as unwanted commentary: It was as if what he was witnessing dumbfounded him. The child's presence raised the level of the photograph from grim to devastating.

"You're not saying anything," Charley said when he decided I'd remained quiet for too long.

"What do you want me to say?" I replied, "That it's a good likeness? That it's not a good likeness?"

"You don't have to say anything," Charley said, "I've heard enough smart remarks already."

I must have arched an eyebrow, because Charley raised his voice and said, "Oh, yes. Oh, yes. I haven't gotten to that part yet – the part where I listen to what people say about Hart and me. That's right, Danny. I found the photograph only after looking at hundreds of examples of Diane Arbus's art. Carole hadn't told me it was in one of the larger rooms towards the end. And when I walked into the room, I knew the instant I spotted the photograph that it was me – is me. I knew from fifteen feet away. Hart Warner and me, forever linked. Two men friends placed between a photo of four world-weary swells at a fancy ball they now probably wish they'd never bought a table for and a photo of three sisters sitting on a bed in communion outfits and looking like a recessive-gene festival.

"After I got to this large square room with what? – sixty photographs arranged in a line around the four walls, I took a good long look at myself nearly forty years ago. Then I stepped back while other people – the lucky ones who'd been spared Diane Arbus's attention – filed past."

"Did you overhear anything worth hearing?" I asked.

"Depends on what you mean by 'worth hearing.' Is 'Look at these two saps!' worth hearing? Because I heard it." I tried not to react. How about 'That baby sucking his thumb has the right idea'? My favorite were the five school girls in short skirts and showing their *pupiks* the way all school girls do today – uniforms or no uniforms. They remained quiet as they passed the photographs on the way to mine but completely broke up when they saw me and Hart. They never said a word – just gales of laughter.

"This went on for minutes. Every time they seemed about to pull themselves together, one of them would point at the picture, and they'd all three collapse again. Holding each other up, putting their hands over their mouths to stop themselves. There's more, if you want to hear it."

"How much more?" I said. "How long did you stand there?" I had to agree with Charley that the Arbus photograph was not, um, flattering. But I didn't want to put it in so many words. I could tell he wanted me to agree with him about it, yet also to disagree. I was in a lose-lose situation. I didn't want to mention his vigil was masochistic, but it was.

"I was there for about fifteen, twenty minutes."

"That long? Did anyone notice you and connect you with the photograph?"

"I tried to make myself as inconspicuous as I could. So I stood back from the photograph as if I were analyzing it. I kept my hand over my mouth, as if I were serious about the scrutiny. Nobody paid attention to me. Well, there was one young woman, who I think was with her husband or boy friend. When she finished looking at the photograph, she looked over at me. Something registered. As she was walking away, she whispered in the boy friend's ear, and he looked back at me. Then the two of them chuckled. They definitely knew I was the *shlemiel* in the photograph."

"Maybe they were just commenting on the way you seemed to be paying such close attention to it," I said, making a stab at a soothing observation.

"They weren't," Charley said. "They were laughing at me. The whole world is laughing at me."

"Don't be dramatic," I said. "The whole world has not seen Diane Arbus's entire *œuvre*. I've seen plenty of Arbus's photographs, and I've never seen this one." I still had the catalogue on my lap and open to the incriminating page. "It's obscure. And of those who have seen it, most of them have forgotten it. Nobody can retain that much."

"It doesn't matter. I've seen it," Charley said. "And I remember the slogan they used to put above fun-house mirrors. 'See yourself as others see you.' I have seen myself as others see me. The camera doesn't lie."

He paused, obviously giving me an opening to observe that the camera does lie. Or at least the opportunity to say something that skirted a Pollyanna-level reply but was nevertheless comforting. I thought I might expound on Arbus's work being exhilarating – as all genuine art, no matter what the content, is exhilarating. If you could think of it that way. But I knew Charley couldn't.

I thought to say, "Maybe forty years ago you looked like the man Arbus shutterbugged in Central Park, but you've changed, you've matured." But I kept mum, because as the remark was forming in my head, I realized that Charley still looked enough like himself four decades earlier – and knew he did – not to believe me.

It's not that the camera lies. If it did, we'd all be off the hook. It's that at minimum it tells partial truths, and there's the rub: Partial truths can be mistaken for whole truths.

As I sat looking at Charley and he sat looking at the ground inconsolably, I knew nothing I offered would convince him that Arbus had committed a miscarriage of photographic justice. So I changed the subject – clumsily, I'll admit – and shortly thereafter we parted, Charley to go his way, I to go mine.

This all happened only a few months back. Ever since that sullen, stunning afternoon, whenever I arrange to see Charley or bump into him, he finds some point in the conversation to look at me and moan, "The Diane Arbus photograph, the Diane Arbus photograph."

When he says that, what do I say? What can you say to a man who's seen himself as others see him? Or thinks he has and concludes it's not a pretty picture. Literally. What can you say to a man who's been captured for posterity? Who believes he's been trapped for posterity? Who shares with most of us that most dreaded fear – the fear of being found out – and now believes he has been. If that's where he's decided he is – where he's always worried he irrevocably is – here's what you say:

You say nothing.

Stanley Konig writing as Conrad Stamp

i.

"What I'm about to tell you is strictly confidential," my old friend Stanley Konig was saying at the first of two recent lunches we had. He wasn't sitting across from me, as he usually did, but next to me at a ninety-degree angle. I thought it was odd when we'd sat down but hadn't attached too much importance to it.

Initially.

We'd polished off our fancy papaya salads and were waiting for coffee to arrive – his regular, mine decaffeinated. And I was well into thinking there was something curious about the conversation so far. It wasn't the content that raised the red flag – the usual mix of politics, the arts and updates (some of them racy) about mutual friends and acquaintances.

It was the manner in which we were having it. There was something halting in Stanley's delivery, the brief but noticeable pause before he'd respond to a remark or a slightly longer pause before he introduced a subject.

Something was definitely weighing on his mind, and I surmised rightly that the lull between the *entrée* and coffee would be the segment of lunch designated for my being let in on what it was.

(Neither of us ordered dessert after a unison stomach-patting.)

I also sensed that whatever he had to declare was tied in with why he'd chosen the day's uncharacteristic seating arrangement. As he made his statement about confidentiality, he was leaning so closely into me I could smell his after-shave lotion or cologne or whatever the slightly cloying aroma was.

That was a new note, too; so was, it suddenly hit me, his hair-cut, which seemed more – is "shaped" the word?

Other minor alterations in his appearance were kicking in. Stanley was wearing a tweed blazer that looked more expensive than he normally went in for. His shirt and tie looked new as well and decidedly more luxuriant than I was accustomed to seeing on him. He always dressed well – I knew he cared about clothes – but never nattily.

Stanley's appearance now was unmistakably debonair – if anyone is debonair anymore – and so was his affect.

Debonair!

Stanley!

As I was registering these only somewhat perceptible changes – perceptible to me because I knew Stanley a while, but perhaps not perceptible to everyone of his acquaintance – I must have gone quiet, because Stanley repeated himself.

"What I'm about to tell you is strictly confidential."

I still didn't respond; I didn't understand I was expected to. He added, "Or I can't tell you."

"Of course," I said, "strictly confidential" – and added for emphasis,

"Absolutely confidential." I put the 'absolutely' in verbal italics. "Got it."

"I'm not kidding," he said and looked to the right and left and even twisted around in his chair to get a good view of the tables behind him. "Tell me you won't repeat what I'm about to say."

"I won't repeat what you're about to say," I said.

I was getting a bit annoyed. I'm not what you'd call a *bona fide* blabbermouth, and I felt Stanley should know that. If anything, he was the one whose trust was in question. After all, he – not me – was the one who'd written three novels containing barely veiled accounts of the lives, or incidents from the lives, of a number of his friends and family.

The novels had been respectably received by reviewers but had only done so-so at the cash register. But I didn't say as much to Stanley. Instead I said, "How do I know that what you're about to confide so confidentially is even worth repeating?"

That jarred him into rapidly stirring half-and-half into the regular coffee that had been placed in front of him. "Believe me," he said, "when I tell you, you're going to think it's worth repeating." He caught himself. "Only you absolutely must not. Must not repeat it."

"Will you please get on with it?" I said. "Through this entire meal you've been waiting to tell me whatever it is you're going to tell me. Whatever it is has been preoccupying you so much, you've barely been a participant in the conversation. Every time I asked you a question, I've had to supply my own answer."

"You have not."

"Okay," I relented, "it only seems that way, but you have to admit you've had something on your mind you were only biding your time – and wasting mine – until you could get to. So get to it, for pity's sake."

"All right, I'm bringing it up," Stanley said. "In a second." Again, he gazed surreptitiously around, as if he were Aldrich Ames about to slip state secrets to a foreign agent.

Seemingly satisfied for the moment that no one was eavesdropping, he leaned in even closer – giving me another strong whiff of his amusing, expensive scent – and said, or perhaps I should say whisper-hissed, "What do you know about *The Cocksman's Tale*?"

Not whisper-hissing in response, I said, "I know what everyone else knows. It's a giganto best-selling novel, and nobody knows who wrote it. Apart, I suppose, from the author and his – or her – editor."

"Have you read it?" he asked

"I'm ashamed to say I have," I said. "Have you?"

Stanley let that go by but not without giving me a dyspeptic look. He pressed on. "What did you think of it?"

"Odd you should ask," I said, "because I expected to think it was pure trash, but I was surprised to find it was fairly well written by this Conrad Stamp guy, whoever he – or she – is. I guess I came away from the couple of hours I spent on it with my opinion altered. I can now say with some authority that it isn't pure trash. It's well-written trash."

"But you think it's trash?"

"Don't you?" I asked.

"Yes," Stanley said, "I suppose I do."

"So you've read it," I said.

"In a manner of speaking, I have," he said and shot another of his high-security gazes around the room before leaning into me again to allow – after a pause long enough for me to have taken any soiled shirts I might have had with me to my cleaner three blocks from where we were sitting and then returned – "What I mean is, I wrote it."

Having unburdened himself of that revelation, he leaned as far away from me as he had been leaning towards me. It was as if he were giving me sufficient space in which to absorb the immense piece of information he'd just imparted. In this new and expansive pose he took on the aspect of a pasha revealing the breadth of his holdings to a supplicant.

But along with the satisfaction, there was in his eyes a flicker of concern, of fear even.

It didn't take me an instant to respond to him, but during that instant I packed in plenty of thought about *The Cocksman's Tale*, which for those who don't know – or are lucky enough to have blotted all knowledge of it from their minds – purports to be the confessions of a modern-day, that is to say post-AIDS, libertine.

Steeped in non-stop accounts of erotic triumphs with easy-virtue women and easier-virtue men and heavily implying, if not broadcasting, that easy virtue is rampant in our amoral world, it's pornography lent a literary sheen.

It's Frank Harris's *My Secret Life* slapped up-to-date.

When I read the libidinous work – after having removed the dust jacket on which an unsheathed sword points upward and dangles a lace thong from its tip – I won't deny I had a certain salacious interest. It's an interest I apparently share with its other readers, which the bestseller lists – and Amazon.com rankings – would have you believe are legion. When I put it down, I felt a shower was in order – a cold shower followed immediately by a hot shower.

"You're Conrad Stamp," I said, more loudly than I wanted. I said it first as an incredulous declarative sentence and then a second time as a humor-laced query. "You're Conrad Stamp!?"

Stanley whipped around to see whether anyone had taken in the news flash. Satisfied that in this single incidence people had other things to occupy them than Stanley Konig's life and times, he leaned towards me again and reiterated with a downturned mouth, "I said, 'Strictly confidential.'"

"No problem," I responded, "since I don't believe you."

But even as I spoke and even the instant before I saw chagrin cross the flat planes of Stanley's wide face, I knew I'd better believe him. I knew what he said must be true. I even recalled that when I was reading the book in question and was trying to see if I could recognize a writing style, I'd had a fleeting intimation that Stanley might have written it. There were a couple of neatly-turned phrases in it that I thought I'd recognized from one of those first three novels.

(Don't ask which neatly-turned phrases. I've conveniently forgotten.)

But just as quickly as the thought came to me, I dismissed it, thinking that anyone might have used such phrases – might even, for all I knew, have lifted them from Stanley's work. You're stretching, I said to myself at the time and gave up the guessing game, figuring that eventually the author would be exposed – just as authors writing as Anonymous or under names publicized as assumed are almost always brought to light.

So now all had been vouchsafed but in a more direct and one-on-one way than I'd imagined. I'd expected the information would break in the papers, or someone in casual conversation would say, "Oh, did you hear they've identified the author of *The Cocksman's Tale*? It's blah-di-blah." And I'd say, like a wag at a dull soirée, "Have they? That's almost interesting.'" And change the subject.

But this was a whole other kettle of fish. "I take it back," I said to Stanley. "My apologies for doubting your honesty. You did write it, didn't you? You'd never take credit for *The Cocksman's Tale* if you hadn't written it. If you hadn't written it, you'd be the first to condemn it."

"I suppose I would," Stanley said. "I still can. Contractually, I can't. I'm forbidden to discuss it at all in the press."

"It's starting to make sense now," I said. "When you were working on the project last year that you said was hush-hush, it was this book, wasn't it?" Stanley nodded. "And the clothes you're wearing, the hair-cut, whatever the cologne is that you've taken a bath in – they're all *Cocksman's Tale* bounty."

"Ermenegildo Zegna jacket, Jean-Paul Gaultier's Le Mâle," Stanley said, still in *sotto voce* mode. "Everything thanks to the first royalty check. On top of the sizable advance. I've never seen this kind of money. What I made on my first three novels put together is chump change next to what I've already made on *The Cocksman's Tale*. If it keeps up, I'll make the kind of money where I'd never have to write another book, and I'd still live like a king. Or know I could. The problem is the publishers and their lawyers tell me that suddenly spending a lot of money calls attention to myself, and that mustn't happen. I'm risking their wrath by telling you today." He let that settle. "Now do you understand why the conversation goes no further than this table?"

Again he executed the swiveled gaze.

"I understand all that. What I don't understand is why you told me."

"Frankly," Stanley said, "I had to tell somebody. I'm having the unexpected success of my life, and nobody knows."

I don't like it when people say "frankly". For one, it implies that nothing preceding what they're about to say has been frank, and, for two, it throws suspicion on what follows.

"I always wanted to write a best-seller," he said. "That's how crassly small-minded I am. Now I have, and no one knows it. No book tour, no signings at Border's or Barnes & Noble. I can stand in stores and watch people bring my book up to the counter – sometimes with abashed looks – but I can't say anything. I can see people reading it on their Kindles, but I have to keep mum. I can buy myself a few nice things, but I can't overdo it. Only my accountant knows for sure, and the IRS might figure it out if they got interested enough.

"The last time I spoke to my mother, she actually said to me, 'Why don't you write a book like *The Cocksman's Tale*?' When I asked if she'd read it, she said, 'Yes. The author's mother must be very embarrassed.' I feel as if I made a pact with the devil. I'm beginning to know what Faust went through. Half the time I'm exhilarated, and half the time I'm depressed."

With that, he fell silent, and it was my turn. So I asked the first of the obvious but as yet unasked questions. "Why did you write it?"

"It wasn't even my idea," he said, becoming animated again. "It was my editor's. We were having one of those editor-author lunches, and I said only half jokingly, 'I wouldn't mind having one best-seller – just one – but I'd have no idea how to write it.' And he said, also only half jokingly, 'Sex sells.' 'All right,' I said, still with the half jokes, 'I'll write a book in which there's nothing but sex.' 'You write it, I'll publish it,' he said. 'Is that a promise?' I said. 'Yes,' he said, 'but you won't be able to do it. It takes a certain kind of non-literary writer to do it, and you're anything but that.'"

The planes of Stanley's broad face were getting flush, as if a wildfire were sweeping across them. He was het up. "Sam was telling me I was too literary just at the time when I was sick of the whole idea of literary fiction. It's the equivalent of satire in the theater. It's what closes on Saturday night. It's what doesn't get read on Saturday night. So what he said about my inability to write such a thought-free manuscript struck me as a challenge. If he'd thrown down a gauntlet, he couldn't have jolted me into action more effectively."

"Isn't the whole idea of throwing down a gauntlet already too literary?" I said.

Stanley lobbed a tolerant look my way. "I've written the book now. I can return to being literary. But at the time I just wanted to see what I could get away with. I threw myself into it."

"I'll say you did," I said. "Feet first. So to speak."

"'Erect cock first' is what you want to say," Stanley said.

"That's right," I said and for the first time noticed I was the one looking right and left. When I put a fast stop to that foolishness, I said to Stanley, "How did you do it? If the damn book has anything going for it, it's how real the episodes are."

"Thanks," Stanley said, with more satisfaction than I deemed fitting.

I said, "What I mean to say is, some of what goes on you just don't make up." I was referring to sex scenes of such imagination and detail that you'd have to have lived through them, at the very least as an observer, to believe they could really happen. I was referring to Conrad Stamp's protagonist, Rory Wilde, and partners indulging themselves in orgiastic behavior that would have flabbergasted the most decadent Romans.

"All made up," Stanley said. "Okay, I concede a few of them are flights of fancy based on milder forays of mine. Much milder. Much, much milder. Tame."

"I'm not going to ask you to elaborate."

"Right," he said. "I've done my elaborating. Now I'm faced with the consequences."

I wanted to hear Stanley elaborate, of course. I was especially interested in learning what mild "foray" he'd inflated into a brothel scene involving a leather-and-lace dominatrix, a Latvian aristocrat, a twelve-year-old Eurasian virgin and four bulldogs. But reading *The Cocksman's Tale* was enough concession to prurience on my part.

Instead, I said, "You mean, you're faced with the consequences of remaining silent after spending seventy-five dollars on a haircut rather than twenty and buying yourself three-hundred-dollar shirts and six-hundred-dollar shoes? The consequences of putting fifty thousand dollars into improving your kitchen instead of ten thousand?"

"How did you know I'm redoing my kitchen?" he asked with a certain amount of awe.

"Lucky guess," I said.

"Well, yes, there's that," Stanley went on, "but that's not the worst of it. I wish it were. When I started this albatross of a book – 'albatross' is another literary allusion, I know – I was so caught up in the game I'd decided to play with my editor that I never considered the breadth of the potential repercussions. I thought no further than writing the dirtiest book I could muster with an overlay of enough socially redeeming value for a reputable publishing house to release it not as outright pornography but as, according to the introductory advertisements, 'a parable for our neo-pagan times.'" He put his fingers up to indicate the quotation marks around "a parable for our neo-pagan times."

"It never occurred to me," he went on, "there was a problem with trying to write as convincingly as possible – and that the problem was people would be convinced the book was autobiographical fiction."

"I fail to see the problem," I said. "It's Conrad Stamp's autobiographical fiction. As long as nobody connects you with the book, you're safe as houses. Anyway, you've just told me you're the estimable Conrad Stamp, and I'm not shunning you. Yet." I had to throw in the "yet," figuring that nervous as Stanley was, he wasn't so nervous he wouldn't get the joke.

"Yes, but you're not Andrea Shadwell."

"Who's Andrea Shadwell?" I said.

"I haven't told you about her, have I?" he said and his broad, soft face went broader and softer. "She's the woman I want to marry."

This revelation set me back farther than the earlier one.

I could believe Stanley Konig was Conrad Stamp more easily than I could believe Stanley Konig had found someone he actually wanted to marry. Part of what made Stanley believable as Conrad Stamp was a certain disinclination he shared with his fictional cocksman: Neither found it easy to make a commitment to any one person, let alone any one sexual preference.

To that extent, yes, Stanley's novel was a randified imitation of his life. It was Stanley who years earlier had taken the adage about not buying a cow when you can get milk through the fence and rephrased it as "Why decide between buying a cow or a bull when you can sit on the fence?"

"Excuse me if I act surprised," I said, "but you haven't mentioned anyone named Andrea Shagwell before now."

(I knew what I was doing when I said "Shagwell.")

"Shadwell," Stanley corrected me and blushed, which wasn't something I knew him to do very often. To wit: He hadn't blushed once when discussing his authorship of *The Cocksman's Tale*, which I would have considered a fine time for blushing. "I only met her a few weeks ago," he said. "I haven't talked to you since then, except when I called to make this date."

"You might have mentioned it on the phone," I said.

"I was saving it," he said.

"You were saving an awful lot for one humble lunch," I said. "And now I'm confused. At first, I had the impression you were eager to tell me about your candle-stine connection with The Cocksman's Tale. Now that you've introduced Andrea Shadwell into the discussion, I get the feeling you're eager to continue keeping your status as the latest publishing phenomenon under wraps."

"I am," he said, scraping his chair even closer to me. Which made me realize the restaurant's tile floor was a smart decorating idea. It made the surroundings noisy but at the same time obscured conversations. Everyone added to the din, but no one was heard above it. "That's just it. I'm conflicted."

"Said the cardinal to the hooker."

"No time for pleasantries," Stanley said. "On the one hand, I'm having this amazing success and want to tell everybody, and on the other hand, I'm in a position where for more than the publisher's interests, I want no one to know. The whole thing is literally giving me nightmares."

"Where does Andrea Shadwell figure in all this?" I asked.

"The way she figures in is, if I'd met her before I wrote the book," Stanley said, "I'd never have written it. You can guess why."

"I'm going to say that you've set yourself up with a real problem by writing a book full of sexual exploits so all-fired convincingly."

"Give the man a silver dollar," Stanley said. "Everything you come across about the book includes some remark like – and I quote verbatim from one review – 'Conrad Stamp writes about debauchery as if he has studied it up close and very personal.' The upshot is everyone, maybe with the exception of you, believes that Conrad Stamp lives the life he writes about in his tome. Or lived it."

"And the everyone you speak of includes the mysterious Andrea Shadwell."

"That's right," Stanley said. "Except she's not mysterious. That's what I love about her. She's not only beautiful in a way not everyone would think is beautiful but I definitely do, she's extremely straightforward. I've never met a woman with less guile. At the same time, she's very far from being naïve."

"If she isn't naïve," I said, "she realizes that everyone who's reached your age comes with a certain amount of experiential baggage."

"A certain amount of experiential baggage, sure," Stanley said, "but not as much as Rory Wilde has amassed in Conrad Stamp's *The Cocksman's Tale*. That's not baggage. It's tonnage."

"You're protected, though. She doesn't know you're Conrad Stamp."

"That's just it. She doesn't know I'm Conrad Stamp, but I know I am. And I sit there or lie there knowing the incontrovertible fact the whole time we're together. It's as if I'm living a lie. I am living a lie." He shook his well-coiffed head. "We were having dinner the other night – she can cook, too – and somehow the subject of *The Cocksman's Tale* came up.

"Believe me, I didn't mention it. She just suddenly asked if I'd read it. I sputtered for a few seconds and then said I had. She took my awkward response as embarrassment at having read it. 'It's one thing to read it,' she said, 'but an altogether different thing to have written it.'

"She wanted to know what I thought of it. That put me on the spot, didn't it? I said, 'It's not my favorite novel,' which was dissembling on some exalted level, because I was thinking, 'It's not my favorite novel of those I've written.' But of course I didn't say the 'of those I've written' part.

"I might just as well have had my fingers crossed behind my back. I asked if she'd read it, and she said she'd read enough to know it's a disgusting book no matter how well written it is. Not because of all the sex, she said, which is puerile enough but because Conrad Stamp, whoever he is – that's what she said: 'whoever he is' – thinks his puerile fantasies are worth recording for others to salivate over.

"Then she delivered the *coup de grâce*. Whether or not he's actually had the experiences he's shmeared onto the book like rancid cream cheese on a bagel, I wouldn't want to know him.' She said it just like that. 'I wouldn't want to know him.'"

"Uh-oh," I said, not having anything else handy to say.

Stanley, having repeated her remark twice, was looking as if he'd just heard it for the first time – wounded. "What could I do then?" he said. "I've fallen in love for the first time in my life. Forget all the other times I told you I was in love. They were nothing. And the woman I love turns out to have sufficient cause not to love me. She just doesn't know it. I can keep the truth from her – and from everyone else but four or five people on the planet, you now being one of them – but I can't keep it from myself. What kind of heel am I for not letting her know? But if I do, I'm almost certain to lose her."

I was listening to this, and as I was, something was beginning to come into focus. I was starting to understand I hadn't been asked to meet Stanley simply because he was bursting to tell someone – anyone – his news. I was there, because once he'd filled me in on his – I was about to say "little secret" – but it was a big secret, a huge secret, a secret with a thick publishing house contract behind it.

Anyway, once he'd filled me in on his secret, he was going to ask something of me, something that, whenever it's asked (by Stanley or anyone), makes my blood run cold.

He was going to ask what he should do, and I had no idea.

And yes, Stanley's request came, bald as an egg. Once again, he leaned my way so precariously I thought he might fall of his chair. "What do I do?" he asked.

What a sad little plea it was, too. Oliver Twist begging for more gruel couldn't have been half as poignant. But, trying to remain unmoved as a Victorian school master, I opted out with something I consider cleverly evasive. "I see the bind you're in, Stanley," I said, "but I don't know what to tell you to do. I might if I knew more about Andrea Shadwell."

Stanley was having none of it. "But you must have some reaction to what I've told you," he pressed.

"All I'm saying is, you may be right that if Andrea learned you're Conrad Stamp, she'd drop you. You've only been together for how long? Four, five, six weeks?"

Stanley said, "Just under two months. But long enough for me to know this is the real thing."

"Be that as it may," I said. "Maybe you don't know her long enough yet to know what she means by a phrase like 'I wouldn't want to know him.' Maybe all it means is, she wouldn't want to know the man she thinks Conrad Stamp is from reading the book. She knows you, though – at least well enough to begin a love affair. Maybe if she learned it was you who wrote the book, she'd have an altogether different take."

"You think so?" Stanley said. His apprehension altered into the expression an eight-year-old takes on when told that if he's good from now to Easter, he might get to spend spring break at Disney World.

"I think it's possible," I said. "As I say, I don't know this woman. For all I know, the prospect of the easy life your windfall promises would be compensation enough for your being Conrad Stamp."

"Andrea isn't mercenary," Stanley snapped. "Don't think she is for a minute."

"I don't say she is," I said. "I'm sure she isn't." I wasn't at all sure – I didn't know the woman. "I'm only saying that from where I sit, anything is possible."

"So you think I should tell her?"

"If you feel you ought to. So far you seem very uncomfortable not telling her. How long can you live with that?" I had another germane thought. "On the other hand, you don't want to confide in her if this is just a fling and within a couple of weeks there's some ex-girlfriend out there thinking she could have a shitload of retaliatory fun spilling the beans on you."

"You haven't met her yet and I know you know my long history with women," Stanley said, "but this isn't a fling."

"If you say so."

"I do say so," Stanley said. He bit his lip in thought. "So you think if this isn't a fling, I should tell her?"

"I didn't say that," I said. "You're putting words in my mouth. I said you should tell her if you think you should tell her."

"That sounds as if you're telling me to tell her," he said.

The line of argument was getting up my nose. "We're going around in circles here, Stanley," I said.

Because it hit me we were going around in circles, I decided that nothing short of stating my position flat out would get through to him. Even then it might not. "I'm only telling you what I'd do if I were in your fine-leather shoes."

I could just as well have been trying to sell a liberal agenda to a Rush Limbaugh conservative, so I let it ride, and with a short resumption of our earlier and less fraught exchange on the miserable state of the world, we finished our lunch and settled the bill.

Stanley insisted on paying, by the way, and I was still riled enough to give him no argument – even though I figured my meal was courtesy of the cursed *Cocksman's Tale*.

When we parted on the street – Stanley to tread his troubled path, I to tread mine – I had to suppress the urge to shout after him, "Look, everybody, there goes Conrad Stamp!"

ii.

I mentioned that there were two recent Stanley Konig lunches. The second was three months later. That's recent enough. It was a different venue, where the house specialty of the day wasn't papaya salad but squid salad with broccoli *rape*. The service was exquisite, although perhaps not so exquisite for the other patrons, since there had been a development between lunches that affected how Stanley and I were treated.

I should say there had been a development that affected how Stanley

Konig was treated: He had been revealed as Conrad Stamp. Yes, the big bad news had come out. For a while, it even seemed to Stanley that I'd been the spoil-sport, because for one damning thing, the news had come out only a day or two after he'd let me in on his gnawing secret.

What happened apparently is that early one morning Stanley picked up the phone to a gossip columnist wanting him to confirm the rumor that he'd written *The Cocksman's Tale*. He denied it, he told me, with a curt "I don't know what you're talking about," hung up and dismissed the intrusion.

He had had a few calls like it in the past – as, by the way, had many other authors. But within an hour of the first call, there was a second and then a third and then a half dozen more. By the tenth call, to hear him tell it, he stayed on the phone long enough to inquire how the reporter had gotten such an outlandish tip and was told it had arrived as an untraceable email.

That's when I got the outraged call in which I was verbally battered with all sorts of names, among which "traitor" and "Judas" were the few printable ones. When I was able to slide a word in, I denied any such disloyal activity, of course.

To no avail. Stanley was convinced I had to be the conduit, and after saying so and telling me our friendship was as much a thing of the past as the Peloponnesian War and making a don't-darken-my-doorstep-again warning, he came as close to slamming down his cell phone as he could.

(Which wasn't very close, given the unslammability of cell phones.)

There was nothing for me to do but stare dumbfounded at my landline for a minute and then go on with the day.

I'd kept mum, but only I knew I had. Since I'd told no one, no one could know I hadn't told.

I'd hardly found time to think about whether or not it was worth trying to call Stanley back to reiterate my innocence of the heinous crime when, mid-afternoon, the phone rang. It was Stanley with abject, heart-felt and terribly sincere apologies.

He'd discovered who the malefactor was. Who the malefactors were, that is: The executives at his publishing house.

He explained that although he was contractually forbidden to discuss his authorship of *The Cocksman's Tale*, the publishers were under no similar restriction. And they'd decided that while sales of the book were still snowballing – and international translations were well underway – they could give an added goose to the momentum by taking the wraps off Stanley.

His editor, a Sam Somebody, told him it was a recent decision, but Stanley suspected (with no way to prove it) that the theatrical step had been part of their strategy from the git-go. He believed the anonymous email campaign had been in the works for months, and he was pissed.

That's what he was saying when his other cell phone tootled its particular melodic phrase and he excused himself, promising to be back in touch shortly.

Shortly turned into an entire calendar season, because Stanley Konig instantly became the toast of the town.

(Only at lunch did I learn that in some fashion he regarded himself as "the burnt toast of the town.")

He gave interview after interview, showed up on magazine covers, did the talk shows. He submitted to a gentle ribbing by David Letterman and was a good sport about Letterman's Ten Ways to be a Failed Cocksman list.

Through all the press attention, he insisted that *The Cocksman's Tale* was completely fabricated. Yet, he always managed to phrase his denials coyly. It was clear to me he was going along with a high-level marketing decision and having a helluva time doing so. The thinking had to have been that were his denials of all the libido-demonstration totally convincing, they might hobble the exponentially gathering sales. By appearing as if he might be as licentious as his protagonist, he was boosting revenue.

The publishing house powers knew what they were doing, all right: Stanley was their spinning top.

Therefore, what with the demanding schedule, Stanley Konig as Conrad Stamp was out of touch with me, and I kept my distance.

When he finally called one cool morning, he said he was free that day because Barbara Walters had to postpone, and he wanted to take me to lunch if for nothing else, as an apology for his unfounded and presumptuous accusations.

I wondered what I was letting myself in for by accompanying him to a public place, but I also knew that saying no would be churlish. It would seem as if I were still sulking. And although I'd never registered very high on the sulk meter, maybe to some extent, I was sulking. If so, I figured I might as well sulk over a pricey meal coming out of someone else's wallet.

It was a very pricey meal, too, which would have been even pricier if Stanley had had to pay for the add-on freebies an adoring *maître d'* and a company of smiling servers lay obsequiously on the table – the champagne, the extravagant dessert that looked as if it had been designed by Santiago Calatrava.

Stanley was abashed by none of it. It didn't take more than a few seconds for me to see how grandly he reveled in it. I do mean he regarded all the reverence paid him to be part of some glorious unfurling of new and fully entitled revels.

When we walked down the carpeted stairs into the main dining-room where Stanley was greeted by *maître d'* Oscar with a florid "Good afternoon, Mr. Stamp, er, Mr. Konig" and a vigorous handshake, the nod he gave in response was unmistakably imperious, picked up, I imagined, from newsreel footage of actual royalty.

I also was treated by Oscar to a handshake only minimally less vigorous. I was also offered Oscar's toothy smile for being cunning enough to associate with someone of Stanley's caliber.

We were immediately led through the entire room to a table in the corner where there were sufficient glasses and cutlery to accommodate a large dinner party. The fawning Oscar explained that he assumed "Mr. Konig would prefer this more secluded area," but it was obvious to me and I'm sure to Stanley that Oscar thought it good for business to parade the man also known as Conrad Stamp in front of as many patrons as possible.

So our room-threading retinue was Oscar, Stanley and me bringing up the rear. From my vantage point I couldn't see Stanley's expression(s), but I could see him turning his head slowly to right and left, as if taking the room in out of curiosity but actually making sure his full face was seen by one and all.

In a short time he'd come a long way from surveying a dining-room to make certain he wasn't overheard. Now when he did his full-frontal beam, which he did frequently during the following couple of hours, it was with the slow rotation of a monarch acknowledging the admiring rabble from a gold coach.

And there definitely were admirers. We were in the restaurant *du jour* – I'm not mentioning the name, because I don't want to be part of the promotion campaign – and because of this, none of the patrons, many of them public figures themselves, stared outright. What they did was look over from time to time, smiling half-smiles that said, "I know who you are, and I'm registering with approval that we're in each other's presence."

I received a few of these tacit welcomes myself.

It's a funny thing about celebrity, isn't it? It doesn't matter what you have come to be celebrated for – or whether your celebrity is in actuality notoriety. Among those who've made their mark and their millions (or billions), it's as if a celebrity fraternity is understood to exist and its arcane entrance requirements to have been met. You, too, have caught the elusive brass – no, platinum – ring, and, as the old song goes, you have ascended from the commonplace into the rare.

Stanley was now a member in good standing, and I – because I was sitting with him – was recognized as a possible future applicant to whom club privileges are to be accorded on a temporary basis.

When I had last seen Stanley, he was nowhere as sanguine as he was over this lunch. He put away his squid with merry élan and just as jauntily quaffed the wine recommended by the sommelier.

Nowhere in his manner was the suggestion that anything had gone despairingly amiss during the recent change of affairs, although I again intuited that the preliminary banter about what we always bantered about was intended partially to confirm that fact, the fact that nothing had changed between him and me.

Perhaps needless to say, there was a barrage of additional apologies for his ever thinking I could have been the one to expose his cover. His profound regret was the reason, he said, for our lunching in such splendor. He wanted his conciliatory gesture to be special.

I thanked him for his consideration and assured him that, as he had reasonable cause to think I was the informant, I'd never held his remarks against him.

I didn't say that I was also aware that our eating in such a hoity-toity beanery was a convenient chance for him to show off his new and exalted ranking in the show-business end of bestsellerdom.

I also said nothing about his now being outed as Conrad Stamp freeing him to spend his money so profligately that were Thorsten Veblen still with us, he could add a new chapter to his revered volume on conspicuous consumption.

One reason for keeping my counsel was that I wanted to hear too much else about Conrad Stamp's coming-to-light.

Stanley didn't hold back.

"At first," he began, "I was sore. I felt as if I'd been betrayed by the publishing company, manipulated. They'd forbidden me to admit I was – am – Conrad Stamp, but whenever they decided it was salutary for them, they could throw open the floodgates. Which, by the way, was something they'd never in the least indicated they might do. But I had no recourse. The contract was the contract. I had my rights, and they had theirs."

While getting current over the apricot soufflé, Stanley was, it may come as no surprise, not leaning in to me to maximize privacy. Oh, no, he was sitting upright as a soldier and speaking in tones that varied, I noticed, according to how important he judged it was that what he was saying be overheard at neighboring tables.

"But it didn't take long for me to realize the publishers were probably right," he went on. They – that is, we – had derived maximum benefit from the Conrad Stamp mystery. And I had been griping about the bind I found myself in when I was unable to be open about my having written the blessed book. Well, you bore some of the brunt of that frustration, for which many thanks and additional apologies. So I realized it was childish to complain that they'd jerked me around. Their tactic was very, very cagey, because suddenly there was a second wave of publicity that felt bigger than the first.

"Why wouldn't it? I had had to sit out the launch with mouth zipped. Now it's all about me. And I have to admit I've enjoyed every moment of it. Did I tell you I had to take on a secretary? I've never had an assistant before, screening phone calls, fielding requests. The publishing house has even assigned me my own twenty-four-seven publicity person. With my previous literary fiction novels..." He put a sneer into the term 'literary fiction novels," as if they were now an aberration he deeply regretted. " ...I had to share the publicist and never felt I was getting my fair exploitation share."

He put down the fork and spoon with which he was dismantling dessert and spread his arms. "Look at me," he said in moderate voice – and appended in a voice he knew would carry, "I'm having the devil's own time."

I was reminded of the previous lunch and his comment that it was as if he'd made a pact with the devil. I didn't think it was the right time to recall it to him, however. Why be a wet blanket to a guy who was feeling flush for perhaps the first time in his life?

In his stylish suit and his stylish shoes and his stylish everything else and with the cognoscenti and the literati and the glitterati and the whatever-otherati in the immediate vicinity to validate him, nothing I might venture in the way of a reality tug was likely to mean much anyway.

There was one thing I wanted to know, though, in light of the tangle we'd had three months earlier. In as off-hand a manner as I could muster, I said, "You haven't mentioned Andrea Shadwell."

"Oh, her," Stanley said. "What do you want to know?"

"You were so concerned that should she find out you, Stanley Konig, are also Conrad Stamp, she'd nip your budding romance in the bud. I'm assuming that if the rest of the world discovered the truth, she did, too."

"Yes, she found out," Stanley said. He muted his voice for this but still held himself as if he were on display. What am I saying? He was on display.

He continued, "By the time I had the ninth or tenth phone call that morning, I had to tell her – because she was there – what the calls were about, and that the worst was true – that even though I was still denying it to the callers, what they were calling about was so. I was – I am Conrad Stamp. I told her I know what she thinks of Conrad Stamp, and I'm sorry if she thinks I'm disgusting. But I wrote the book, and there's no getting around it."

"What did she say to that?" I asked.

"She said the damnedest thing," Stanley replied. "She said she already knew. She'd been looking for envelopes a week or so before and had opened a drawer where she thought I might keep them and found a manuscript that had no title page. It had never occurred to me to hide the thing. She started reading it, recognized it immediately and could tell by the corrections and additions I'd made in the margins that I had to be the author.

"Then she said what you told me she might say. She said she now thought of the entire situation as funny. Throughout the length and breadth of the country, people were thinking about how stupendous Conrad Stamp's sex life had to be, and she was it. She said she'd come to know me well enough to know I wasn't disgusting, that as far as she was concerned, I was a great guy and that although *The Cocksman's Tale* would never be her favorite book, she loved me enough to understand every book I write can't be on the same literary level with the best of them. Besides, she said, she didn't want me to think she was judging me on my novels alone. I was bigger than that, and she was bigger than that."

I was impressed. "Wise girl," I said. "So the two of you are together and better than ever."

"Don't jump to that conclusion," Stanley said. He gave out with what I can only call a hearty laugh. "No, we're not together, as you so quaintly put it. Andrea and I decided to call it a day – and a truly beautiful day at that – about a week and a half ago."

"I don't get it," I said. "What went wrong?"

"Nothing went wrong," Stanley said and took time to flash an all-encompassing smile around the rose-and-gold room with its spray of exotic flowers on every table and, at every table, its array of smart-looking people. "Over the past few weeks, my life has changed considerably. I don't have to tell you that. I had no idea how much it would change. Everywhere I go, I'm recognized. People go out of their way to get my attention. They trip over their feet to do things for me."

As if on cue, a waiter silently set a tray of complimentary cookies in front of us. Stanley nodded at him, and I can attest with certainty that, although nothing was said, a laser streak of some kind of sexual recognition passed between them.

"Men, women," he went on. "They want to know what I think. They want to know what I feel. They want to know what I'm wearing, eating, doing. Everywhere I go, they practically throw themselves at me. Many of them do – literally – throw themselves at me. Believe it or not, I'm running up huge bills at my cleaner and my tailor, even though I have enough disposable swag to throw out damaged clothes and replace them. I don't have to tell you I had sexual opportunities before, but nothing like now, after I've written the book.

"Millions of people out there think I am the book. There are just too many temptations at the moment for me to limit myself to one person in my life. Andrea's an understanding woman. She understands I need latitude and plenty of it. It was her idea that we give each other space and maybe see if there's a viable future somewhere down the road. I had to agree with her. It just seemed better to give in to temptation than try to fight it. We're both mature enough to regard that as a recipe for resentment."

Stanley stopped to see how I reacted to that much of his current public and private *persona.*

"I thought you loved her," I said. "You said she was the first woman you ever loved. She was it."

"I did love her," he said, "but that was the old Stanley. I'm a different man now. By the way, I don't remember if I mentioned on the phone that I've begun work on my next book. The publishers think a sequel is in order. *The Cocksman's Extended Tale*, I'm calling it."

He looked over at a table nearby, where a young woman whom I thought I recognized as a starlet of some sort was looking back. "I'm researching it now, you might say," he said, keeping his eyes on the starlet. "So I'm continuing to write as Conrad Stamp. The byline on *The Cocksman's Extended Tale* will be Stanley Konig writing as Conrad Stamp."

He downed the last of his dessert and sat back with a look of total self-possession on his face. And I recognized – with a *frisson* of only slightly adulterated admiration and maybe even a *soupçon* of envy – that now he was not only Stanley Konig writing as Conrad Stamp, he was Stanley Konig living as Conrad Stamp.

Off on the wrong foot

According to Stewart Kahn, it was a harmless remark. He meant nothing by it. He was just passing time. He thought he'd interject something cute.

So he'd said it: "Nice feet."

One of the ironies – and in time there were a number of adjunct ironies – was that when he said it, he hadn't been heard. Not heard exactly. By the other three. Arnold, who Stewart once said was "often preoccupied," had asked, "What? What did you say?"

To that query, Stewart could have replied, should have replied, "Nothing. Forget it." How often had he wished his response had been just that? But if he had a nickel for every unrealized wish, he'd be rich as fill-in-the-blank. He didn't, however, and he wasn't.

Anyway, he hesitated just long enough for Mark, whom Stewart called "tough but worth it," to say, "Something about feet."

That's when Marty – said by Stewart to be "an all-round nice guy and way gullible" – addressed him directly with, "I thought you said, 'Let's eat.'" Another convenient out that Stewart could have seized on.

But he didn't grab that chance either. Again he let one second too many elapse.

Just enough for Mark to say, "No, he said something about feet."

"Feet?" Arnold asked and turned to Stewart again, "What about feet?"

Marty said, "Feet? Not eat? Too bad, I'm getting kind of hungry. I guess you hear what you want to hear."

"No," Mark insisted, "Stewart said something that sounded like 'nice feet.'"

Arnold asked, "Why feet?"

Right there was when Stewart sealed his fate. Still committed – like a *putz* – to the comment by which he only meant to be cute he said, "Sting's feet."

Marty asked, "Sting's feet? What about 'em?" Apparently, Marty doesn't enunciate the "th" in "them."

Stewart said, "That poster we passed – the one with Sting on it."

Arnold said, "The ad for the radio station. Lite FM, whatever. Yeah, I saw it. A picture of Sting. So what?"

"Since when do you like Sting?" Marty asked Stewart. "I thought you hated Sting."

Stewart said, "I never said I hated Sting. I don't think about him one way or another."

Arnold said, "You like 'Ev'ry Breath I Take,' don't you? It's a great song."

Stewart said, "It's an okay song. I can take it or leave it."

"I can leave it," Mark said, "but if you don't care about Sting one way or another, why are you bringing up his feet?"

"The poster," Stewart said.

"Sting in a tub," Arnold said. "They think that's going to make you want to listen to the station?"

Mark said, "Let Sting keep listening to FM Lite in his tub if he likes it so much, and leave me out of it. What's he doing listening to the radio in a tub anyway? Doesn't he know what could happen if it fell in? Doesn't he know about showers? With all his money he could afford a built-in waterfall."

"Sting's in the tub with his feet sticking up," Stewart said, ignoring Mark's outburst, "They're nice feet."

"Let me get this straight," Mark pushed in. "You don't care for Sting one way or the other, but you think he's got nice feet."

"Well, yes," Stewart said. "Normally, I think feet are ugly. You don't see good-looking feet very often, and Sting's aren't bad."

"Where is this poster?" Marty asked. "This I gotta see."

"It's back there a couple blocks," Mark said, "and we're not fucking going back to look at a pair of feet. Unless Stewart wants to gaze at them some more."

Stewart said, "I don't want to 'gaze' at them. I didn't 'gaze' at them before."

Arnold said to Stewart, "I didn't know you had a thing for feet."

"Men's feet," Mark added.

"I don't have 'a thing' for feet," Stewart said.

"But you make an exception for Sting," Mark said, "It's a Sting thing?"

"Stewart's into feet," Marty said, "Wow. But, hey, whatever gets you through the night." Arnold said, "I'm a leg man myself, but I stop at the ankles. Hairy legs, but not too hairy."

I'm repeating all this not because I was there. I wasn't. I repeat it because Stewart told me. A couple of times. And he seems to remember the event verbatim, since he repeated it pretty much the same exact way every time he told it: who said what – down to the least "But, hey!" – and with what inflections. There was more, which I won't go into at the moment.

What's important – to Stewart, certainly – is that's how it started. One night after going to the movies with flick pals Mark, Marty and Arnold, he'd passed a poster of Sting being used as part of a campaign to get listeners for one of the local radio stations. On the poster Sting is lying on his back in a tub with his legs sticking straight up in the air.

I'd seen the poster, too. Who besides Marty hadn't, since it was spread on subway shelters throughout Manhattan for a couple months some time ago. All you see of Sting is his head and his legs from the calves down. Or from the calves up, since the former Gordon Sumner's legs are aimed towards heaven. His feet are flexed. I remember looking at the poster and thinking Sting wore an expression akin to the one babies take on when they've only recently discovered their toes.

But unlike Stewart, I just made note of it and moved on without having to comment aloud to myself or anyone else.

Stewart, who maintains he thinks feet are ugly and always has, noticed that Sting's feet looked unobjectionable, shapely even, which surprised him. He wouldn't have considered himself someone who'd listen to a radio station because he was intrigued by the sight of a rock star's feet. Who would?

He wouldn't become a regular listener, but on the other hand – on the other foot? – he wouldn't make a point of not listening, which he might have done if Sting's feet had been as unappealing as he considered most people's, including his own.

And so, since the Mark-Marty-Arnold *après*-film conversation had hit a momentary lull, he'd made his unfortunate lull-filling pronouncement: "Nice feet."

Stewart had no idea it would only go downhill from there – and at an accelerating pace.

At the time, he didn't appreciate the ribbing he'd taken about having a thing for feet – the accompanying jokes, the plays on words (e.g., about his footing the bill at dinner, et cetera), and it continued for another ten or fifteen minutes, with Stewart saying a half dozen times to no avail, "Can't we move on to another subject?"

Finally, also to no eventual avail, the topic shifted. When the four of them broke up for the night, the pangs of near-mortification Stewart suffered had died down to a dull ache. Stewart vowed to himself never again to refer to Sting or feet and pledged to take a hiatus from even mentioning anything that might trigger feet associations – like shoes and socks. Having done that, he assumed the foot idyll was history.

That, I suppose, is why I didn't hear about it immediately. Stewart, you see, is one of the people who consider me, for one reason or another, a reliable confidant.

I've known him for some years. Ever since we almost had a date. Or was it that we had a date, but it didn't work out? Or was it that I thought we might be on a date and he didn't? Or vice versa? It's unclear, because it was one of those situations where you're introduced by friends you have in common who are being very sensitive to everyone's feelings and sense that if they told either party, or both parties, that the little get-together was meant as a pairing-off introduction, either or both introducees might balk and bail.

So Bets and Oogie Frank – for that's who the upper-class Yente-the-Matchmakers were who brought us together for drinks – contrived an excuse for leaving us alone to figure out what was up. By the time we did just that, we realized that if there was chemistry at work, it wasn't the romantic kind.

It became apparent when we noticed that most of our talk had been about other people we were seeing. Nonetheless, what we liked about each other was how similar our likes and dislikes were in relation to the other people with whom we were involved and about whom we hadn't bothered to update Bets and Oogie.

As a result, we struck up a friendship without becoming integral parts of each other's crowd. We talked on the phone every once in a while, saw each other occasionally. I'd met Mark, Marty and Arnold. Stewart introduced us, but I didn't hang out with them or join them for their movie nights (actually I did once: disaster), which explains – if explanation is needed – why I wasn't around for the Sting conversation.

It doesn't explain why I was moved to pun at Stewart that the colloquy had 'sting' in more ways than one before I had grasped the gravity of his complaints. I certainly would never have made the feeble quip at a later date when stories began piling up.

I only heard about the intensifying situation a few weeks later when Stewart called to ask if I had a minute. Ordinarily, when people ring merely to gab or to propose getting together for a meal or a Yankee game, they barrel directly into the burden of their plain song. When, on the other hand, they ask if you've "got a minute," it always means two things: 1) that there's a real problem they need to lay out in hopes you can come up with a workable solution; and 2) that it's going to take longer than a minute.

I had the minute. I had more than the minute. I had the morning and suggested we meet at the Starbucks around the corner from me. (Of course, we had to establish whether I was suggesting the Starbucks around the corner from me three blocks south or the one around the corner from me three blocks north. But for the purposes of this story, that's neither here nor there.)

Stewart arrived before I did, which goes to prove how eager he was to talk. Usually, he's five to ten minutes late and has some excuse involving traffic and/or transportation. He'd taken off his six-button camel-haired coat – he's the last person I know who wears one – placed it on an empty chair neatly folded and was sitting over coffee in his crew-neck sweater, khakis and loafers. When I got to the table, he looked up at me with such need, I had all I could do not to reach in my pocket for some spare change.

"I'll get my coffee and be right back," I said to his round, expectant face with its couple-days stubble. "I'd ask if I can get you anything, but I have a feeling whatever you want isn't available at the counter." He only nodded, tacking on a weak, gap-toothed smile.

"Okay," I said, when I returned with my over-priced latte, "what's the problem? I'm assuming there is a problem."

"There is," he said, "but you're going to think this is silly."

"I don't think anything is silly," I lied.

"You'll think this is," he said and grabbed a moment to compose himself for the revelation. During that moment I took Stewart in. He's a big fellow, who always strikes me as slightly unformed. 'Blob' is an unfair description, but it goes some way toward indicating the physical type. Were he a dog, he'd be something of a German shepherd mix – shaggy, shambling, likeable. But aren't all people with a gap between their front teeth somehow appealing? They are in my experience.

Stewart was ready to divulge. I knew by the large intake of breath. He began by telling me what I've already covered, including details I've left out to save time. I'll continue to disregard them, because while it's amusing to know that Marty kept up a sing-song litany of "so Stewart's into feet" as underscoring to the attenuated Sting repartee, it doesn't add much substance to the larger saga. Instead I'll jump-cut to the next segment, which Stewart related with chagrin so palpable it practically joined us as a third party.

"I figured that after that night it was over," he said, picking up from where he'd left off. "That is, I'd hoped it was over. And I had reason to think it was, because the following movie night, we met at the Clearview Cinemas – don't ask what movie; I haven't got time for that – stood on line, saw the flick, came out and went to The Food Place for a drink. So far, nothing was said about me and feet. We were talking about the movie, and then we were talking about the people around us. But just when I was seduced into a false sense of security, Mark said, 'Does it bother you they're all wearing shoes, Stewart?'

"'I'd pushed the foot business so far to the back of my mind I didn't understand at first what he was getting at. I said, 'Of course, they're all wearing shoes. It's the middle of winter." I noticed Marty and Arnold snickering. Mark said, 'You can't see their feet.' I got it then. 'I told you I'm not into feet. I'm anything but into feet. Ask me what I think is the ugliest part of the body, and I'll immediately tell you feet.'

"'Stewie," Arnold said, giving the syllables of my name an annoying nasality, 'We're all friends here. You like feet. There's nothing wrong with it.' Then Marty asked, 'Is it just bare feet, or are you also into stockinged feet? Or socks and shoes? Cordovans, maybe, Bass Weejuns, Nikes. I see you looking around.' I said, 'We're all looking around. That's what we do here. We look around.' Then Marty said, 'Yes, but you're looking down, isn't he, boys?' There was a declaration of 'yeah, he's looking down' in two-part harmony."

Stewart took a break there to catch his breath and – from the looks of him shaking his head side to side – to replay the scene on his mind's Imax. That gave me an opening to ask what I'd been wanting to know since he launched into his tale, "What was it about Sting's feet, anyway?"

"Don't you start, too," Stewart said with pathos originating somewhere deep in his gut. I knew to stop.

"But, look, Stewart," I said, "they're just pulling your – uh, ribbing you. Why can't you laugh it off?"

"If it was funny," he said, "I could laugh it off. But it's not funny."

"I didn't say it was funny," I said, "It's really kind of lame, but they're your friends, and they think it's funny. They found a button, and they're pushing it. My guess is, the more you protest, the more you're going to be kidded about it."

"Kidded about what?" Stewart said, took a swig of his coffee and gave such a sour turn to his lower lip I thought for a second that perhaps the Starbucks java was as stale as the Mark-Marty-Arnold joshing. "Kidded about saying Sting has nice feet? I mean, the irony here is that not only do I not like feet, I do whatever I can to avoid looking at them. I've been known to drop potential lovers once I got a look at their feet. Long, gnarly things, toes going every-which-way."

"Known to whom?" I asked. "Not to Arnold, Marty and Mark. Far as they know, you do like feet. Sting's feet anyway. Or they're pretending to think you like feet?"

"Believing, pretending," Stewart said, "what's the difference? It's all coming out the same. Now, every time I see them, they're going to make some crack about you know what. I can't even say the word. Or the singular of the word."

With that his shoulders fell, and he stared into his empty coffee cup.

"Listen, Stewart," I said, "if I were in your shoes..." He looked up from the cup and fixed me with the dazed stare of someone who'd just been hit with a plank. "Whoops!" I said, "I didn't mean that. Honestly. I wasn't thinking. I'm on your side."

He relaxed the stare and said, "If you were in my unmentionable lower-limb coverings, what?"

"This isn't advice, you understand," I began, "I'm just saying if I were in your place, I would let it ride. You only think this is going to come up again. For all you know, your trio of ageing boys has had its fun, and that's the end of it."

"You think so," Stewart said, evincing the first signs of relief I'd spotted. "Okay, I'll try that." He fell silent again and sat that way for the next while, tacitly attempting to convince me and himself that he would let things go. I don't think he convinced either of us, but we talked no more about it.

Not that day anyway. Next time I received the got-a-minute phone call and obliged, it turned out I'd been – I admit it – wrong. "The other night when we went to the movies," Stewart blurted after extremely truncated amenities, "Mark was carrying a wrapped package. Nothing was said about it. Nobody referred to it. I noticed it but didn't pay much attention. Occasionally, people carry packages. That's all I thought. But when we'd seen the movie – the new Scorsese; It's not very good, but I don't want to discuss it – and were sitting around at The Food Place and had ordered and were waiting for the orders to arrive, Mark picks up the package and hands it to me. 'This is for you, Stew,' he said. It wasn't my birthday. There was no reason for him to be giving me anything, so I was instantly apprehensive. Plus I notice that Marty and Arnold are sitting there like the cat who ate the canary – like two cats who ate a canary each. Marty said, 'It's from all three of us.'"

Stewart looked at me then to see what I was making of this, but as yet I wasn't making anything of it. He intensified the gaze into something close to accusatory but went on. "The package is covered with brown paper and tied with string, and it's heavy – a couple of pounds heavy. For all I know, it could be a loaf of thick bread. Pumpernickel or something. Gee, I just thought of it. Loaf, loafers. Now they've got me doing it. But it wasn't.

"'I say to all three of them, 'Do I want to open this?' Arnold said, 'Of course, you do. You'll love it.' That worried me more. But I pulled off the string and pulled off the paper, which had been crudely scotch-taped. And there was a shoe box. A shoe box! But I'm thinking of you, Daniel, and what you said about letting things go." He gives me another piercing look. "I think that the choice of a shoe box could be harmless. Lots of people wrap objects in shoe boxes. They're handy. So I say nothing. I'm thinking – hoping – this is some kind of conciliatory gift. I remove the top and look at what's inside. Do you know what it is?"

He stopped to let his question settle. Inherent in the pause, it seemed to me, was his conviction that I should know the answer and that if I concentrate hard enough, it'll come to me. His dark German shepherd-mix eyes fixed on me. But of course, I didn't know what was inside. I wasn't getting any gap-toothed smile display either and realized I hadn't in some time.

"Do you?" he pressed.

"No, I don't," I said, as neutrally as I knew how.

"'Well, I'll tell you. What's. Inside.'" It was as obvious as a Kansas tornado that Stewart wasn't happy about what was inside, and his manner was hinting at more: that a good part of his unhappiness had to do with me. He did one of his big breath-intakes and said, "It's a plaster foot. That's what's in there. A plaster foot. And when they see me see it, the three of them are sitting there like three cats who've stuffed themselves with three canaries.'

"'After a second, Mark says, 'Aren't you going to take it out?" And Marty says, 'We didn't know whether to get you a right foot or a left foot, because we weren't sure whether you might have a preference.' 'We didn't want to get you off on the wrong foot,' Arnold says. 'Get it?,' Marty asks, 'Get you off? On the wrong foot?' 'So we got you a right foot,' Mark says.

'Looks like a gladiator's foot, doesn't it? We wanted to get you a replica of one of Sting's feet. We thought we might scare up a plaster caster who by some stroke of luck would have one.' Arnold says, 'Remember plaster casters from the Sixties? We looked into whether they're still around, but they're not, and near as we could find out, they always stuck to penises. Not even a Mick Jagger foot could we turn up. Or Charlie Watts, who after all is a drummer and has talented feet.'"

All the while Stewart went on about this, I was picturing him sitting at The Food Place holding a plaster foot in a shoe box. I wanted to laugh. I didn't, of course, which was smart, because the next thing Stewart said darkly was, "And you told me they'd forget about it." The implication was that if I hadn't told him to forget about it, he would have devoted more time to preparing for a plaster-foot humiliation or something along those lines and wouldn't have been caught as off guard as he was. In other words, I was responsible for compounding the ignominy.

"I thought they might let it go," I said. "Might forget it. I hoped they would."

"They didn't, and that's not the end of it," Stewart said. "In my shock and surprise, I was kind of rendered speechless. And motionless. And as I'm sitting there with this plaster right foot in a shoe box on the table in front of me, some guy walks by with a drink in his hand and says, 'Hey, a foot.' 'He likes feet,' Mark says to him, pointing at me and winking. Winking! 'Why the fuck not?' the guy says.

"'No, I don't,' I say to him like I care what a stranger thinks. But the truth is, I do care. 'Don't pay any attention to him,' Marty says, 'he's just shy about it. He's scared people will be judgmental.' 'Who has the right to judge?,' this guy says, and he's very good-looking. 'We all have our quirks. I like licking assholes. Long as they're clean. I didn't used to admit it, but then I realized it's just another thing to do. A very human thing. And we're all human, right?'

"Then he reaches into the box, taps the foot on the instep three times with his knuckle and walks off to join his friends." Stewart mimed the knocks. "I watch this self-avowed asshole-licker say something to his chums, and they all look over and give me the thumbs up. One of them raises his shoe at me and wiggles it." He waited for that to register. Then he said, "And you said it was probably over. It's the farthest thing from over. Now I can't go into The Food Place without wondering if everybody there knows me as the one who loves feet. And I hate feet. More than ever."

The next time I heard from Stewart, he didn't hold his update for a face-to-face encounter. The phone rang, and when I picked it up, Stewart said, without acknowledging my hello, "Mark and Arnold and Marty fixed me up on a blind date last night. They said they wanted to make it up to me for their going on about feet. They gave me the number of someone they'd met who they thought I'd like. Since I wanted to trust them, I called him up – Hal – and we talked for a while. He sounded like an okay guy. Interesting. He works at the Central Park zoo. A zoologist with hands-on experience. He loves animals. You gotta love an animal lover, right?

"So I asked him over Saturday night. He arrived on time. Cute, thirty-ish, receding hairline, big smile. I show him in, offer him something to drink. He just wants whatever juice I have in the house. I give him a choice of orange or apple-cranberry. He opts for the apple-cranberry. I tell him to make himself at home, and I go into the kitchen. When I come back with the juice, he's laid himself on my sofa with his bare feet facing me. 'I hear you like it like this,' he said and jiggled his toes.'

"'You heard wrong,' I say so he'll know I mean it. To his credit, he got very embarrassed and reached immediately for his shoes and socks, which he'd put neatly under the end table. 'You've been taken advantage of by my so-called friends,' I said. 'The truth is, I think feet are genuine eyesores.' When I said that, the guy – Hal – looked so injured, I had to say, 'Not yours. You've got okay feet. More than okay.'

"'I almost gagged on the words. Hal got up to go, but I felt so sorry for him, I asked him to stay awhile so we could talk. Which we did – as a zoologist he knows a lot about feet and paws – and then I let him go. Not long after he left, the phone rang. When I picked it up, someone asked in a low voice, 'Is this the guy who services feet?' I said no, and asked him how he got my number. 'From the bathroom wall at The Food Place,' he said. 'I had to go right over there with a magic marker and obliterate it.' I couldn't tell whose handwriting it was. I figured it was Mark's or Arnold's. I don't think Marty would go that far. Now are you satisfied?' He yelled that so loudly, I had to move the receiver away from my ear."

"I don't think it's a question of my gratification," I said. To empty air. He'd already hung up.

I knew Stewart was pissed off at me, but I suspected he wasn't so put out that he'd remain out of touch. I reckoned that I was the only person he could talk to about his on-going crisis and that if, indeed, it was still going on, he'd alert me out of desperation. This is why I wasn't surprised at the desperate tone in his voice the next time he phoned. Just before midnight on a Tuesday a few weeks later. Could he come over? He wouldn't stay long. He just had to "get it off my chest." Needless to say, I suppressed the urge to ask, "Get what off your chest – someone's foot?"

When I let Stewart in, he looked like a man afraid he was being followed. Before he unwound the blue-and-white knitted scarf he had on or unbuttoned the camelhair overcoat, he went to my window and peered down at the street. "Don't you think you're being a little too dramatic," I asked, as I signaled him to give me the coat and scarf.

"I don't know what to think," he said and sat on my sofa with his coat still on. "What do you have to drink?"

"You don't drink," I said.

"I drink juice. I drink water."

I got him some Pellegrino with ice, while he sat there distractedly ruffling his unkempt hair.

"Now what?" I asked.

"Today's mail," Stewart said. Since I had continued gesturing for him to hand me his coat, he was taking it off and passing it my way. "I received a copy of a magazine – *Big Foot*. It has one of those banners on it that reads 'Complimentary copy.' There's a slogan under the title – 'For men who admire feet.' I take one look and drop the magazine like it's a squirming rat. When it hits the floor, it falls open to a page where a corner has been turned down. I pick it up and look at the page. At the bottom, an ad is circled. It says – all in small letters – www.feetfellas.com. No hyphen in feetfellas. Something tells me I need to go to the website. I fight the urge. I throw the magazine in the trashcan in the kitchen. It's the first time I've ever regretted I took out the compacter. But I keep thinking about that web address. So I give in."

I have to confess that by this time, I was on tenterhooks. Wouldn't anyone be? But Stewart was having trouble finding the energy to get the words out. When he spoke, it was as if words were cannonballs, and he was hauling them up a steep slope. "I get online," he said, "and go to www.feetfellas.com. The home page comes up, and it's what you expect. If that's what you expect. I expected it. It's a website devoted to... I don't have to tell you what it's devoted to. There are pictures and headlines, and smack in the middle under a banner that says, 'New Feet in Town,' there's a close-up of two feet, the bottoms of blunt toes and wrinkled soles forward. They're crossed, as if the owner is relaxing, and they're as ugly as sin. And you can tell they're flat feet. Under the picture is a caption. Do you know what it says?" I shook my head. I had an inkling, but I didn't want to confirm his fear that his disgrace was apparent. "It says, 'Stewart P, New York City, 13Cs, try us on for sighs. Size is spelled s-i-g-h-s."

I have to allow here that while there was something indisputably amusing about this, Stewart's crestfallen appearance was so acute, there was no chance of my betraying even the hint of a smile. I knew it was my turn to say something, and so I said faintly, "I guess there's no possibility it's referring to another Stewart P?"

"From New York City? I don't think so," Stewart bellowed – he'd found his vocal strength. "I don't see another one in the phone book."

"How did they get the picture to send in?" I asked. "I know you didn't give it to them."

"What picture?" Stewart howled. "Those aren't my feet! I don't wear a size 13 shoe. I don't have flat feet. I wear a size 11 shoe, and I have high arches. High enough. They sent in a picture of someone else's feet. Who knows how they got it or where they got it from."

"Can you do that?" I asked.

"What do you mean, 'Can you do that?'! They did it. There it is – a picture of what are supposed to be my feet with the irrefutable implication that I like showing them off when I'm kicking back. I don't like showing off my feet. I never show my feet. I've had long-term lovers who have never seen my goddamn feet."

Stewart was now so wound up, I thought he was going to lift off. I wondered if I could lighten the atmosphere. "Ah," I said, "so you're a guy who likes to make love with his boots on."

No atmosphere got lightened. To the contrary, additional consternation gathered on his brow. "This is no time for comedy," Stewart said.

"Maybe," I ventured, "this is time for nothing but comedy."

"Believe me, it isn't." Stewart parried. "My feet – or two appendages purporting to be my feet – are on a website for all the world to see."

"All the world isn't going to see it," I said.

"No, only the drooling-over-feet percentage of the populace. In a world population of a few billion, that probably only means a few million foot-lovers. How about if someone from work sees it?"

"You're safe there," I said, "anyone who finds you there and talks about it is admitting something about himself."

"I'm not in the mood to be thanking God for small mercies," Stewart said. He had picked up his scarf and was twisting it around his hands. I took him to be wringing surrogate necks. "My question is: What do I do now?"

"You could try to get the photo removed."

"How? By contacting the website. That's the last thing I want to do. Besides, presumably I have already contacted them. As far as they know, I'm the one who set himself up to be flavor of the month. Pistachi-toe."

"Get in touch with Mark or Marty or Arnold. Tell them you got the joke – ha-ha-ha – and now it's time for them to get your picture off the Internet."

"Do I have to remind you it isn't my picture?" Stewart said and, for an instant, smouldered. "Furthermore, I'm not going to give the three of them the satisfaction of knowing I saw it and then calling them with a feeble plea."

"That's my boy," I said, "make them wonder. Give them a little of their own back."

Looking like a Renaissance portrait of misery, Stewart stood up to go. "I guess that's what I have to do." He didn't seem wedded to the idea, and his spirits didn't improve as I showed him to and out the door. I watched him go down the stairs, shoulder sagging and scarf around his neck like a knitted boa constrictor.

I didn't hear from Stewart for at least a month, and I didn't think I should call him. If he'd gotten any website-induced offers, I probably would have heard. If he had anything dire to tell me or any further complaints about Mark, Martin and Arnold, he'd have called. When I thought about it, which I did from time to time, I wondered what they could do to top the Internet prank. I couldn't think of anything. It did occur to me they could rent digitalized Times Square billboard space and run a 'Stewart Pekin Wants Your Feet' ad, but the expense would have been prohibitive for those anything-but-big-spenders.

Not hearing from Stewart, however, didn't mean I wasn't curious. I was. I also worried some. How about if he were so traumatized by his association with the foot lovers of this world that he was sitting in his house, catatonic. Staring at the walls; worse, staring at his feet. I fantasized his taking an axe to those high-arched size elevens and then realized I was getting as bad as he was. So I turned my mind to other things.

And then I did hear news. But as the playful gods would have it, I didn't hear from Stewart. I heard from Mark. And quite by accident. (Or is anything accidental?) I was walking across West 23rd Street one spring Saturday afternoon after taking care of a few chores, when I passed Mark. I didn't see him; he saw me.

"That's you, isn't it, Daniel?" he said. I allowed as how it was, although I won't say I was pleased to see him. Actually, my gorge rose more than I might have imagined it would have when I thought of how he and his chums had been making a pigeon of poor Stewart. It rose even farther when I thought of how I'd had to listen to a time-consuming series of accounts of their extended practical joke and the mild havoc it had wreaked.

I let none of this on. Far be it from me to offer more grist for their Stewart Pekin-baiting mill. As a matter of fact, I switched tone-of-voice gears from the cool one I had affected when acknowledging his greeting –

to something decidedly more casual. This was on the suspicion that if he detected distance, he might have ascribed it to my knowing about Stewart and the foot caper. We knew each other so little that nothing else would be likely to leap to his mind as explanation for the chill.

I had another reason, which was that were I sociable during whatever chat we were about to have, he might try to probe whether I knew anything of what had been going on and where I stood on the matter. I figured that toying with his curiosity was revenge enough for the ear-bending he'd indirectly subjected me to.

Considering what transpired, I'd figured out rather well. "Yes, it's me, Mark," I said, with what I considered the appropriate dose of unctuousness. "You probably weren't sure, because of the goatee. I've had it for a couple of months, and you're not the first to be confused. So how is everything?"

Mark is on the thin and short-ish side but wiry. He has struck me – the few times I've been in his company – as not knowing what to do with all the energy packed in his prominent biceps. When you're talking to him on the street, as I was doing, he shifts from one foot to the other. He was doing that now. "Oh, fine, fine," he said, "Can't complain. Work's going well."

He stopped short there, thinking, I assume, it was my turn to jump in with a brief report on the state of personal affairs. I didn't. Instead, I continued smiling approval at him. He was forced to keep the conversation going.

"So," he said, and I liked seeing him visibly conjuring nonchalance, "have you seen much of Stewart lately?"

I hesitated a couple of seconds to do some grinding action with my mouth and teeth that would suggest I was thinking this over. "No, I haven't," I said, as if I'd just realized I hadn't. "Not in a couple of weeks.

Maybe a month. Actually, now that I think of it, maybe even longer."

"Haven't even talked to him, huh?"

"Not for a while," I said. "I guess you've seen him much more recently. Your movie night. How is he?"

Mark stopped shuffling. "Got a minute?" he asked.

The familiar got-a-minute was when I knew something intriguing was about to come at me. "I have more than a minute," I said but made sure to temper anything that sounded like enthusiasm. "And you know, it's foolish to stand out here in the elements when there's a Starbucks not a hundred yards from here. In any direction."

Mark indoors was as restless as he was outdoors. I'd forgotten this from the one night I'd been out with the movie club. He continually shifted his own position as well as the position of his coffee cup. He also has a tendency to talk out of one side of his mouth. It was my surmise, given the circumstances as they unfolded, that he was probably even more restless than usual.

When we settled down (i.e., when I settled down and Mark settled down as much as he was going to), I said, "Stewart's all right, isn't he? I had the impression from what little you've said that maybe he's in trouble."

Mark rocked his chair towards me and said, "We don't know." He paused for that to register; I merely widened my eyes and gave my head a tell-me-more shake. "He's been acting strangely."

I ought to mention here that I don't think Mark is an objectionable guy. I bought it when Stewart said he was tough but worth it. And I could see from the look in Mark's eyes that somewhere in there was a tinge of genuine concern along with the tinges of who-knows-what-else. "'Strangely,'" I said, "Stewart? How? There are many ways to act strangely."

"I'm not sure I should say," Mark said. "It might come out sounding like gossip."

Taking into account what I knew of Mark's recent activities in regard to Stewart – his evident collaboration with Marty and Arnold to manufacture gossip about the put-upon fellow – I had to smile inwardly at his show of delicacy. "Surely," I said, masking my amusement, "if two friends are discussing the welfare of a third friend, their exchange can't be categorized as gossip. What do you think?"

"Perhaps you're right," he said.

"Although," I stuck in, because I was determined to derive my share of fun from the serendipitous meeting, "I don't want to twist your arm into betraying confidences." I could see from the glint in Mark's eye – coming not from that concern I'd detected only moments before – that no arm-twisting was necessary.

"No, no," Mark said, perhaps a beat too quickly, "you're a friend of Stewart's, and maybe you ought to know about this."

"If you're sure," I said.

Mark nodded vigorously that he was sure. "Okay," he said, "you know our movie club?" I shook my head in assent. "How we meet every couple of weeks – flexible night. Last Thursday we arrange to see the Clint Eastwood movie..."

"Oh," I said, interrupting him mainly because I knew he didn't want to be interrupted, "I've been wanting to see it. Is it any good?"

"It's okay," Mark said, clearly irked that I'd changed a subject near and dear to his conniving heart. "But about Stewart. He meets us – Marty, Arnold and me – at the movie, and he's got someone with him. Someone I know – Hal Bradley."

"Hal," I said as neutrally as I knew how. "Bradley. Uh-huh."

"Marty and Arnold know him, too – works at the Central Park Zoo.

So we all say hello and good to see you *et cetera*. It's obvious from the way Stewart and Hal are looking at each other that something's going on between them."

"You mean early-stage Significant Other?" I said.

"From the look of things, not such early-stage," Mark said.

"Is that so?" I said, "I haven't heard a word from Stewart about a b-f coming on the scene. I wonder how they met."

"I'm not sure," Mark said, "but I think I may have even mentioned Hal to Stewart as somebody I know that he might find interesting. They shared some interests."

"Really," I said, "what are those?"

"Oh," Mark said, "I don't know. Interests. Things in general."

"Uh-huh," I said again, "but nothing specific you can think of at the moment."

"No," Mark said, making a couple syllables out of the one-syllable word. "So the five of us go into the movie, and on the way across one of those long stretches of hideous carpeting you have to travel before you get inside the movie you're seeing, Stewart and Hal are holding hands and making goo-goo eyes at each other."

"Wow, our Stewart," I said and gave a low whistle, which is something I do very well. "Tell me more."

"I thought you'd be interested."

"I am," I said, "but so far there's nothing strange about Stewart's behavior. Well, aside from his not having had a boyfriend in a while."

"I'm getting to it, I'm getting to it," Mark said, annoyed with me again. He hesitated to see if I'd quiet down. I did, and he resumed his story, though not before shooting me a warning glance. "We found seats just as they started those fucking awful ads they're throwing up on movie screens now, and then the trailers come on. We're sitting Hal on the aisle,

Stewart, me, Marty, Arnold. Do you get the picture? The seating order is important."

"I've got it firmly fixed in my mind," I said, very benignly.

"The previews are rolling on – one after another after another. They're really boring, like they always are, and I become aware that Stewart and Hal are leaning into each other, whispering sweet nothings, if you can believe that."

"I'm trying to," I said.

"And although I know they don't want to be overheard," Mark said, "I'm beginning to pick up words and phrases about how they are so lucky to have found each other and they can't wait for the movie to be over so that can go home and make out. Then they're whispering that they want to kiss each other all over and lick each other all over." He halts to make sure I'm getting the strength of all this.

"Yucky, but still not strange," I said.

"Not strange, huh?" Mark said, "you don't think so? You want strange. Are you ready for it. Here it comes. Then I hear Stewart say to Hal, 'I want to suck your toes,' and Hal says back, 'And I want to suck your toes...'"

'No," I said, "you must have heard wrong. After all, they were whispering and you knew they were talking soft enough so you wouldn't hear. Maybe Stewart said something like – oh, I don't know – I want you to shuck your clothes or – I don't know – I'm stuck on your cute nose."

Mark was shifting even more animatedly. "I know what I heard, and it was all about toe-sucking. Marty and Arnold heard it, too."

"Let me get this straight," I said, now playing this for all it was worth. "Marty and Arnold heard this, too, even though they were sitting on the other side of you, and Stewart and this Hal guy were whispering so's not to be heard?"

"Marty and Arnold heard, because, one, they were leaning in," Mark said, underlining his report with matching body movements, "and two, Stewart and Hal were in that lovey-dovey frame of mind where they'd forgotten there was anyone else around to hear. They're saying, 'I want to suck your big toe and each toe right down to the piggy.' The piggy," he said. "On both feet."

"You're right," I said, "This is strange. This does not sound like the Stewart I know. The one who thinks feet are ugly."

"That's what I thought," Mark said. "That's what he always said, but now I see it was just to throw us off the scent."

"Are you referring to foot odor?" I asked, thinking maybe I could interpose a little mischief.

"Not yet," Mark said, "but I'm getting to that. You didn't know Stewart had a thing for feet. I didn't either, but we were all fooled. Because if you think I was imagining the part about sucking big toes and piggies, what happened next will clinch it for you. The movie starts, but Marty, Arnold and I are hardly aware of that, because of what happens next. I hear Stewart say something like 'I can't wait until we get home to suck your toes and kiss your arches, and I see him start to bend over. And Hal is bending over, too. And they're grabbing at each other's feet."

That Stewart! I thought. I wouldn't have guessed he had it in him. That's what I was thinking, but what I said was, "Right there? Out in the open. They were going for each other's feet?"

"They were oblivious to everything and everybody." Mark said.

"Other people were aware of them?" I asked.

"People were turning around to look at them," Mark said. "By this time, Stewart was contorted and Hal had Stewart's foot in his lap and was removing his loafer. It was disgusting. It was beyond disgusting. Two grown men acting like that. All three of us were disgusted. I'm cringing now just remembering it."

"Who wouldn't cringe?" I asked gravely. "Even if you happen to subscribe to a to-each-his-own policy? What happened then?"

"Who was sticking around to see what happened then?" Mark said. "It was too vomititious. I gave Marty and Arnold the high sign, and we all got up and pushed past the two toe-suckers and ran up the aisle. We didn't even stay to see the movie and be pointed at as the guys who were with the foot fetishists. We sneaked into one of the other theaters."

"And you're convinced they just continued their podiphilic practices?" I asked. I made the word up on the spur of the moment. I couldn't think of any other way to phrase it.

"If that means feet, yes, I'm convinced," Mark said. "You weren't there. You didn't see how prepared to munch they were."

"Yes," I said, "it definitely sounds as if popcorn wasn't going to satisfy the appetites of that ravenous pair. But Stewart of all people, a foot man. He never seemed the type."

"What's the type?" Mark begged.

"Now that you ask," I said, "I suppose Stewart is, but I just would never have known."

"I didn't either," Mark said, "even though maybe I should have."

"Why on earth should you have?"

"The signs."

"What signs?"

"Well," Mark said, suddenly getting very confidential. "A couple of weeks before this took place, the four of us were together – Arnold, Marty, Stewart, myself, movie night – and we passed a poster on the street. I don't know whether you've seen it. It's for one of the radio stations, and it's got Sting in it. He's in a tub with his feet sticking up in the air. Do you know the one I mean?"

Why should I have come clean at that point? "I don't think I do," I said.

Mark said, "Take my word for it. And when we passed the poster, Stewart said something I didn't make much of at the time."

"Oh," I said, "what was that?"

Mark drew himself up, "He said, 'Nice feet.'"

"'Nice feet,' you say?" I said, pretending to think it over. "Sounds like a harmless remark to me."

"That's what I thought," Mark said. "So I didn't make anything of it at the time. Neither did Arnold or Marty."

"And now," I asked, "what are you going to make of it?"

"Marty, Arnold and I talked it over," Mark said, "and decided we're not going to make anything of it now either. It's Stewart's life, but we also decided that while it's up to him whether or not he goes for feet, we don't want to encourage it. Certainly not when we're around him. Personally, we're never going to bring up the word 'feet' or 'foot' around him ever again."

"Sounds like a wise decision to me," I said, "and perhaps I'll adopt the same approach. Maybe we should all start campaigning for the long postponed switch to the metric system, too, so we can avoid using 'foot' and 'feet' in that context."

"Now do you understand what I mean by strange?" Mark said.

"I do," I said, "so strange that I think we should keep this conversation just between the two of us, don't you think?"

"Absolutely," Mark said. That agreement triggered the conclusion of our business, and we left shortly thereafter.

When I got home, I phoned Stewart to congratulate him. (I don't have a cell phone, or I would have rung sooner.) Also to chastise him for not notifying me about his night out with Hal and the boys.

"I've been meaning to call," Stewart said in a voice slightly lower and more resonant than I'd always associated with him, "but a lot has been going on. Meet me now, and I'll fill you in. I need a change of venue, though. I'll be at the Starbucks near you that we haven't gone to.

Stewart was already there, when I showed up. He'd taken off the camelhair coat, and it was across his knees like a lap robe. It was probably too warm a day for the coat, but I knew Stewart was wedded to the dated garment. I waved away the thought of my getting coffee and said I'd be happy to watch him enjoy his latte.

"I'm told you and Hal Bradley put on some charade at the movies last week," I said to Stewart when we'd settled in.

"I can tell you it started out like a charade," he replied. He took a nice pause and rearranged himself into something seriously straightforward. "After I spoke to you last, I was determined to get those guys off my back, but I wasn't sure how. For some reason, it occurred to me to call Hal. I think because they'd also played a dirty trick on him, and although I had no way of knowing whether he was interested in getting back at them, I thought at least he'd understand my inclinations."

"I see," I said, although I didn't see entirely.

"We met that night for a drink. My idea was that I'd explain why I'd called and what I had in mind, vague as it was. But a funny thing happened. The longer we talked – we were having dinner by then – I realized I was losing interest in Mark and Marty and Arnold and becoming interested in Hal."

He sipped his latte and then looked over at me. I got the gap-toothed smile. "There's a simple way to fill you in on everything you need to know about our behavior on the night in question," he said. With that he pushed his chair back from the Starbucks table, pulled his overcoat up, swung his legs out. He was right. I got the complete picture of why Hal and he had devised the false foot-fetish frolic(k) for the boys and the part said hoax played at their finding each other in this zany universe: Although it was still early April, he was wearing open-toed sandals. I had the urge to say “nice feet” but stopped myself.

Blue Beard

Oh, to be young and foolish again!

Not.

When I was young and foolish, I knew for sure I was young (and reveled in it), but I didn't have the vaguest inkling how foolish I was. Less so the unfortunate forms foolishness can and will assume.

Nor did I have any insight – wouldn't have wanted it – into the problems, not to say the damage, a young man's unexamined and unchecked foolishness can cause.

On the contrary, like so many other young men with whom I was acquainted then, I believed I knew it all and if I didn't know it all, I certainly believed I knew enough of it to be pretty sure of myself and my effectiveness in almost any situation.

As the saying goes, I thought I was hot stuff. As the vulgar spin on the saying goes, I thought I was hot shit.

And why wouldn't I be? I'd had a relatively privileged upbringing, I'd been born with a snappy intellect (and the absence of any understanding that intellect isn't all), I'd gone to the best schools and sailed through them with an oddball combination of conscientiousness and insouciance, I'd come to the world's best city where in green-apple-quick-time I'd located an affordable apartment to rent and landed, hot off the swanky streets, a hotsy-totsy little position at a well-read magazine where they liked adding new old-school-tie boys at the low end of the masthead.

The world was my erster, so to speak.

I also found a use for a small unexpected and unlooked for talent I'd discovered I had.

This goes back to bright college years where I roomed in the same entryway with a funny (both funny ha-ha and funny peculiar) guy who fancied himself a composer. Terry Woodside was his believable enough name. He stood about yea high with pudgy arms and legs, a round face that resembled the crescent moon and talked six to the dozen whenever you ran into him.

He could be something of a nuisance, he was that gregarious, that garrulous, but you couldn't really dislike him. Okay, some of the fellows did, but most didn't and said things about him along the lines of "Terry's all right – I get a kick out of him."

That was pretty much my take, and whenever we bumped into each other or ended up sitting together in the Commons, we more or less talked easily.

It was during one of these early senior-year conversations when Terry gave out with there being a school tradition of senior class songs that over the decades had been more honored in the breach, but he was damned if in his – in our – senior year he was going to breach it. Cole Porter hadn't, and Terry figured he, at twenty-one, was just as good and as promising as Cole Porter was at twenty-one.

That's the kind of confidence he had, which I racked up to his having a mother who repeatedly told him, he said proudly and often, how "gifted" he was.

While we all scarfed down our tuna casserole, Terry said he'd been fooling around on the piano in the Commons lobby for a while and had come up with a few tunes he liked. Now all he needed, he said, was someone to write the words.

He admitted he wasn't so good at that.

We were eating with four or five other guys who encouraged him – half-seriously, half-jokingly, some winkingly – to follow through on the class song(s) idea, but when he mentioned needing a lyricist, they shut up and looked at each other.

I was looking from one to the other just as they were and sensing the urge to roll my eyes, too, but after several seconds of this eye-shifting, I thought, "What the hell!"

I turned to Terry and said outright, "I'll give it a go. Why not?"

I knew a few Cole Porter songs, and, by gum, I knew his fight song – "Boola Boola." I thought to myself that if I couldn't come up with something as good or better than Porter's "Boola Boola" – how simple-minded is that, for Pete's sake? – I'd be a sorry excuse for an Ivy Leaguer.

(Only decades later did I learn Porter was not, as most people believe, the song's author. Allan M. Hirsh, class of 1901, was, but by then, the light bulb going on above my noggin changed nothing.)

So immediately after we finished lunch, Terry – being the eager beaver he was – got me to the piano and played the first of his melodies.

I can't say what came over me, but when he did, I began hearing phrases for which the names of various campus landmarks fit, and, figuring proleptic nostalgia was the way to go – since that's how so many college songs rattle on – a lyric hewing to something like "oh, those long ago golden days of yore!" would be just the ticket.

Thus, after a certain amount of backing and forthing with Terry, a song was born, was precipitately played for the graduation committee, passed muster, and was sung by a dozen graduating seniors with good voices (not, I hasten to say, The Whiffenpoofs) during one of the graduation weekend ceremonies.

The song was even finished early enough to be published in the yearbook, where it can be found today, were anyone intent on giving it a backward-longing sight-read.

I can't say Terry and I labored very strenuously over it, nor will I say he didn't tweak it somewhat into its final shape. Nor can I say it forged a sudden unbreakable bond between him and me. My circle of friends wasn't his, and vice versa, and, although we were both around for rehearsals of the one-time-only performance, the numbered days of senior year and undergrad life essentially skipped along as previously.

I can only say I did wrote the words (or most of them) to 'Thinking Back on Campus Life (I Think of Magic Years)' – boasting rhymes like "cheers," "souvenirs," "beers," "engineers," "laughs and tears," "queers" (excised from final draft but retained for parody version) – and I enjoyed the brief notoriety attached to the song.

Nonetheless, I thought little of it in the couple years after we'd left school. Moreover, once we'd departed those dear old ringing, hallow'd halls, I never thought one way or the other about keeping in touch with Terry. I knew he was also in New York City, because I saw Bucky Steadman one day on 57th Street, and he said he'd seen Terry in a different part of town "swinging along, crazy as ever, too into himself to see me."

Otherwise I knew nothing of him. That's until, one day out of the blue, I got a call from him at work.

At work, no less!

I'd thought so little about him and I was so entrenched in the editing I was doing when I picked up the phone that he had to say his name twice before I realized who it was. This, despite his having the kind of buzz-saw voice it's hard to forget.

"Oh, hi, Terry," I said – or something vague and flat as that, my mind still on what I was supposed to be doing. (Deadline days have that effect.) "How are you, old bean?"

Why I'd addressed him as 'old bean,' I'll never know. Maybe I do know. Maybe I thought it was a slightly irritating salutation, and he'd retreat from it.

He didn't. "I'll come right to the point," he said voice buzz-sawing away and completely letting the 'o-b' sobriquet slide.

He did come right to his point, it being that he was still pursuing composing as a career – although for a survival job he was selling clothes at a downtown department store everyone knew – and he'd recently been asked to contribute to a small satirical revue some friends with a do-or-die theatrical bent were putting on.

He'd tried to write with a couple of them but didn't like what they were turning out – or "not turning out well," as he put it. He wondered, since we'd had such an instantly successful collaboration at the revered alma mater (my words, not his), whether I'd be interested in having "another whirl."

Not meaning to be curt but also aware I needed to be closing my section of the upcoming issue in no time flat, I reminded him our success was based on one song and, at that, was probably a fluke.

He said maybe, maybe not. What's to lose by trying again?

As much to get him off the phone as anything else, I said I'd give it some thought and dictated my home phone number, asking him in future to reach me there and not at the office.

He reached me at home about a week later, asking if I'd given it the thought I said I would give it, and if so, would I do it? His friends had raised the little money they needed, had nailed down a small, run-down but serviceable West Village venue and were getting ready to go into rehearsal.

Truth to tell, I hadn't given it any thought. His initial phone call had just about slipped my mind, but I didn't want to admit it outright. I fumfered and said I had given it a little thought but didn't have any ideas, unless – here's where I made either my first mistake or my first smart step – he was talking about making fun of things like the boring Nixon administration, you know, things like Pat Nixon's cloth coat.

"There's your title," he screeched so loudly through the phone that I had to hold it away from my ear. "Pat Nixon's Cloth Coat," I heard him yelling. I put the phone back to my ear in time to hear him say, "I knew you could do it. When can we get together?"

Somehow I didn't feel I could put him off, and in all honesty, I was tickled at the prospect of writing a song about Pat Nixon's cloth coat and everything it represented about the false humility of the wretchedly unfolding Nixon years.

I told Terry I could meet him the following Saturday morning at his very far west (read tenement) West 47th Street apartment, where he'd informed me he had a Yamaha piano thanks to a small trust fund that had come his way on graduating.

When I arrived at the address he'd given, I was no sooner in the door – had no sooner taken in the clutter amid which he lived so that getting to the piano was an adventure – than he sat down and played a melody he'd come up with, a jaunty item, I must say.

"What do you think?" he asked suspiciously in what over the years I learned was his typical query after playing a melody for me the first time.

"It's good," I said, noting the suspicious glint in his narrowed eyes.

"Just good?" he asked – also, although I didn't know it at the time, a standard Woodside rejoinder.

"Really good," I said.

"You realize the first phrase is where we put the title phrase, 'Pat Nixon's Cloth Coat.'"

"Yes," I said, "and in the almost identical phrase right after it, we put 'Not even some fur at the throat.' So it's 'Pat Nixon's cloth coat, not even some fur at the throat.'"

Fast as that, it had come to me.

Terry looked at me wide-eyed, the previous glint turning into a flare. "That's great," he said, "I knew you were the person for this. Let's keep going. We can finish the whole thing today."

That's just what we did. The song practically wrote itself, although it really didn't, and the next day, Terry had me come with him when he played it for the rest of the revue team, who loved it, asked if we had more. "No," Terry said, "but we can come up with more."

Yet again, I took the "why not?" attitude.

We wrote three more songs that were incorporated into the show, which, when it opened to encouraging notices, reaped us a couple of genuinely nice mentions.

Since there had been little money to promote *The Underfed Revue*, it took those favorable notices (for us and the other writers and performers) and, more importantly, good word-of-mouth for the enterprise to start building. When it did, more and more people started coming downtown to catch it. That gathering rush, that flush included producers, casting directors, the usual on-the-prowl-for-new-talent show-biz ilk.

The result was that all of us whose names were on the credits began to get nibbles for work elsewhere. Corby Whitaker was probably the first to hit it big, cast, as he was almost immediately, in the Broadway revival of Eugene O'Neill's *Ah, Wilderness*, which led to the screen test, and the rest is film history.

Since nightly 'Pat Nixon's Cloth Coat' was getting big laughs and applause, Terry and I were approached, too. Nothing came our way fast enough for us to quit our day jobs, but we were having meetings with some mighty intriguing and intrigued people, many, though not all, of the appointments plotted by our recently acquired agent at – wait for it! – William Morris.

So one Saturday when we were working on the imminent second edition of *The Underfed Revue* in the flotsam and jetsam, the yin and yang, the *sturm und drang* of Terry's apartment, the phone rang. Terry left the piano to answer it, picked up the receiver, said hello and then listened with dropping jaw and popping eyes to whatever was transpiring on the other end.

Finally, he said into the phone, "He's here now. I'll have to ask him." He put his hand over the speaker and said, "You'll never guess who this is."

I said, "If I'll never guess, you'd better tell me."

It was a director we'd never met but who we knew was young, hot and out of town – in New Haven, no less – with a new musical. They were having trouble, little surprise with a new musical on the road. It was imperative that comic songs be supplied for a show that was ostensibly a comedy, but the show's songwriters were apparently having difficulty supplying enough of them.

Our names had come up as possible score doctors. More than one person connected with the production had seen *The Underfed Revue*, had liked our material and recommended we be contacted.

Would we fast get on a train to New Haven – all expenses reimbursed, of course – so we could meet the producers and director between the matinée and the evening performances. They'd like us to play some of our songs for those who didn't know our work and then, if we liked and they liked, we could watch the evening performance, which starred – we knew this very well; who didn't from the advance publicity? – the great stage and sometimes television and movie clown Diz Frawley.

Who, by the way, would be sitting in on our meeting.

"We'll be with you in a minute," Terry buzzed into the speaker, while I, dazed, perched on his poop-brown couch.

Hand over the speaker again, Terry said, "We have to go, don't we?"

The "why-not" response had worked for me before. I didn't see any reason it wouldn't again.

"Sure," I said. "I have nothing else to do today, unless you think we need to finish what we're working on."

"The hell with it," Terry said, letting volume get away with him.

It was only 12:30. You can bet we got to Grand Central Station and up to New Haven and into the lobby of the Taft Hotel – next to the Shubert where *Funny Is as Funny Does*, starring Diz Frawley, was playing – in plenty of time to meet the *FIAFD* contingent at 5:15.

Were we nervous? Yes. We were two kids about to audition for some of the most recognizable names in show business.

Then again, we were young and foolish, had a few good reviews behind us and were catercornered from the campus on which not that long ago had been trumpeted our class song, faint echoes of which had begun to soothe my inner ears.

Neither Terry nor I had particularly outstanding singing voices, but Terry had his inimitable buzz-saw edge and the courage of his conviction that he was the next Cole Porter, and I had my handy "what's there to lose?" *modus vivendi*.

We sang three songs, leading off with "Pat Nixon's Cloth Coat."

We had played material for others of this stripe – or almost as prominent – in recent months. So we weren't completely undone by the reception as it unfolded. We knew that their not laughing heartily didn't necessarily mean they didn't like what they heard but that they were thinking about it.

(As is well known, show-business people think it adequate if, on hearing jokes or songs, they merely say an uninflected "That's funny." The concession excuses them from actually having to laugh. It identifies them as Mavens of The Joke, rather than as your average lay laughers.)

Also, in these situations, people can be waiting for others to endorse what they've heard. That saves them from being caught out on a limb, alone, abandoned and egg-on-faced.

As we sat there grinning and waiting, that's what was going on – with one exception:

Diz Frawley.

He had chuckled through the three songs and had even let out a single wall-shaking yuk during one of them. As those who remember Diz will know, he was a big and burly man, a man whose humor was predicated in large part on the delicacy with which he moved his bulky body around. For a man with a fleshy face and features that could have been lifted from steeplechase billboards, he had unusually tiny hands and feet. He also had bulging eyes, an ample nose and a mouth so rubbery his lips could have been two eels teasing each other.

When we finished and got our grins in place, Diz looked at the others, sized up what was going on and after less than a minute that felt like an hour had elapsed, said, "I don't know what's with the rest of you bozos, but I think these guys are terrific. I'd do their material any day of the week."

That's all they needed to hear. Diz had hardly finished his remarks when they were in competition to see who agreed with him more. The producers Harley Goodrich and Augie Fiedler asked us how soon we could write them at least two songs. That hot, young director, Ellis Simpson, said they'd better wait until we saw the show and decided what we could do for the score and where. The designers, there for the heck of it, nodded like bobble-heads in the back of a speeding sedan.

Terry and I felt as if we were the men of the hour. We left the production suite, flanking Diz, his heavy arms around our shoulders like a boxer leaving the ring and his attendants after the knockout round.

We were in like Flynn.

Better yet, we were in a win-win situation. *Funny Is as Funny Does* was a show in trouble, all right. We knew it the minute we saw it that night. Both of us had witnessed enough Shubert try-outs in our four New Haven years to recognize poor-bordering-on-unsalvageable fast enough.

When we were finally alone, we wondered to each other how this high-toned cadre had gotten themselves immersed in something with so little obvious promise.

(It took us much longer to learn that's a question you never ask of, or about, theater people: The best of them lose objectivity some of the time, maybe even most of the time.)

But we were in the cat-bird seat. We could – and did – write a couple of comedy numbers for Diz Frawley, and he delivered them as if he were in the middle of *Fiddler on the Roof*. One catchy ditty, 'People Are People,' was choreographed by Wiley Hooper so amusingly and Diz danced it with such a twinkle in his banjo eyes and a buoyancy in his little cat feet that it stopped the show just about every night – most strategically on opening night.

He consistently spun within-the-proscenium gold of "People are people, and don't you forget it/Because if you do, you'll forever regret it/You'll give them an inch, and they'll sure take a mile/And run you aground with a sickening smile/And leave you in worse shape, Remember I said it.")

For Terry and me this virgin Great-White-Way experience was a thrill, but when the reviews came out, it didn't extend much beyond Diz and Wiley Hooper for their contributions and us for ours. The lack of minced words for the overall quality of the production sealed the fates of too many, and *Funny Is as Funny Does* closed – "shuttered" in the vernacular – after nineteen previews and thirteen performances.

What didn't shutter was our friendship with Diz Frawley, who came away from the flop with a mere blip on his career. Were movie and/or television work not to accrue in the immediate future, he had his stand-up act to return to.

That's where Terry and I became instrumental.

You see, Diz came to believe we two – "the college boyos," as he called us to his confederates – were precisely whom he needed to write new special material for him and in time to write the score to the new musical he had in mind that would make *Funny Is as Funny Does* nothing but a bad dream.

At least, that's what he said, and we believed him. He'd been relying, he reiterated, on what he termed "middle-aged hacks" to give him jokes and ditties, but now he had "two Ivy League geniuses" – as he also crowned us – to do for him.

We ate it up. Here we were, not yet a quarter of a century old, still wet behind the ears (although we didn't see it that way) and palling around with one of the acclaimed comic actors of the day, of the decade, of the age.

Here we were, dining at fancy restaurants with him. When theater fixtures about whom we had only daydreamed came up to his table, we'd be introduced as his "two best writers ever." We'd be billed as "the guys who are going to write me the best ever-lovin' show in town."

What did it matter to us that when he introduced us with all those blared encomia, he never included our names? What did it matter that we weren't even sure he knew our names? No, I'm lying. He knew our names were Terry Woodside and Lionel Caplin. It just wasn't clear if he knew which name went with whom.

What sank in with us two Ivy League geniuses – I say it with tongue in cheek and therefore lisp – was the notoriety.

What didn't register – until much later in some cases and much, much later in others – were the knowing looks some of the table-hoppers exchanged.

What didn't register so rapidly was the discrepancy between the talk about what we'd be writing for him and the ensuing actions not being taken in the way of new material written and/or a score composed for that snazzy-jazzy musical that was going to run for years and make all of our fortunes.

What didn't register was that Terry was still selling clothes at the lower Manhattan emporium and I was still editing like a mad fiend at the newsweekly and those Diz rendezvous could only occur when we could get ourselves free, which was often enough to keep the big guy satisfied.

During our confabs, there was, yes, a certain amount of unspecific "how about this?" and "how about that?" chat. There was talk about ideas for songs, not necessarily what those ideas were but that the three of us should and would be putting our thinking-caps on and coming up with them.

When something struck Terry and me, and we mentioned it – such as his surely being able to include 'People are People' in any act we all put together – Diz would say "fabbo" and change the subject, promising, of course, to come back to it.

There was chat about what kind of tuner would take advantage of Diz's boundless abilities, about whether we should look around for material to adapt or come up with an original concept. When Terry and I would refer to a book we deemed right for adaptation or said we had the germ of an original plot, Diz would say "gonzo" and change the subject, promising, of course, to come back to it.

But above all, what was not registering in the miasma of things not registering was that serious discussion for this three-way collaboration never took up more than a small percentage of our time together – not more than, say, ten or maybe twelve minutes (if that) per meeting.

There was, you see, an ever-present and significant distraction. It wasn't the food we were eating at the establishments Diz favored. Nor the traffic we encountered getting to them when Diz, driving his well-appointed Saab, picked us up or dropped us off at our separate buildings. It wasn't the meal-time interruptions by chums wanting to say hi and then having to shake our hands and listen to Diz give his spiel about us. It wasn't the fans sidling up to our table to ask for Diz's autograph and getting it – but in the bargain having to take Terry's and my autograph, too.

What it was was a young woman called Ina Goldsmith, although sometimes she was called Penny Eversholt.

But who was Ina Goldsmith, who was Penny Eversholt?

Who was this nubile twenty-two-year old with the cascading auburn hair and the blue eyes seductively blue-eye-shadowed and the moist red-red lips and the kind of body men often likened to the proverbial-but-rarely-spotted-in-real-life brick shithouse?

And why did she have two names?

No answer was ever forthcoming on the latter question.

On the former, we had some lowdown we initially thought reliable. Ina/Penny, Diz explained, was a family friend. She was the daughter of someone (never identified, certainly not as a Goldsmith or an Eversholt) from his Cleveland childhood. She hadn't been in New York City long, had come to make her way in the garment industry and didn't know too many people. Diz felt, he said, "an obligation to look after her while she's settling in."

It was, he said more than once, the least he could do for an old school mate.

From what we could tell, he was fulfilling his obligation conscientiously. Sometimes, he'd pick Terry up first and then me and say off-handedly, "I hope you don't mind, but I've asked Ina to join us – you boys don't mind sitting in the back, do you?" and we'd say it was fine by us. Sometimes he'd pick Terry and me up and she was already in the front seat, and he'd say, "Penny was able to come along tonight and said she'd like to see you two again," and we'd say the more, the merrier.

How truly merry was it?

Not exactly unmerry, non-merry, but the situation also wasn't what we'd bargained for. The first half dozen, maybe dozen occasions, on which Penny-Ina – as between ourselves Terry and I had taken to calling her – made up our fourth and gabbed mindlessly about nothing through dinner while Diz watched her as if she were dispensing epigrams worthy of Dorothy Parker, we thought he was being commendably generous to a family friend, to the daughter of the family friend.

We thought, What a swell guy, What a *mensch*!

Yup, that's how young and foolish Terry and I were.

But we'd both graduated from one of the best colleges in the land, and eventually what was instantly obvious to others was sooner or later bound to hit us pair of ten-o'clock scholars like a big kahuna breaking on the shore.

We began speculating to each other about wool possibly being pulled over our eyes and that if it were, we maybe should give it a freeing tug. We should be giving that tug, we reckoned, if only because it was possible, just possible, we were operating under false pretenses – or, rather, Diz was.

We thought we were going to be riding to further songwriting acclaim on his coattails, but the glue meant to secure us there wasn't solidifying.

What if we college boys were merely along for the ride – were, literally and figuratively, being taken for a ride?

What if we were really – and only – serving some other purpose, the term for which (find below) we'd never heard before we'd gamboled into ultra-sophisticated Manhattan like lambs to the slaughter?

What if instead of being Diz Frawley's new and exalted writers, we were nothing of the kind? What if there were to be no new songs, no new musical – not even a musical written entirely on spec that kept threatening to be produced but never was?

What if (horrors!) we were being used, what if we were there to disguise Diz's – well, there's no other word for it – philandering?

(Okay there are other words for it I needn't go into.)

What if we were not just wet behind the ears but sopping after several months of these evenings, at the end of which we were always deposited at our apartments before Penny-Ina – or Penina as we'd abbreviated her even further – was deposited at hers?

What if we were there as plants to ward off speculation that the female member of Diz's convivial foursome was present under questionable circumstances?

What if we were – new term (see above) to Terry and me – his "beard," his co-beards.

No two ways about it: Our thoughts added up to a lot of what-ifs – the sum total of which led us to admit to our aghast selves that there was no "if" about it.

Right here, I have to give credit where it's due: to Terry. I haven't said much about our relationship since we started working together regularly and collecting modest kudos as well as modest attention. I'd say we'd become professional partners, who continued to keep our lives otherwise separate.

That hadn't stopped us, almost needless to say, from getting to know each other as well or better than we knew other people in our disparate circles. One aspect of Terry I'd taken in over the four or five years I'd known him is that he was more observant about certain things than I.

I thought I knew why. As I recognized from our undergraduate stretch, Terry was aware he was – if far from an out-and-out laughing-stock in some quarters – a frequent source of amusement. At times, he couldn't care in the least; at others, particularly where people whom he wanted to impress were involved, he was as sensitive to which way the wind was blowing as a tin weather vane. He was on the alert so consistently that he frequently registered tangential signals.

It was Terry who first said to me, "I'm having my doubts about Penny, Ina, Penina, whoever the hell she is, and people I've talked to say I'm absolutely right." From that, we came to the indisputable decision about Diz and his "family friend" being more than family friends – or, put more exactly, less than family friends.

We'd been duped, were being duped.

We were dupes, dopes.

But on our behalf, I have to submit there was a mitigating factor to our stupidity. You see, we had had the opportunity to meet – and to become charmed by, smitten with – Mrs. Diz Frawley, and in Terry's and my estimation, she was a dish in her own right.

She was *cordon bleu*, threu and threu.

There was much Terry and I differed on, but we didn't on this. Stood up against Ina Goldsmith/Penny Eversholt (which I have no doubt she ever was), she would have won our vote in any election year.

To get specific, we hadn't met Lorna Roth Frawley in New Haven. We'd heard she'd been there opening night, had departed rapidly the next day without saying much to anyone and wasn't scheduled to return, on the belief (on the pretext, I've come to think) that within such a pressure-cooker atmosphere, she'd only be in the way. Besides, there were the three Frawley children – twelve-year-old Allie, eleven-year-old Marcie and nine-year-old Joey – to be parented.

As a matter of fact, we didn't meet Lorna Roth Frawley until the night *Funny Is as Funny Does* opened on Broadway, when, as a matter of another fact, Penny/Ina wasn't on hand – or if she was mingling anonymously with the crowd (perhaps masquerading as someone else's date), we were never introduced to her.

That came later.

The party was held on the second floor at Sardi's – as openings still were back then. We'd raced over the couple of blocks directly after the curtain call, which had been more enthusiastic than I'd expected, although there are reasons for that – demonstrative backers, a partially papered house meant to guarantee what *Variety* used to call "heavy mittage.")

For a few minutes after we'd arrived, we swapped nervous small talk with the designers we'd befriended and especially with Hershel Strang, the ebullient pint-sized orchestrator-arranger who'd been almost as big a fan of the songs we added to the show as Diz and who was, even more to our liking, an enthusiastic gossip. Hershel always had a few lip-smacking items to pass along – although, curiously, never about Diz.

Because, however, Terry and I were billed in the program under an "additional material by" tag but were not the composer and lyricist of main record, we eventually sensed it was only polite for us to quit the others and fade to the walls where, with drinks in our hands, we'd look properly abashed and unprepossessing.

I now see we didn't have to look that way. By nature and the specific circumstances, we were nothing less than abashed and unprepossessing.

From that obscured vantage point, we heard the heavy mittage Diz received on entering before we saw him. We knew it had to be for him and so stopped saying whatever we'd been saying to each other and maneuvered to get a better view.

Diz knew who he was, of course, and what was expected of him. For the occasion, he'd put on a brocade dinner jacket midway between high fashion and sight gag. He'd also affected a garish woven cap that could have been something he'd purchased at a Moroccan souk. Acknowledging the response, he was doing one of his crowd-pleasing mincing walks through the parted celebrants.

Only a few feet behind him was a tall woman in a tailored suit of burgundy velvet with a burgundy velvet rose on the left lapel. She also wore burgundy gloves. The only jewelry she wore were gold earrings and a thick gold bracelet on her gloved right wrist. Her straight black hair was parted in the middle and cropped just below her ears. She had deep-set eyes above high cheekbones, a narrow straight nose and a wide mouth, a cleft chin.

My first impression was that she looked as if she'd stepped out of the pages of *Vogue* or off its cover, more like. My first long-winded but insistent question to myself was, "This has to be the Lorna Roth Frawley we've heard not a lot but something about, and how in the world had Diz landed someone so statuesque, so traffic-stopping?"

I concluded she had to prize humor and intelligence over looks and had to be recognized the wiser for it. She could be a gold-digger, I thought – she was wearing gold – but she didn't at all give off that vibe.

When after no more than a minute, the star's welcome subsided and the Frawleys were absorbed in the assemblage, Terry and I noted what a looker she was but far from the much more *zaftig* looker we'd imagined.

When we'd established our shared awe at the revelation and shook our heads over that for a couple minutes, we resumed speculating what the reviews – due within the hour – were likely to say.

So I was taken by surprise when some minutes later I felt a tap on my shoulder, turned and saw Diz standing there with fashion-plate Lorna at his side.

"I want you boys to meet my wife," he said with an imposing flourish of his brocade-clad arm and a tilt of his capped head. "Lorna, these are the two college boyos I've been telling you about, Woodside and Caplin." (No mention or motion to indicate which was which.) "These are the Ivy League geniuses who are going to take my career to new heights. Maybe not tonight but sooner than anyone in this room realizes."

Without removing the gloves, Lorna extended her hand, and, speechless as dummies in a store window, we each shook it.

"I've been hearing a great deal about the two of you," she said with a measured smile, "and when I heard the songs you wrote in the show tonight, I knew why. Diz has been humming them for weeks, but from that I couldn't tell what they were."

Diz said, "You couldn't tell, because you wouldn't listen."

She looked at him and said nothing, looked back at us and said, "Between you, me and the lamppost here" – she indicated Diz – "your songs were the highlights tonight. Without a doubt."

"Shh," Diz said, looking around grandly. "You know it's true and I know it's true, but others here don't."

"Others here should," she said and indicated the room with a nod. "Of course, there is evidence that some of these others come up short in the recognizing-solid-laughs department." She and Diz exchanged a conspiratorial look filled on both sides by enjoyment and another ingredient I couldn't quite pinpoint but I took to be less sanguine.

"But you two," she said, taking Terry and me in with a glance both warm and piercing, "are talented."

As she was saying that, Diz had turned and was headed back into the party's swell. All three of us watched him go.

I expected her to follow, but she didn't. Instead, she said in a tone I wasn't sure how to interpret, "He's working the room. If there's one thing Diz knows how to do, it's work a room."

With that, she turned back to us, and said, "I don't know how to work rooms, perhaps because I'm not interested in working them." She flashed us a smile Richard Avedon could have been in another part of town attempting to get from Jean Shrimpton and said, "Why don't you boys tell me about yourselves."

Terry needed no further encouragement and recounted our joint *curriculum vitæ* almost without stopping to catch a breath. Since I decided he was doing as well or better than I could, I made little attempt to slip in words edgewise.

I was more interested in observing Lorna. She was the most stunning woman I'd met or, when I thought about it, had seen since I arrived in Manhattan. Then, I was convinced I'd do nothing but run up against stunning women and accomplished men – the sort of men and women with whom ambitious, full-of-themselves college graduates have no doubt they'll be able to consort with as soon as they get off the train, bus or plane and start poking around the big city.

Lorna made good show of listening to Terry, nodding every once in a while, but as I watched her bestowing the occasional encouraging smile on him and me, I had a feeling I couldn't pin down that she was preoccupied, that she was thinking something else over.

Of course, she never said what it might be, and she never took her eyes from either of us to scan the room as people at show-business fetes are all but compelled to do for networking purposes. I never saw her look up from us to see where Diz might have gotten himself.

When our colloquy had gone on for maybe ten minutes, maybe a few minutes longer, and Terry had run out of credits to roll going as far back as the sixth-grade Christmas play in which he sang the first song he'd ever written (about the three shepherds), Lorna finally said with a lovely sigh, "I wish I could keep talking to you boys, but there are some star-of-the-show's-wife duties I suppose I ought to dispatch. I hope I'll see you again. Diz has big plans for you, and I'm glad he does."

Then she leaned towards us and said in something just above a whisper – her voice was like a series of low notes bowed on a cello – "You do realize, don't you, that besides Diz, you're the two most talented people connected with the show? For better or worse, I've always gravitated to talent. It has an obliterating charm."

("Obliterating charm." What a phrase, I thought, but had no idea what she meant by it. That understanding only came with time, much time.)

She stood upright and again held out her gloved hand. Too taken aback to do anything more than simper like Campbell kids, we both shook it and watched her walk away – she had a regal gait – to join Harley Goodrich, Augie Fiedler and what I assumed were some of their backers.

"Wow," Terry said when he regained whatever he had of composure.

"'Wow' is right," I said. "She's amazing."

"She's right about us, you know," Terry said.

I agreed, but I wasn't thinking about whether she was right or wrong. I was thinking about her – the fantabulous, frabjous Lorna Roth Frawley.

Restrained agreement wasn't enough for Terry. He repeated more insistently, "She's right, you know."

I realized I had to say more or we might have to continue a conversation about how good we were that Terry kept up more often than I liked. He expounded the belief – sometimes expressed, sometimes implied – that I took too off-hand an attitude towards our accomplishments. Unless I agreed with everything he said about our abilities and prospects, he felt my commitment was shaky.

That was hard for him to handle.

The truth was, I thought our songs were fine, but what there had been of them so far was come by so easily that I figured true greatness, or anything approaching it, demanded much more effort.

I've never resolved the issue acceptably for myself, but I knew the best thing to do was give Terry the answer he wanted – if only to get back to my real interest at the moment: more concentration on the cosmopolitan dream that had just come true in my still young and abidingly foolish life.

I gave Terry even more than he'd bargained for. "Oh, she's right, all right," I said. "We are better than these other *shlubs*." I waved my hand specifically at the bookwriters, who were standing not too far from us. I turned the casual wave into something much firmer when I realized one of them had caught my eye. "And working more with Diz will give us the chance to prove it for real."

"You got that right, partner," Terry said, satisfied.

With that he also walked away. I knew what he had in mind. He wasn't so abashed that he wouldn't eavesdrop on other conversations to determine whether any of them might be about us, and our gre-e-e-a-a-at talent. He might even – I'd seen him do this before – position himself in front of some revelers, announce he was one of the "additional material" guys and see if that elicited any compliments he'd then milk for all they were worth.

I was glad for his departure. It gave me the freedom to stand right where I was and watch Lorna. I wanted to watch her every move. I wanted to observe her walk. I wanted to glimpse the way she held out her hand on introducing herself to people and the way, when she laughed, she bent her head back slightly and let out only two bursts of muted laughter. I wanted to take in how she negotiated the party without a drink, without smoking, how she treated everyone with whom she came into contact with the same give-nothing-away *politesse*.

She may have said she didn't know – or want to know – how to work a room, but that was patently not the case. In her own right she was a first-class room-worker.

I knew what was happening to me, of course. I wasn't that unself-aware: I was infatuated. She was a married older woman – I estimated late thirties, maybe early forties – but so what? For the time being, I only wanted to become her friend. I couldn't imagine myself hoping for more. She was Diz's wife, and Diz was our pal and benefactor, but I did hope – since we would be working as closely and for as long as Diz reiterated we would be – that I'd get to know her better.

I – and Terry, of course – might even be invited to the Frawley home in removed-from-show-business-hurly-burly West Orange, New Jersey, where Lorna would interrupt our sessions to ask if we wanted anything to eat, perhaps a bacon-lettuce-and-tomato sandwich, some iced tea. If Diz were called to the telephone, she might chat with us about ourselves and herself until he returned. I'd get to see how she dressed when she was at home, what she was like with her children. Maybe she'd get to the point where she felt a social kiss was appropriate on our arrival and/or departure.

Maybe I'd get to the point where I'd become a confidant.

So with unsipped drink in hand, I clung to the wall and my expanding fantasy for some time. Once, as Lorna went from one group to another, she looked my way and, I think, caught me staring. I tried to pretend I hadn't been, but I felt my face flush – probably the same color as her suit.

She give me a half-smile and the monarchic wave.

I figured that whatever I was doing, I'd better cut it out.

I didn't need to, since just then the show's publicist ran into the room with Harley Goodrich, Augie Fiedler and the early editions of the newspapers. (These were the days when reviewers still attended the opening night performance.)

Group by group, everyone fell silent. The publicist handed the papers one by one to Harley, and Harley handed them to Augie, who read them aloud.

Other than for its recognizing Diz's amusing gallantry and – in three of the five reviews – for the freshness of our songs and Wiley's whirligig choreography, the prose Augie mouthed was hardly uplifting. A headline in the *Daily News* put succinctly what the others uniformly expressed: "'Funny Is as Funny Doesn't.'"

Terry had found his way back to me, and, since we had come out all right and the production wasn't really ours, we were in the position of being spectators as much or more than participants. We shrugged at each other, Terry saying *sotto voce*, "We're going to be able to make something of this, you know – am I right or am I right?"

We watched everyone else. The blanket thrown over the party was flood-conditions wet. People looked at each other with sad eyes and little hopelessly hopeful smiles. Then they were doing things with their shoulders, hands and shuffling feet that said it must be time to leave, and they did.

I looked around for Diz, who was standing on the other side of the room. I was looking for Lorna, too, and she was with him. Her expression hadn't changed. She had the positive, ladylike smile on her exquisite mouth and her left hand on Diz's right forearm.

It was the only time I'd seen them touch all night.

Just then she leaned over to say something in his ear, never allowing the smile to fade. He was concentrating on the floor with an unreadably neutral expression. When she'd finished, they both nodded, and now Diz was displaying the puckish grin for which audiences go wild.

Throwing her gaze around the room as if to ascertain whether anyone has been paying attention to them, Lorna saw me, and, if I'm not greatly mistaken, raised her eyebrows meaningfully. She held them there for, what?, for two seconds, and I took the look to be a non-verbal way of saying, "You're a bright boy – what do you think now?" I saw it as a sign that this show might be doomed to close soon but not Terry's and my association with Diz.

And with her.

Of course, I wasn't prepared for Ina Goldsmith/Penny Eversholt, Diz's obligation to whom when he was with us apparently took precedence over our expanding friendship. Furthermore, when he was with us, Diz never so much as touched on a developing acquaintanceship with Lorna. He barely ever mentioned her, and if we asked after her, he brushed us off with a quick "She's fine, the kids, too."

Moreover, visits to West Orange never materialized, much less anything like tunafish sandwiches and potato chips prepared by Lorna with loving hands. The closest Terry or I came to renewing our short but oh-so-gratifying association with her over the next several weeks were a half-dozen telephone conversations I had with her.

Diz had given us his home phone number but requested we use it sparingly and to stick to business, to logistics.

(Only much later did it hit me that that was his way of telling us – without telling us – we weren't to bring Penny/Ina into any discussion.)

More often, he said, he'd be getting in touch with us, which he did at least twice a week during the next three, four months. When I called him to reconfirm or to get times pinned down, Lorna answered or took the phone from a maid called Zona and said she'd get Diz.

One time, while waiting for him to pick up an extension, she asked me how the work was going. I didn't know what to say. After a seconds during which I could hear children in the background, I said, "Pretty good. You know how these..."

I never ended the sentence.

"You writers," she said, "you don't like to talk until you have something you're completely ready to show."

"That's it," I said and felt as if I were being disloyal by dissembling to this woman for whom, over a single ten- or fifteen-minute conversation, I had launched a fervent young man's admiration society.

She chuckled at the other end of the line and said, "I look forward to hearing whatever you come up with. I know it'll be good."

That's when Diz picked up the phone. "Hello," he said and then, "you can hang up now, Lorna." "I'm just about to," she said, "I was telling Mr. Caplin I look forward to hearing the material he and Mr. Woodside are writing for you." "You will," Diz said, "you will. All in good time."

There was a click as Lorna left the line.

Terry and I had written nothing for Diz. More than once we'd mentioned putting "People are People" into his new act and adding topical references to it. We'd mentioned a couple of songs of ours written for *The*

Underfed Revue and its successors that we thought he could do.

He'd expressed interest, but we hadn't played him any songs of ours he hadn't already heard. We'd only quoted a few lines of the lyrics. His reactions were fabbo-gonzo inconclusive – he'd said they "sounded possible," "promising," "a good start."

It was about then or shortly thereafter that the Penina dime dropped with more than a metallic clink, and Terry and I begin to suspect the miserable "beard" designation was undeniably applicable to us.

We were smarting, all right – not sure how to proceed, whether to try to pin Diz down on his plans for us, whether to confront him about Penina, whether to just play along for the time being and then extricate ourselves, whether to figure out what the issue was with him and then force it.

So when one late Saturday morning I got a phone call at home from none other than Lorna Roth Frawley, I was... well, what was I? Flustered isn't an entirely inaccurate way to begin describing what I was.

But that's only the start. I had talked to Lorna before – addressed her as Mrs Frawley – but always when I was the one phoning. She'd never called me. Our exchanges for the most part had been, as I've said, what Diz had requested they be – short and to the point.

So hearing her at the other end of the line – though no Allie, Marcie or Joey audible – had me mildly tongue-tied at first.

But I rallied, if what I got around to saying can be called rallying.

After exchanging hellos – Lorna speaking in a cooler manner than I remembered from the opening-night party or previous telephone exchanges, more oboe than cello – she said, "I'm sorry to interrupt you, Mr. Caplin, but I need to talk to Diz."

"Diz," I said and hesitated. "Diz isn't here."

"When he gets there," she went on, "will you tell him to call me immediately? It's a matter of some urgency." She added, "Otherwise, I would never bother you when you're working."

"But," I said, trying to think fast but not thinking fast enough, "Diz isn't here, and I'm not expecting him."

"Oh," Lorna said, "maybe he meant to say he'd be at Mr. Woodside's. I'll try him there."

That might have made some sense, since Diz still got us wrong way around and Terry was the one with the piano, at which we might have been working had we ever worked at that Yamaha with him, which to Terry's and my chagrin we had yet to do.

But that particular day, it didn't make sense, since Terry wasn't in town. He'd gone to the Cape to see his parents.

What was I to say? What I said was, "I don't think he's there, Mrs. Frawley." (How I longed to call her Lorna.) "Terry's away for the weekend. We're not working today. Or tomorrow, for that matter."

There was silence at the other end of the line.

I'd like to say that I don't know what got into me then, but I know damn well. What got into me, what got the better of me, was my anger at being used in the way Terry and I were being used. What got into me was my resentment at not getting to work with Diz on new and strong material that would help build our name. What got into me was my dismay at having to admit to myself that I'd thought I was having a bravura first few years in New York but, on the contrary, I'd allowed myself to become a metropolitan cliché – a beard, of all blasted things.

So taking advantage of the momentary silence, I said – only after a split-second dismissing the option not to – "You might want to try him at Ina Goldsmith's."

"Ina Goldsmith," she said, her inflection indicating she wasn't so much asking about the name as taking note of it.

“Yes,” I said. “I think that’s her name. Your family friend. From Cleveland. I may have it wrong. The name might be Penny Eversholt.”

“Penny Eversholt,” Lorna repeated. “Oh, yes, I know whom you mean. Thank you, Mr. Caplin. I’m very sorry to have bothered you.”

There was a click.

Although I knew the call had ended, several seconds passed before I replaced the receiver. I was trying to decide whether I’d detected continued coolness or incipient warmth in her parting words.

I couldn’t decide.

Which is completely beside the point.

The cogent point is that Lorna’s phone call marked the last time but one that I ever spoke to her.

It also represented the end of any contact Terry or I had with Diz.

He dropped us like a couple of hot potatoes.

It wasn’t clear to us at first. Although we were in the habit of hearing from him weekly, we didn’t attach too much importance to the lapse the first couple of weeks. I might have attached more importance to it than Terry, to whom I had never mentioned Lorna’s Saturday morning phone call for reasons I can only call cowardly.

But when over two weeks had gone by and Terry suggested perhaps it was time to get in touch with Diz just to see how he was doing, I knew I had to fess up. And, yes, I knew it was a confession. I knew, or at least deeply felt, I’d committed some sort of sin. I didn’t know what sort – a social sin, maybe?

A social sin against Lorna.

Maybe a sin against Terry as well.

All the same, I told him about Lorna’s call, expecting him to fly into a panic over my failure to safeguard the relationship by fudging Diz’s whereabouts. I thought that when he learned I suggested Lorna might try phoning somewhere else – and someone else – he'd fly into a panic over my so deliberately imperiling the Diz relationship. I thought he'd be mad as hell at what increasingly appeared to be my bringing a premature end to our most promising meal ticket.

Quite the opposite. He surprised me when he said that although we'd gotten any number of great meals out of the situation, he'd already begun to accept that the many-course career meal wasn't going to materialize – "meat-erialize," he even said, leavening the baleful development with a pun.

I saw with relief that I'd forgotten Terry's unshakable confidence in our future. As Terry imagined those sunny days, if they weren't going to meat-erialize courtesy of Diz Frawley, they were bound to arrive via some other marvelous opportunity right around the next corner.

With that we commenced to put the out-of-sight Diz Frawley out of mind, and I tried to come to terms with my also having to consign Lorna Roth Frawley to a file marked closed.

This nearly had been mine, but nearly wasn't anything like all, and I'd have to live with it.

It became more difficult to live with when one day, walking down Broadway, Terry and I ran into Hershel Strang, who was just coming out of the Brill Building with the usual stack of sheet music under his arm.

Since he, Terry and I had had such a good time *shmoozing* throughout the *Funny Is as Funny Does* episode – while just about everyone else was having a God-awful time – we were ripe to catch up. And I would have been riper if just about the first thing out of gossipy Hershel's mouth was the only dish I would have chosen not to hear.

Looking at us with glee spread like raspberry jam on his craggy face, he said, "I guess you guys have heard that Diz's marriage broke up."

We hadn't, of course, and the news hit me right between the eyes.

"Yeah," Hershel said, "Lorna left him and took the kids. She finally found out what everybody else knew all along. He'd been running around on her for years. You guys must have known. Didn't I see you having dinner once with him and the latest bimbo? You know, the one he had shacked up in New Haven at the Taft."

That shocked us, because we'd never spotted her – not once. And maybe I was jolted just as much for Hershel's never before having referred to it – to her, to the Hotel Taft shacker-upper.

"That was going on back then," I said, "and you never mentioned it?"

"I didn't?" Hershel said, genuinely nonplussed. "Gee." He shook his head at the uncharacteristic oversight. "Anyway, poor Diz. He got what he asked for. He's gone to Hollywood now. He'll get plenty of work. That's probably where he should have been all along, instead of doing a stinkeroo like *Funny Is as Funny Does*."

The three of us had something of a laugh over that, and after Hershel's asking us what we were up to and our asking him the same, we parted.

When Terry and I continued up Broadway, he said, ironically, I know, "Hmm, I wonder what gave Lorna the fatal clue."

"I guess I know," I said.

"Yes," Terry said, "I guess we both know."

It was another time Terry surprised me. He looked at me, gauging how lousy I felt. Perhaps also intuiting how guilty I would continue to feel for some unlimited time to come, he started talking about something else.

After that, we rarely spoke about Diz – or Lorna. When our careers began to take diverging paths from the once-beckoning bright lights of Broadway, we never really looked for the opportunity to reminisce.

Those young and foolish – ha! – years were devoured by the succeeding decade, and I – I can't speak for Terry – had no regrets. I neither needed nor wanted any reminders of my irreversible rash act and its unfortunate consequences to Diz's marriage, to Lorna, to their kids, to heaven-knows-what-else.

But I have said that Lorna's phone call to me was the last time but one I ever spoke to her.

The final time took place about twenty years later, and as the result of an accidental meeting. I'd been invited to a dinner party given by a couple I knew through a fellow I'd been seeing for a few months. I didn't know them as well as he did, of course, and when he said they'd asked him to bring me along, I welcomed the chance to spend time with them and with other friends he and the couple shared.

Perhaps like many people, I find it informative to learn about the people to whom I'm attracted by sizing up their friends. These two, Hilly and Joan Prentiss were media consultants, living in a *soigné* Lexington Avenue high-rise in the Seventies. Henry and I arrived there well into the cocktails-and-*hors d'œuvres* segment of the evening. The Prentisses welcomed us and immediately led us to others of Henry's acquaintance.

As I was greeting them, I noticed a woman in another group who for an instant struck me as familiar and who in the succeeding instant I knew had to be Lorna Roth Frawley.

When I'd first seen her those two decades past, I knew she was unforgettable, and this was confirmation.

For the next few minutes, I feigned interest in the conversation Henry and I had entered but kept sneaking looks towards Lorna – yet not so sneakily that Henry didn't pick up on them.

When the chat we were having with – I think they were called – Paul and Anita Marx ended, burly, bookish, astute Henry took me aside and asked in his gruff baritone, "Whom do you keep looking at?"

"I didn't realize I was being so obvious," I said.

"'Obvious' is an understatement," he said, "You might as well have been waving flags."

"If she's who I think she is," I said, "and I think she is, I knew her in another life."

"Then maybe instead of staring at her," Henry said, "you should just go up and say hello."

"I'm not sure I can do that," I said.

"Oh, and why not?" Henry said.

Before I could figure out a response that wouldn't take at least five minutes to plod through and then might have put me into a relationship-ending pickle, I saw Lorna detach herself from the people to whom she'd been talking and head towards Henry and me.

I recognized the regal walk. I recognized the stunning looks and bearing, though she was now a woman in her late fifties or early sixties. The hair was still parted in the middle and cropped just below her ears, but it was silver. The midnight-blue dress she wore was a tasteful matter of pleats and fine tailoring.

She extended her hand – I recognized the grace of it – and said to me while taking Henry in, "I'm Lorna Roth. I believe I know you. You're the songwriter Lionel Caplin, are you not?"

Right then I may not have wanted to be, but I was. There was no denying it, certainly not with Henry standing at my side – perhaps wondering about the songwriter designation, which hadn't been much a part of the personal history I'd given him when we met.

"I am," I said, "and this is Henry Rieger."

She and Henry shook hands.

"I thought it was you," she said to me, "even though we only met once before, if I have it right."

"That's right," I said, "only once." I thought I might add "but we've talked on the phone several times." I thought better of that.

Whatever was conveyed to Henry in these succinct sentences I couldn't say, although I understood he understood something sub-textual was afoot when he interrupted to say to Lorna, "I hope you'll excuse me. I see some people I need to say hello to."

He gave my right biceps a manly squeeze and left.

I hated him for that and loved him, too.

He'd picked up that he was in the presence of two people with uncompleted business to attend to, but because I didn't know what I wanted to say when he left us alone, I said nothing for the first few seconds.

Not acknowledging that I seemed to be temporarily at a loss even for small talk, Lorna said, "Let's step over here out of harm's way."

She moved to an unoccupied sofa, sat down and patted the cushion next to her.

I sat.

Was this the moment when I was supposed to ask absolution for my transgression towards her? I knew it was but rummaged around in my mind for an acceptable way to ignore the damned invitation.

So I was shocked when Lorna – as beautiful and desirable as she was when I first saw – said with a beneficent smile, "I'm happy to have met you here, Lionel, for I fear I have to offer you a long overdue apology."

"An apology," I said. "What for?" She couldn't have startled me more if she had leaned over to lock lips. "An apology for what?"

"You wouldn't know, would you?" she said and took my left hand in both of hers.

Why couldn't this have happened twenty years ago, I thought, and looked around to see if anyone was watching us. Henry was. He gave me a fast thumbs-up for whatever was transpiring that he knew would make a good story later. Facing away from Henry and therefore not privy to his gesture, Lorna said, "I suppose you might remember that when you were working with Diz all those years ago, I called you one day looking for him."

I knew this was my goddam opening and said, "Yes, and I'm sor..."

She cut me off, saying, "I said it was an emergency and needed to speak to him immediately."

Again I tried to speak, but she went on. "The truth was, there was no emergency. If Diz had gotten on the phone, I would have come up with something – I don't know what – but I knew I wouldn't have to. If I'd really thought Diz was there, I never would have phoned. But I was fairly certain he wasn't. He wasn't at Terry Woodside's, either. You explained Terry was out of town, which was neither here nor there, as far as I was concerned. Then you suggested I try someone named Penny Eversholt or Ina Goldsmith."

Guilt weighing on my head like a heavy metal object, I said, "I never should have given you those names, Mrs. Roth."

"Ms. Roth," she said. "I went back to my maiden name after the divorce. Anyway, after all this time you must call me Lorna."

"Lorna," I said.

"Giving me those names, Lionel," she said, "was what I wanted you to do, what I counted on you to do. Not those names perhaps, but some name or names. This is where my apology comes in. You see, I was taking advantage of you. I regret those words, but it's what I was doing. I knew something not on the up-and-up had to be going on with the two of you and Diz. He was off to Manhattan to work with you week after week, but I knew no work was getting done."

By then my face must have been a bulletin-board of confusion.

"You're wondering how I knew that," she said. "Simple. Diz gave himself away. Sometimes – and this was one of them – he was so transparent. I knew that if you and Terry were writing any new songs for him, he'd be humming them around the house. He always did when he was learning songs. His humming was so unintelligible I could never figure out the melody, but the humming told me enough. When I didn't hear it, it was clear to me you and Terry were serving some other purpose.

"Diz was using you the way he used so many of his middle-aged writers over the years. But I'd never been able to get them to divulge anything. They were all in cahoots – honor among scoundrels. You boys were so fresh-faced, so right out of college and impressionable, I decided if Diz was going to take advantage of you, I would, too. I'm sorry to put it that way, but there's no other way."

The dinner party was swirling pleasantly around us, but Lorna Roth and I had moved into a parallel party of our own.

Lorna went on, "I knew if I played my cards right, I could get you to give me the information I sought, whatever it might be. This is going to sound terribly vain, but in those years I knew the appeal I had for young men. I've undoubtedly lost it by now, but the night I met you, I knew I still had it."

"Yes," I said, "you did. You do."

"I wasn't fishing for the compliment," she said, "but I appreciate your giving it. That's why I'm all the more contrite. I decided the night we met it might be through you boys I'd confirm what I'd already suspected – and had suspected for far too long. And that's exactly what I did."

She let go of my hand and continued, "It's occurred to me that over the intervening years you might regret having told me what I already knew. You mustn't. You were being played, and for that I'm repentant. They say the wife always knows, and they're right. Once I knew for certain about Diz's sad dalliances, once I had a name to put to my assumptions, I had no qualms about divorcing him and giving myself the right to go on with my life and my children's lives elsewhere. I knew he'd have his career and whatever or whomever else he wanted, and I knew I could always go back to the law, which I've done.

"But if I have no qualms about Diz, I have had qualms about you and Terry, to whom you must also relay my apology. Please tell me I have your forgiveness."

Lorna Roth wanted my forgiveness. Sensing something pounding in my heart, I said, "You do. Have it."

"I'm glad," she said. Then she rose, smiled and said, "Now I think we'd better rejoin the others. By the way, your friend seems extremely nice. I hope the three of us will talk more later."

We did – about the kinds of things informed New Yorkers talk about at sophisticated dinner parties. When this one was over, we said goodbye and shook hands one last time, her grip leaving an impression I still feel.

Yes, over the years I did attain a certain degree of Manhattan-brand sophistication but never enough to excuse myself fully – as Lorna Roth Frawley wanted me to – from having blurted, one day when I was a bare-faced boy with cheek, the names Ina Goldsmith and Penny Eversholt.

Why did I have to? Why did I have to say what I wanted so adamantly to say – and what Lorna Roth Frawley, when she was still Lorna Roth Frawley, wanted me to say?

Oh, to be young and foolish again!

But only, of course, if in that miraculously regained youth and foolishness I could know what I know now.

Not talking

the intro

After a busy week swinging perilously on the prickly-friends grapevine, I think I've got this straight:

i.

Janet is not talking to Diana. You see, Diana expects to be telephoned, makes it a policy not to be the one who telephones. According to Janet, Diana actually says this in so many words. "It's hard for me to find the time," she says, "but feel free to call me whenever you want." For a long while, Janet was happy to be the caller not the callee. She accepted it as Diana's way. It seemed to work. Whenever Janet did call Diana – at home, on her cell phone – Diana was her friendly self, eager to make plans and then, their having gotten together, full of fun and confidences. But, come on, there's a limit. As Janet explains it, it eventually dawned on her that what Diana was implying by her actions was this: My life is too important, my time too valuable, for frivolities like telephoning friends any old time. Furthermore, Diana's attitude unmistakably posits that those whose lives are less important, whose time is less valuable, can do the calling. What else do they have to do anyway? So Janet finally put her foot down and stopped telephoning Diana. What really got Janet's goat, however, is that it occurred to her after a couple of weeks of not calling Diana that Diana might not realize Janet wasn't calling. Or if she did realize, might be assuming that Janet wasn't calling because, like Diana, she was busy, had seen her life take on some importance. Temporarily, of course. So Janet decided the only way to make sure her gesture registered was to call Diana and announce outright that she was not talking to her. Having had to do so, though, made her even angrier. So subsequently she was that much more adamant about not talking to Diana.

ii.

Rollo is not talking to Buzz. Because Rollo had pulled Buzz aside at The Vertical Club to tell him about a problem he was having with his boss. The details aren't significant; something to do with workloads and deadlines, holidays coming up. Buzz listened with head lowered until Rollo indicated he was ready for feedback. "I see your point," Buzz said, "but I also see Forester's point." That wasn't what Rollo wanted to hear. "I see what he's saying," Buzz went on with maddening disregard. That's when Rollo flew off the handle; within seconds his face, under the sweat he'd worked up working out, went from his usual pallor to blotchy red. "I don't need you to take his fucking side," Rollo said. "You don't think he's got a point?" Buzz pressed. "Yes, I see he's got a point," Rollo said, "but the fucking point is I don't need you to fucking point out his fucking point." He headed towards the Nautilus-room door. "Stay the fuck away from me, Buzz," he said. "I've got fuck-all to say to you." Everyone agrees that Buzz had a right to say what he'd said – that, moreover, Buzz was absolutely right and Rollo, being irrational, was wrong. Which, of course, couldn't be expected to have any effect on Rollo's behavior.

iii.

Miranda is not talking to Janet. She's begun to notice that everything Janet says to her is a subtle dig. Okay, not everything, but enough. And she's not imagining it. Shirl and Rollo, to name just two, know how Janet can be and support Miranda. There was the remark Janet made about the matronly dress not more than twenty-four or maybe forty-eight hours after the remark about the blaring shade of lipstick. And that came on the heels of the comment about blue not being Miranda's color. Where was that coming from? Just because Janet spent a fortune on a personal color consultant doesn't mean she's become some kind of expert. Janet also knew Miranda didn't have time to shop for a different suit before her Burson Marsteller job interview. Why would Janet say what she did? Couldn't she have just said it's a great suit and left it at that?

iv.

Gracie and Buzz are not talking to Miranda and Corby. The summer house thing. The four of them agreed going in that house-sharing can be fraught, but they all swore that as long as they were aware of the pitfalls, they could – and would – steer around them. Gracie and Buzz are now telling friends what Miranda and Corby are telling friends: You can swear all you want, but you can never fully prepare for the way small things accumulate until they no longer seem small. To cite one example: the CDs and cassettes. That Corby likes heavy metal is not the issue.

(Even though it hardly seems age-appropriate: Why is a man with a career on the Street and two girls in grade school listening to such dreck, even if he more or less ungrudgingly acquiesces to headphones?) No, too much Metallica and Black Sabbath wasn't the problem. What was was that every time Corby went to play a CD, he would remove whichever of Buzz's CDs was on the turntable and fail to put it back in its case, would leave it lying wherever, often in the sun's direct rays. How many times do you ask civilly before you realize that asking civilly isn't going to work and what you really have to do is ask uncivilly? Who goes on vacation to be uncivil, Gracie and Buzz beseech. And that was only one of many irritating things. Don't even ask about kitchen obligations. By the end of the summer Gracie and Buzz knew too much they didn't want to know about Miranda and Corby, and *vice versa*.

v.

Prez and Shirl are not talking. Prez is tired of Shirl's opinions. It's not that Prez disagrees with Shirl, although he frequently does. She's certainly entitled to her opinions and as free as the next person to make an ass of herself. What gets on Prez's nerves is how she states her opinions: as if they were facts. Haven't you noticed, Prez would like to know, that whenever Shirl says something about something, that's that? There's no begging to differ. One day it finally dawned on Prez that he was getting snarky at Shirl's reactions whenever he – or anyone, come to that – disagreed with her. More often than is necessary, he realized with a start, her face hardens into a smile at once superior and patronizing and she says, smugly, "You're wrong." Doesn't she know, Prez implores, it's bad manners to tell someone flat out, "You're wrong." And over what? I say, Prez says, the *X-Men* series isn't very good, but it's certainly harmless. To which Shirl says, "You're wrong. *X-Men* is as political in its way as a Costa-Gavras film." Film, she says, not movies, film. She says, "Look what all four *X-Mens* hold up to celebrate – disregard for life, violence, male bonding to the exclusion of women." Yadidah-yadidah. How much do you take – about *X-Men* and contemporary male-bonding comedies, for Christ's sake! – before you get fed up? It's like a tic with her. You say day, she says night. And that's the end of it. Night, it is. "You can't talk to her," Prez says, "so I've given up trying."

vi.

Hector is not talking to Rollo. It's really not Rollo's fault. Then again it is. Rollo knew Hector was, well, romantically interested in him and took care to make it clear that, while he didn't reciprocate Hector's "warmer" feelings, he was more than willing to be friends: The two of them did have a great time when they were together. Hector accepted the conditions, all the while thinking that in time Rollo would come around, would realize he is reciprocally interested in Hector; is only holding back because of a chronic resistance to any kind of relationship. Furthermore, Hector felt that Rollo's understanding of his own secret interests was implied in his eagerness to build up a friendship where both of them would spend so much time together. Yet, many movies, plays, dinners, tennis matches, phone calls, lunches, strolls, privates jokes later, Rollo is still maintaining that friendship with Hector is his sole purpose in their constant companionship, whereas all those good times – the delight, for instance, Hector takes in Rollo's accurate and biting imitations of mutual acquaintances – had only served to render Hector more and more infatuated. In love would actually be no exaggeration. Not only that, but Hector was becoming increasingly convinced that Rollo's refusal to see that he, too, is enamored is an indication of some perverse psychological impulse. Hector began to suspect (and had even tried the theory out on Miranda and Sarge, who allowed it was possible) that Rollo has an unexamined need to reject anyone who gets too close to him. Hector was forced to conclude that the only way to spare himself being hurt any more was to stop talking to the person causing all the pain. So he has. He's stopped talking to Rollo.

vii.

It's the gifts that finally put paid to Shirl's talking to Gracie. Gracie and Shirl were born the same day, the same year, and once they discovered that fun fact – back when they were in grade school together – they established a tradition of exchanging birthday presents. Going on three decades, when they opened their presents – at the same moment – they would gasp with surprise at the other's having gotten maybe not exactly what they necessarily wanted but definitely what they were thrilled to have. The subtext was that their ability to anticipate each other's desires in silk blouses or perfumes new on the market meant they understood each other through and through. It was a good feeling. For some time, however, Gracie had ceased intuiting Shirl's needs or tastes accurately. Quite the contrary. The gifts had begun to strike sour notes. One year, for instance, there was a carved wooden frog. How come? Gracie had no reason to think Shirl collected frogs or in any way got a kick out of them – even if this one was the handiwork of a Bahian peasant. Another year there was an arcane board game. Gracie knew Shirl hated board games. Or should have known. Shirl realized she had begun feigning enthusiasm when she ripped the wrappings away from these oddball gifts. She found herself being effusively grateful but wondering, What makes her think I'd want this? And also wondering, Do I have to leave this *recherché* object out every time she comes over? Here was Shirl, continuing to give time and thought to what she bought Gracie, listening to Gracie's remarks on stores she'd passed through and items that had caught her eye. Shirl assumed her own care and perspicacity was still paying off: Gracie's excitement over what she received seemed abidingly genuine. But she could only think that somehow Gracie's getting wider and wider off the perfect-gift mark had a more serious implication. And it didn't have to do with Gracie's also spending considerably less on the gifts she gave than Shirl did. Consistently. Shirl prided herself on not having a tit-for-tat mind. It wasn't the price; it was the thought. Either Gracie wasn't considering what she picked out or she was considering and no longer had a clue. Or she was considering and then acting on some ulterior motive Shirl couldn't fathom, some psychological twinge Shirl didn't get. Whatever it was, it suggested that after all these years she and Gracie had grown apart. This year Gracie gave her a paperback copy (trade paperback, but still paperback) of *Women Who Love Too Much and the Men Who Love Them*. It was the last straw. What the hell did she mean by that? Now Shirl can't bring herself to talk to Gracie.

viii.

Corby stopped talking to Sarge when he acknowledged that much as he enjoyed Sarge's company in the morning and at the end of the day (the easy camaraderie, the sharing of business-related information), Sarge was, in the final analysis, selfish. Neither of them liked public transportation, so both of them, despite the expense, kept cars in the city. What made sense to them, however, was to use only one car to drive to Wall Street every day. The arrangement was that they split the cost of one garage space in lower Manhattan and alternate weeks driving. What with traffic and unpredictable weather, there were days they were unavoidably detained. When Corby was driving and there had been some delay, Corby would drop Sarge at his building and then park and walk; when Sarge was driving and they were late, Sarge always managed to beg off dropping Corby at his office, insisting that they park first and then both walk. It was true that Sarge had the longer walk to UBS than Corby had to Merrill Lynch, but it wasn't that much longer, two blocks at most. Short blocks. Okay, so some mornings they were really late. Corby understood Sarge's hurry. But every time! Without fail? Couldn't Sarge drop Corby once in a while out of sheer consideration? Evidently not. A few weeks ago – on Sarge's week driving – there'd been a horrendous accident on the FDR Drive and by the time Sarge and Corby reached William Street, Corby was very late for an important meeting. He asked Sarge if he'd mind dropping him off first. He prefaced the request by saying he wouldn't ask if it weren't important. Sarge said he'd like to oblige, but he was also late for an important meeting, and what if he were delayed even further going around the block? Corby acted as he always did – as if he didn't mind. But he did mind. That afternoon, he called Sarge to say something had come up and he wouldn't be driving uptown at their usual time. This happened occasionally, and Corby knew Sarge wouldn't make too much of it. The next morning he called Sarge and said that from then on he'd be making other arrangements for getting downtown. No need for Sarge to feel he had to reimburse his share of the rest of the month's Battery Park garage rental. "Fuck him," Corby said to Miranda as he left the apartment for the subway. He hasn't talked to Sarge since.

ix.

Diana at long last has nothing more to say to Prez. She's sick and tired of his attitude towards feminism. For years now she has tolerated his smarmy manner. She has even – to show that feminists can have a sense of humor now that the century has long since turned – laughed at some of his jibes. She sincerely thought a couple of them were funny. She laughed when Prez made the crack about not seeing the point of using chairperson instead of chairman because chairperson has the word "son" in it. She admitted that accepting "womyn" as a preferred spelling is ludicrous. As is the concept of "herstory". But she didn't agree that these extremes put the lie to the whole movement – or that the movement itself was *passé*. She got increasingly furious with Prez when he baited her by rising grandly whenever she entered or left a room or making big show of lighting her cigarettes. At first she took moderate measures to deal with his not-so-subtle knocks. She tried sneaking cigarettes out and lighting them as quickly as she could when his attention was elsewhere. Somehow she was never fast enough. There he was in her face with Dunhill outstretched. Eventually she gave up smoking in front of him entirely. But bigger affronts stuck in her craw. She couldn't count the number of times she asked Prez not to use the word "girl" around her unless he was talking about someone younger than sixteen. Eighteen at the outside. She tried to explain that men using the word "girl" isn't the same as women using the word "guy." No use. Prez was forever meeting "a new girl," dating "a new girl." Couldn't he see what his attitude conveyed, Diana asked Prez, when he continually dated young women, never anyone over twenty-two or -three? Even though he was well into his forties? If he could see it, he refused to acknowledge it. He didn't even seem to notice that their mutual friends had started keeping arm's distance from the women he brought around. He didn't seem to notice that not only she but all the women in their group felt they were having their advancing years shoved at them by his endless parade of younger women. Or if he did notice, he ignored it. Couldn't Prez comprehend what he was saying to them about themselves, how they might not like it? Prez pooh-poohed the whole thing, said it was pure coincidence that he dated younger women, that if he met someone closer to his age to whom he was attracted, he'd date her in a heartbeat. Diana felt fury rise up in her throat and neck. She mentioned it to Hector, to Rollo, to Corby. They all admitted she probably had something, but they also shrugged and said some version of "What're you going to do? That's Prez." Having to accept that some men appear to understand and still really don't only added to Diana's rage. Ultimately, Prez went too far: the women-want-to-be-raped debate he and Diana fell into. Diana could kick herself for having expected Prez to see the fine points involved in women – some women, she underlined – having rape fantasies. Which she had foolishly conceded in a rash moment over drinks at Gracie's and Corby's. She couldn't make Prez admit that there is a difference between fantasy rape and rape in actuality. Prez insisted fantasies implied real longings that in some situations affect behavior, might very well send unconscious signals. There was no disabusing Prez of the notion. Diana finally had had it up to here with Prez and declared she was through talking.

x.

Sarge isn't talking to Hector since New Year's Eve when he and Shirl had expected Hector for the annual party. Hector didn't show up. Then, when Hector called New Year's Day, he offered a flimsy excuse: Since Hector hadn't heard definitely from Sarge that the party was on, he'd made other plans. It didn't wash. Everyone knew Shirl and Sarge threw the party year in, year out. Nobody needed to wait for an invite; Hector never had in previous years. Besides if he wasn't certain about the party when whatever the other thing was came up, no ceremony needed standing on. He could have called and asked. Sarge's theory is that Hector got a better offer. He'd suspected that was Hector's *modus operandi* anyway. He'd kept a mental account of the number of times he and Shirl had called Hector for dinner or a movie and Hector had said he didn't have his book with him and then asked if he could let them know in a couple of days. Granted, he usually called well within the deadline to say he was free and it'd be super to see them. But once in a while, he'd let them know – not quite last minute – that he'd forgotten totally about it but "I do, as it turns out, have a conflict." Sarge couldn't prove anything, but he had the nagging conviction that something else Hector would rather do had come along in the meantime. So what if it had, Shirl replied to Sarge's complaining. If that's the way Hector wants to conduct his social life, so what? But it bothered Sarge to imagine he was thought of as something to do when there are no other options. Okay, it's silly of him to attach so much importance to having his best friends around him on New Year's Eve, which, yes, of course, was just another night, but that's the way he is. If Hector didn't appreciate that, he wasn't worth talking to.

the outro

Me? Where do I figure in all this non-talking? That I'm talking to all of them makes all of them nervous about talking to me.

Banana nose

At the time, the phone call seemed innocuous. My cousin Sara, to whom I don't speak all that frequently, rang to find out what I knew about Orrin Greenstone. She assumed that since I'm connected to the theater and so is he, I must know something.

It was a fair enough assumption. I write about theater; he produces it.

So, yes, she was barking up the right tree. I do know something – some things – about Greenstone, but not much.

And I'm not convinced "know" is the correct verb. I've interviewed him a few times – usually on productions with which he's been associated. From time to time I've consulted him on breaking stories involving subjects like union strikes. Once or twice I consulted him on think-pieces I was preparing about playwriting trends or changing approaches to acting, that sort of thing.

Greenstone has never been less than civil. Occasionally, he's even been professionally friendly. That's to say, he tacks on a smile at the end of his sentences to suggest he's enjoying himself; he lets breathing space into the conversation, allows the interview to masquerade as conversation. He has even, on occasion, addressed me by first name.

So I think he knows I'm Daniel Freund – or at least remembers for short periods of time.

More often, however, he doesn't address me by name but sits slightly back from his desk – this is when I interview him in person – with legs crossed and hands folded in his lap, answering questions with equanimity. The tacit statement is: You're a reporter, I'm a producer, this is an adversarial situation, you want to find out information I can't or won't or don't want to impart, I'll abide by professional manners so as to dispatch you as quickly as I can without provoking resentment that could turn up in print to my disadvantage.

In my experience this isn't unusual behavior. Many interviewees do some version of the same thing, although Greenstone looks especially good pulling it off. You might call him a handsome man. Many have – handsome in the way that conventions of masculine pulchritude are more encompassing than conventions of feminine pulchritude. He stands over six feet (already a big plus in many assessments). He has a full head of wavy hair that he wears long and into which he undoubtedly douses designer shampoo and conditioner at least once a day. He has an athletic bearing. I've heard he plays tennis but not golf. I've never asked. He has a firm jaw (he's clean shaven) and a wide, though thin-lipped, mouth. He could serve as substantiating evidence that thin-lipped men are more reserved about their emotions than full-lipped men.

I'd tell you the color of his eyes were I the sort of interviewer who notices the color of interviewees' eyes.

Greenstone is always well-dressed. By always, I'm basing the report on my face-to-face encounters with him; more often than not, I've interviewed him on the phone and when I have, I've imagined him dressed as he's been when I've seen him – in a tailored single-breasted suit, blue shirt with white color and tie featuring a small pattern, if any pattern at all.

He's always outfitted thus, I'm guessing, because he believes that a man who wears a good suit is going to raise more capital for a production than a man who doesn't. He's right about that. The man who thinks it's acceptable strategy to appear down-at-heel-arty when looking for funds is probably miscalculating – arty is okay behind the scenes but not at checkbook time.

Orrin Greenstone understands that fact of show business life.

Such knowledge is the sort, of course, that would be imparted in Capitalizing a Broadway Show 101. How much else Greenstone has stored away in his brain that rises above the elemental I can't say. He's never struck me as especially bright, and I've heard others suggest he isn't. But he wouldn't be the first to silence a roomful of magpies because he's shrewd rather than brilliant.

Many of the people who've done well on the Great White Way fall into that very category, and it's its own form of brilliance. Most of them came into the business with fat wallets courtesy of Daddy or Mommy and then figured out how to solidify their standing by talking a good game. Greenstone is thought by many to be one of this happy, well-heeled breed and to have acquired enough smarts along the way to pull the wool over the eyes of wannabes who know appreciably less than he does.

On the other hand, you'd think, wouldn't you?, a man who's had the string of successes he's had couldn't be completely devoid of savvy – *sechel* in the Yiddish, which Greenstone wouldn't likely be caught spouting. You might think it, but that could be where you'd go wrong: Broadway is in every aspect a collaborative effort, and all hits are something of a mystery.

Just who – if any single person – is the guiding force behind a Broadway money-making machine may be impossible to descry. Once upon a time you could, of course. It was the name placed alone atop the bill. But since there are often as many as a dozen names at the top of the credits nowadays – some of them corporations, not individuals – there's usually no hope of knowing who might have thrown what notion into the winning mix.

It's with this reality in mind that I talk to Orrin Greenstone. And not that often, which is why I maintain I know some things about him but not a great deal. There are people in his position with whom I do have the more frequent chat, but one of the reasons Orrin Greenstone isn't in that group is I've had the impression he doesn't hold a high opinion of me.

It comes down to a chicken-and-egg proposition. As I think I've made clear, I don't have a particularly high opinion of him, but who first formed an opinion about whom and then tacitly transmitted it, I don't know.

Often these things are mere chemistry; often we think we have someone else's number, because it's also our own number and instantly familiar. Is that what operated between Orrin Greenstone and me? Maybe, maybe not. Maybe nothing more than reporter and subject operated. Maybe if you'd asked Greenstone about me around the time cousin Sara called, he'd have said he had no opinion of me one way or the other, and he'd have been telling the truth.

There is one other salient comment about Greenstone I've withheld these few prefatory paragraphs: He was handsome – if you regarded him as handsome – in spite of a very prominent nose. I had an Uncle Mickey who would have called it a honker. A "shnahz"–with an elongated "ah" and abundant extra "z"s.

I had a cousin – Mickey's daughter – who would have described the *schnaaaahhhhzzzzz* another way. That would have been my cousin Carolyn, who died some years ago and took with her to the grave a great sense of humor. I hope she's amusing herself with it there.

Carolyn not only had a great sense of humor, she was extraordinarily beautiful. She was the kind of hometown beauty of whom locals said things like "I don't know why people think Grace Kelly is so stunning. She's no better looking than Carolyn Bloch."

Beauty like that often comes at a price, though. Carolyn paid by getting involved with the wrong men. It was easy for her to do. So many men made fools of themselves over her that she took to regarding all men as fools and eventually couldn't tell the less foolish from the more foolish. She turned them away blithely and regularly, often after teasing them, toying with them, stringing them along.

All the while she'd joke about them behind their backs, refer to them by nicknames they never heard. They didn't know they were Thunder Thighs or Flat Foot Floogie or Cobweb Wallet.

Ah, but we family members did.

Another one who probably didn't know what Carolyn called him behind his back – always with a certain amount of affection – was a guy whom much of America knew at the time. He was the emcee of a television quiz show in the early days when there were only a few channels and little choice. The celebrity was the now nearly-forgotten John Burrows, but to Carolyn – whom he dated for close to a year until she tired of him – and to us he was Banana Nose.

Always and only Banana Nose–"Who're you going out with tonight, Carolyn?" "Who else? Banana Nose." Not John or John Burrows or Johnny – "Banana Nose."

I mention this now, because I hadn't thought of Banana Nose for years, for decades before cousin Sara called and asked what I knew about

Orrin Greenstone.

"Tell me what you know," Sara importuned.

"Not much. Why are you asking?"

"A good friend of mine – Nancy Bensky – met him at a fund-raiser, and now he's calling her up. They only met a few days ago, and he's already called her twice a day since."

"He wants to take her out, right?" I said.

"He's dying to take her out."

"Why doesn't she just go out with him?"

"She thinks there's something odd about him. What do you know?"

"What do I know?" It's a figure of speech as well as a direct question – and "know" is the tricky part. I only know/knew what I'd heard, and for many years I'd heard Orrin Greenstone loved to chase the ladies. I'd also heard from a woman friend of mine who'd been pursued by him – but whom he had never snared – that Greenstone was no prize in the boyfriend department. He had a reputation for being persistent but deficient on the follow-through.

In what way was always vague to me. The friend of mine who'd eluded his clutches said a whole lot of snickering went on among the women who succumbed and then recovered their senses. One joke that circulated had to do with a support group supposedly forming – OGA (Orrin Greenstone Anonymous).

But this was all rumor and was wholly unconnected with my direct Greenstone dealings, which were, as I've noted, on a professional level. In the lover-boy end of things, I had no verified facts, and as a journalist, facts are what I'm expected to know or discover. Failing those, I have no story.

Therefore, it wasn't loyalty to Orrin Greenstone or to my fellow men that kept me from choosing to say anything to Sara about what I'd heard, it was loyalty to my reporter's code.

"I can't really tell you anything, Sara," I said. "I know the guy, but I know him to interview him, not to date him. I've heard a few things, but nothing to go on."

"'A few things.' What things?" Sara pressed.

"Nothing worth relaying. He's not married. He dates a lot of women."

"He's not gay, is he? Trying to pass?"

"No, I don't think he's gay," I said, and felt a smirk coming on that she, of course, couldn't see. "Far from it."

"So Nancy should go out with him?"

"For all I know, they could have a great time," I said.

Then I did what I came to regret. Encouraging Sara to encourage the Bensky woman when I had reason to suspect the date(s) mightn't end well, I began to feel slightly guilty. It occurred to me I might lessen the guilt by throwing a small bone Sara's – and Nancy's – way.

It was then that cousin Carolyn and Banana Nose crossed my mind. I suppose because I made a sudden connection – prominent man, sizable proboscis, cousin – that I made what was to become a disputed and, okay, injudicious remark.

As I recall, I said, "Tell her to go out with him, as long as she doesn't mind the banana nose."

Or I said something very close to that.

As Sara recalls it, however, I said, "Tell her to go out with Banana Nose."

It's a fine point, I know.

(Not Orrin Greenstone's nose, but the comment.)

In the way Sara tells it, I referred to Orrin Greenstone as Banana Nose. I outright called him Banana Nose. The way I tell it, I only said his nose is like a banana.

"'Banana nose.'" Sara said and started laughing. "Nancy didn't say anything about that."

"Maybe she didn't notice," I said.

"Oh, she noticed. Nancy misses nothing. She can spot capped teeth or a bad toupee from a mile off. He's got a nose like a banana?"

"Well, yes. It's long and it curves."

"Is it rich with potassium?"

"That, I couldn't tell you."

"So I should advise her to go out with Banana Nose?"

This is where the dispute continues. I say it was Sara who first called him Banana Nose without any prompting from me.

And when she said it, I heard Carolyn and chuckled to myself, because I could hear Carolyn chuckling as she always did when she used one of her nicknames. Never with malice, always with amusement. When Sara said the words, I heard Carolyn chuckling from the grave. She certainly would have if she could have.

Sara, on the other hand, says she only used the Banana Nose term because she'd heard me use it. She maintains she wouldn't have thought to use the description as a nickname. That's not the way her mind works, she insists. I say her mind worked that way at least the one time.

Not that at this juncture determining who said what when would change the subsequent developments.

"Yes, tell her to go out with the guy. What could happen?"

(Three words I'll never utter again without much forethought!)

There was another reason why I encouraged – well, not really encouraged but didn't out-and-out discourage – the date. I don't know who this Nancy Bensky is. For all I know, if I'd said I thought her seeing Greenstone was a bad idea and Sara told Nancy what I'd said, Nancy Bensky could have turned around and told Orrin she'd heard through channels he wasn't a safe bet. If he'd asked what channels, she might have spilled my name, because what did I mean to her?

What actually transpired was worse, but I can't say I wouldn't do the same thing again.

I can say that first phone call from Sara – so seemingly ordinary – was the beginning of a debacle.

To wit: Nancy Bensky apparently had the date(s). Not that I knew about it/them. I didn't know anything about anything until I received the second Nancy Bensky-related phone call from Sara. This was when I'd pretty much forgotten about the whole thing and had gone on my merry way.

I don't want, however, to give the wrong impression: My way is only merry some of the time; the rest of the time it's not so merry. And on the topic of not-so-merry times, a couple of months go by during which I don't give Cousin Sara or Nancy Bensky or Orrin Greenstone a thought.

No, in the service of accuracy – accuracy being part of the journalist's ABCs (accuracy, brevity, clarity) – I did give Orrin Greenstone a couple of thoughts of the professional variety. Nothing that impinges on the matter at hand: An industry controversy arose about ticket-pricing.

Delving into the issue, I figured I might want a quote from Orrin Greenstone. I put a call into his press agent and got a return call saying he didn't want to comment on the matter. I attached no importance to his turndown. I did notice that in other stories on the subject where some of the same people to whom I spoke were quoted, Orrin Greenstone wasn't included. I had no reason to think other than that he'd taken a no-comment position and stuck to it with everyone.

Nor did I see Greenstone to talk to. I saw him across a crush at a few previews. Once was at the press night for a play he was presenting, Matthew Winnick's drama about a dysfunctional family. (So what else is new?) Another night Greenstone was in the pre-theater crowd at Fergus McAndrew.

Fergus McAndrew, by the way, was a typical success story. Fergus McAndrew, the restaurateur who gave his name to the establishment, had made buddies of a few actors with deep pockets. Having announced a couple of years earlier he wanted to open a new spot, he easily got the backing from his pals, plus the promise that they'd spend mucho hours on the premises with their friends. A following materialized. Everybody was going to meet, eat, greet, seat, treat, compete at Fergus McAndrew, where the food was good enough and the view in any direction full of famous or near-famous faces.

Table-hopping took on the aspect of an Olympic sport. You never knew whom you'd see, what they'd say, how they'd carry on, what party would get too boisterous, what brawl would break out. It was, of course, a major destination for the couple of eager gossip columnists feeding, and feeding on, the industry. Paparazzi made the sidewalk in front a standard stop just in case Madonna should drop by.

The night I saw Greenstone there during the post-Nancy Bensky phone-call time-frame, he was at a table with hot playwright Terry O'Malley and a couple of marquee-name thespians, one of whom, Ellen Rich, I'd heard he was taking out. (Greenstone, that is, not O'Malley.) I wasn't facing Greenstone's table. So I couldn't watch his behavior, even if I'd been inclined to. I could only imagine he spent most of the meal pushed back from the table with his legs crossed and his hands folded in his lap. I did hear his laugh – a quick low laugh – which I recognized from the few times he'd meted it out during one of our interviews.

When I got up to leave my table, Greenstone was still seated and happened to be looking my way. He nodded, and I nodded back. It was one of those tacit exchanges that says, Since we know each other, not nodding would verge on the insulting but doing anything more than nodding would be in excess of what either of us wants to commit to.

I do think that in the few moments during and after the nod, the Nancy Bensky connection occurred to me – that Orrin Greenstone might have already taken her out. But I didn't dwell on it for long.

So that was that.

Except that, after all, wasn't that. Out of the blue I got a second Nancy Bensky-related phone call from (agitated) cousin Sara. Many openings and reviews and news stories had passed as well as the few Orrin Greenstone sightings I've pretty much covered.

Sara didn't bother to announce herself. She started *in media res* – with "media" in the other sense and my role in it eventually becoming the crucial part. "Why didn't you tell me about Orrin Greenstone?" she demanded.

"Sara?" I said, fairly certain it was her voice I recognized.

"None other," she said and repeated, "Why didn't you tell me about Orrin Greenstone?"

"I told you what I knew. Why are you asking?"

She ignored the question and said, "You didn't tell me what you knew. You said Nancy should go out with the jerk."

"I told you as much as I know about the guy."

"But you didn't tell me what you heard. You said you'd heard things, but you never said what they were."

"Hearsay. I don't traffic in it." What sounded like a "harrumph" issued from the other end of the line. "Okay," I said, "What happened?"

"I wasn't there to experience it totally, so if I tell you what's happened, it's only hearsay. Nancy has your number. So to speak. She'll be calling. How's everything?"

"Otherwise?

"Otherwise."

"Fine," I said, "How's the family?

"Everyone's fine," she said. "Enjoy Nancy's call." She rang off.

I didn't have to wait long. Funny, Nancy Bensky hadn't phoned to thank me for the Orrin Greenstone endorsement. If that's what it was. I mean, on paper, he could have looked extremely promising. But here she was calling now that he evidently hadn't panned out. How badly he hadn't panned out I was about to learn.

"I'm sure you're busy," she said when right off I explained I was on deadline for a story, "but I'd like to know what you think you're doing telling women they should go out with Orrin Greenstone?"

"You sound very angry," I said.

"I am. Furious," she said. "Did you know there are a whole string of women who've written him off as bad news? A network of them. So many there's been talk of starting a support group?"

"I'd heard that," I said, "but it sounded like someone's idea of a stupid joke. It wasn't my place to pass on gossip."

"Gossip! What is this, some sort of code among men? You don't tell on me, I don't tell on you?"

"If it is, it's unspoken," I said. "We don't get together and take a blood oath."

"No," she said, "it's only the women who get to spill blood. I guess because it's assumed we have a tampon handy for wiping up."

"Nancy," I said, "I'm kinda busy to be having this conversation."

"Then I'll come right to the point." She swung into her point, and that's when it began to feel as if the receiver heated up. "I'll concede that when a woman goes out with a man, it's up to her to decide whether she wants to keep going out with him. But if she's armed with the proper background information, she might have chosen not to go out with him in the first place. And I consider myself deprived of the right information. Thanks to you. The guy comes on strong at first. And he's not half-bad-looking, except for the..."

Interrupting her, I said, "I did say he has a..."

"Let me finish," she said. "When he first started badgering me, I figured he's got an exciting career and a good reputation for it, so I refrained from hanging up on him. Then, on the strength of your say-so, I decided to go out with him. The first few dates were okay. We had dinner. He took me to a play he was producing that I thought was all right and not much more. But I tempered my opinion, since he was obviously proud of it. I'm not going to get into the sex."

"Good, because I don't really want..."

"Let me finish. Except to say there was some. Beyond that, I'm not a kiss-and-tell person, particularly now that Viagra and Cialis and Levitra have to be factored in. Who knows who's doing what to whom under what influence? It isn't the in-the-bedroom part that became the big problem anyway. It was the out-of-the-bedroom part. I find – and I'm not the only one who says so; my single girlfriends say the same thing – there's a kind of man for whom the chase is the titillation. When a women plays hard to get, he's intrigued. He's turned on. He's, 'Ooh, I can't do enough for you.' The minute the woman capitulates, that's the end of it. She's a conquest, and the attitude is, You can treat a conquest any way you fucking well please. Your pal Orrin Gree..."

Pal! Where did that come from? "He's not my pal, he's a professional acquain..."

"Let me finish. Is a prime example of the conquering hero. It's almost as if guys have a kind of weird low self-esteem. They have disdain for any women who would actually be interested in them, and it's important they let the women know it. What's even worse is, it's important they let everyone else know it. Do you realize what your friend did?"

"How could I know any..?"

"Let me finish. He'd take me places, introduce me to people – some interesting people, too, and that was like the lure. Then he'd find opportunities to criticize me in front of them. It didn't happen a lot, because I caught on fast. With a little help from people who were more informative than you fucking were. Women, all of them. One took me aside at a dinner party when she didn't think Orrin was looking and asked how long I'd been seeing him. I said only a few weeks, and she said, 'I don't know you, but I'm just telling you that a friend of mine went out with him, and barely lived to tell the tale.' I said, 'What did she mean by that?' And she said, 'Nothing criminal but not far from it.' Then she shut up. I think she saw him coming our way. Two dates later, we're at another of the endless fund-raisers, where Orrin's paid who knows what – maybe ten thousand dollars – for the table, and so figures he can say whatever he wants to the people shoveling down the mediocre meal on his tab. Orrin starts in on me for something I say about a play I hadn't liked and didn't realize he was one of the producers of. It was a play he'd put on way before I met him."

I was probably imagining it, but the receiver felt as if it were getting too hot to hold. For some time I'd been switching it from ear to ear.

Nancy kept going. "I won't repeat what he said verbatim, but I'll only say he stopped short of using the C-word. Not too short, though. I had about as much as I could take. Partly because I could see the other eight people at the table were wide-eyed – the women particularly, but even a couple of the men. So I picked up my goddamn handbag, my *minaudière* if you please, and said, 'I'm going to go now, but before I do, I've got something to say to you, Banana Nose.'"

"You didn't call him..," I began.

"Let me finish. I couldn't get to what I wanted to say, though, because the minute I said 'Banana Nose,' people started laughing out loud. The women started laughing out loud, I should say. The men were trying not to laugh. Not succeeding for long, but still trying. In the meantime, Orrin – Banana Nose – had this shocked look on his face. Like he's never heard this before. And he puts his hand up to his nose. I thought he was going to try to peel it."

This time I didn't interrupt her. She interrupted herself by laughing. When she stopped laughing, she resumed her horror story. "I said right to him in front of the table, 'Yes, I know everybody calls you Banana Nose behind your back. That's the only thing I knew about you before I accepted the first date. If I'd known more, I never would have said yes. But all my friend Sara could find out when she called your friend Dan Freund – besides I should go out with you – is everybody calls you Banana Nose behind your back.'"

"But I nev..," I began again.

"Let me finish. I said, 'What's it like to go through life being called Banana Nose? Think about that.' And I walked away. All I heard behind me was silence. I didn't turn around to look. I just kept on going. And that's the last I've heard of Mr. Orrin Greenstone. The famous Banana Nose."

Nancy Bensky didn't stay on the phone for long after that. Once she'd let me know what she'd done, her rage subsided. She'd ascribed much of her humiliation to me, and when she'd told me about it, her mission was accomplished.

What could I say in response? No point to my setting her straight on the misinformation she'd passed on. She'd probably only think I was lying to excuse myself. Also I didn't know the woman. There was no possibility that under the peculiar circumstances we'd be friends, much less date in the near future. I begged off by bringing up the deadline I was postponing so I could give her sufficient air time.

Satisfied at last that I'd let her finish, she hung up.

But if she could finally allow Banana Nose to become a fading memory, it came to pass that I could not. The unhappy circumstance was brought home to me at – wouldn't you know it? – Fergus McAndrew. This time it was post-theater. Once again, Orrin Greenstone was there: at the same table I'd last seen him but this time with four people whom I didn't recognize. When I was shown to the table next to him, he was leaning in to his dinner companions and speaking quietly to them. He didn't see me.

I was with my friend Frank Ortiz, and as the *maitre d'* led us to the table, I suggested, as a cautionary measure, that I sit closer to Greenstone. That way, I'd have my back to him. I briefly filled Frank in on all he needed to know –"Orrin Greenstone at the next table," I said, but quietly, "Not a good idea for him to spot me."

Frank nodded that he understood, although the most he might have extrapolated from my hurried remark was that it was related to a news story I was working on or a negative review I'd written of a recent Greenstone enterprise. Had I sat anywhere else at the table, Frank must have picked up, I would have been facing Greenstone, and that wouldn't work.

Sitting at another table altogether would have been much the best idea, of course, but as luck would have it, there was no other unoccupied table in the room. Also, keeping in mind that nuance was noticed at the establishment and maybe even passed on to an importuning theater columnist, I worried that my asking to be seated in another room might have raised some suspicions. Perhaps I'm imputing to myself more importance than is actually there, but, as I say, I was trying to exercise caution.

All for naught. My first clue came from Frank. In the middle of expressing an opinion on some aspect of the (non-Orrin Greenstone) production we'd just survived, he suddenly looked up and then looked at me.

The shifting gaze indicated someone was behind me. I'd only begun to form a question when there was a tap on my shoulder. I was hoping it wasn't what I suspected, but I turned around to see it was.

Orrin Greenstone loomed in his tailored single-breasted suit, blue shirt with white collar and tie with discreet print. Behind him, the four people at his table were watching him – and me. Nobody else around seemed to be paying any attention. His approaching me would have looked to anyone momentarily inquisitive as just another instance of typical Fergus McAndrew table-hopping. If Orrin Greenstone had risen to say hello to, say, David Mamet, that might have turned a few heads. His talking to a reporter didn't set off quite the same *frisson*.

"Mr Freund," he said.

I stood up. "Mr Greenstone," I said. Then, disingenuous as I could affect, I started to say, "Nice to see..." He cut me off and continued.

Loudly.

"Don't say it's nice to see me. Or were you going to say it's nice to see Banana Nose?"

Since he was shouting, I intuited this wasn't the time for polite demurrals. I reckoned I'd better jump in with as direct a response as I could muster. "I'd like to explain..."

"I'm not interested in your explanation. I wouldn't believe it anyway. You reporters can't wait to lie in print. Why should I think you want to do anything else when you're speaking? What I ought to do is punch you out."

As he said that, he raised his right arm to demonstrate what he meant. He gave such a convincing demonstration that I was prepared to believe he was about to follow through on his threat. I raised my left arm, elbow bent, to block him. What I think happened then is: He thought I was about to throw a punch. So he – in his tailored single-breasted suit, blue shirt with white collar and tie with discreet print – rounded with his left fist. I forestalled that blow with my right arm.

Then I, who hadn't been in a fist fight since fourth grade when I was goaded into sparring with Butchie Swigert, let go with my left fist. It was a clean swing, and I caught Greenstone squarely on his substantial beak, on his snout, on his smeller, on his honker, on his unmissable Cyrano de Bergerac, on his *shnaaaaaaahhhhhzzzzzzzzzz* – on the seemingly renowned banana nose.

Well, the damn thing would have to get in the way.

There was the muted sound of bone breaking and gristle ripping, followed immediately by a river of blood that splattered on his tailored single-breasted suit, blue shirt with white collar, et cetera.

I escaped the spray, as did the onlookers whose attention we had attracted.

Stunned, Greenstone put his hand up to his famous feature. "You've broken it," he said to me and sat down heavily in the seat I'd vacated.

A waiter hustled over with a napkin. A second waiter was dousing another napkin in cold water. Fergus McAndrew the person materialized. He threw me a warning glance and joined the employees ministering to Greenstone, whose dinner partners had all jumped up and gathered around him, blocking Frank, who was wearing a look of sheer amazement.

"I could sue you for assault and battery," Greenstone said to me. Or that's what I thought he said, since he had cold napkin compresses covering the bottom half of his face.

"Nobody's suing anybody," Fergus McAndrew said.

Now there's a proprietor who knows the kind of publicity he wants and the kind he doesn't want. He ended the fracas in a matter of minutes – long minutes, but minutes – seeing to it that Greenstone left immediately for the Roosevelt Hospital emergency room. Then he summarily eighty-sixed me from the restaurant, but only for the night.

I left hastily, of course – with dazed Frank in tow – but not before becoming aware of a murmur traveling from table to table about Greenstone's being known throughout the theater community as Banana Nose and the appellation having been hung on him by the reporter who'd just decked him. And not before a columnist on the *qui vive* queried a number of people about what they saw and heard.

(What they saw and heard turned out to be far riper for embellishment by someone with fewer journalistic scruples than yours truly. That's how "decked him" became part of the story, even though Greenstone had come nowhere near to hitting the Fergus McAndrew deck.)

And not before Greenstone was photographed leaving Fergus McAndrew, holding a handkerchief to his face. One of the photographs appeared on page three of the following day's *New York Post* under the headline, "Banana Split." Yes, the *Post* saw to it that Orrin Greenstone acquired a second nickname, one for which I wasn't (wholly) responsible.

So I figure that somewhere there's a headline writer due for a bruising. I also have a hunch I'm not off the hook with Greenstone either – although "hook" may be the wrong word to bandy about at a time like this.

My only comfort is that somewhere Cousin Carolyn is having a good laugh.

Memorial

i.

Not to put too maudlin a point on it, but there is a stretch of Back Street inhabited by gay men. I know about the well-shaded part of town because on a couple of occasions in the past I've held short-term leases on apartments there.

I hadn't thought about this for a long time but was reminded a month or so ago when I reached the *Times* obituary page – I haven't yet gotten to that point in life when the obits are what I open to first, but soon, soon – and saw a notice for Noah Goodman's memorial service. Noah Goodman used to visit me on Back Street, and I used to visit him on Easy Street. Not that any of his neighbors – figurative or otherwise – knew anything about it.

Anyway, I'll drop the metaphor and stick to the facts and feelings as they returned to me, *overcame* me, during the course of that memorial service, which I did attend. An affair at which upwards of one hundred others also appeared – none of whom I knew but some of whom I knew about. A woman called Rosalind Paynter (I actually *had* encountered her in quite another context long after Noah and I had all but lost touch) presided at the event and, in the course of her opening remarks, said something like "I expect each of you will remember exactly where you met Noah, because he always made such an impact."

Like so many who spoke about him in the dimmed auditorium that noontime, she was absolutely right. I certainly remembered exactly where I met Noah: at the Turtle Bay Baths. The summer of 1974. A muggy July night, to be even more specific. (None of the speakers commemorating him recalled a similar meeting.) Did he wander into my cubicle and grab my dick? Did I amble into his roomette and trail the fingers of one hand along his hairy calf? Did we catch each other's eye in the showers? Or pass one another in a busy corridor amid all the libidinous coming-and-goings? *That* I don't remember. I assume we joined up, possibly without speaking at all, in some time-honored way (ironically, rituals at the baths were rigid, considering the supposed liberated setting). Either before, during and/or after engaging in illicit activity, we must have fallen into a conversation during which we became intrigued enough to go home together.

To Noah's home – the snug apartment described accurately by one of Noah's other eulogists as "so full of books you couldn't get from the front door to the nearest chair or from one room to the next without running the risk of upsetting four-foot-high stacks of books." Books, I'll add, of every shape and category. Books with fresh, slick jackets and books bound in crumbling, tooled leather. Books spiked with bookmarks or bits of paper. Books lying open and upside down, one on another. Books never likely to come under the tyranny of anyone's decimal system.

On my entering that unusual library, it wasn't the stacks that fell, however; *I* was what fell. A sucker for books, for reading, for volumes and tomes as insignias of erudition, I took one sweeping glance around the small living-room (I guessed that's what it must be because I thought I caught a glimpse of a leather divan under one especially large-ish and wide-ish pile of books) and told myself I'd hit pay dirt. I'd met the kind of man I'd always wanted to meet, a man who loves books as much as I do. More. Enough to give them the run of the place, which I, in my fastidiousness, could never quite allow myself to do.

The movie in my head cuts to us in Noah's single bed (single brass bed) an hour or so later and Noah saying, "I love you." This with a clarion ring that matched the brightness of the brass posts. This after our having been together so briefly it's possible we were still unsure of each other's first name. Of course, I knew he didn't love me – much the opposite, was exposing suspicious impetuosity by saying that he *did* love me on such short acquaintance. (If you could even stretch our brief meeting far enough to call it an acquaintance.) Yet I thought, while he had his arms around me, while he was looking at me with that gaze only the newly- or recently-infatuated can conjure, that maybe he could *come* to love me, that his saying he already did – intelligent man that he clearly was – was his way of declaring not that he truly loved me but that he expected he could, that he was announcing his intention to give it the old college try.

So there I was – with the four a.m. moonlight falling through the narrow window of his narrow bedroom onto the narrow bed we were so eager to be uncomfortable in – deciding I was happy because I'd found a man who was going to love me and whom I expected I could love back. And so we fell into the fitful sleep of the carelessly charmed.

Morning came. Noah got up, said little, went to the kitchen, came back with two glasses of orange juice and a book of Wallace Stevens's collected poems. Don't you know he read me the very poem someone read during the memorial service? Someone who knew, as I had learned, that this was

Noah's favorite poem. Well, one of his favorites (he'd waffle when asked to commit): "The Anecdote of the Jar." Noah looked around for his rimless glasses, located them somewhere near the bed, put them on without entirely hooking them behind his ears. "I placed a jar upon a hill/And round it was..." His tones as he read were deep and sonorous yet marked by, had at their center, a humor, a lightness, a – what? – a young man's buoyancy. (When we met, Noah was forty-eight, and I was thirty-four.) He finished reading, shut the book, put it on the window sill, took his glasses off, folded the earpieces, placed them on top of the book. "Wonderful, isn't it?" I agreed it was, though I wasn't certain I entirely understood it; I'm still not sure. I said, "Read another one." "Oh, no, beamish boy," Noah replied, getting up, "With poems of that caliber you only read one, and then you think about it for a long time." He took a couple of steps towards the bathroom. "I'm going in here to think. I'll leave you to do your thinking exactly where you are." He took another step, turned around just before closing the door, "Are you thinking?" He was grinning widely; Noah had a great grin, a grin that could light the world. "I'm thinking, I'm thinking," I said, recalling Jack Benny's joke response to the robber's threat, "Your money or your life." "Good Benny," Noah said and shut the bathroom door behind him. When he came out, he barely looked at me, just picked up his glasses and the Wallace Stevens poems and passed through to the living-room. I could hear him moving around. I thought maybe I was still supposed to be thinking about "The Anecdote of the Jar." Instead, I wondered whether I was at the beginning or the end of something. My romantic history would indicate the latter.

A few minutes went by, and Noah appeared in the bedroom door. Dressed. Not *well* dressed – he was never what you'd call *well-dressed*. But dressed. A tweed jacket (keep in mind it was July); an Oxford shirt with a very thin regimental tie (keep in mind wide ties with all sorts of tie-dye prints were the fashion in 1974). "Do you want any breakfast?" he asked. I couldn't tell whether yes or no was required. "Well, I... uh..." "If you do, there's cereal in a cabinet over the sink in the kitchen. Anything else you need is approximately where you'd expect it to be. When you're ready to go, just let yourself out." I was startled. "Are you *leaving*?" He looked at me as if I'd asked an extremely stupid question. "I'm due at my office. I make a habit of getting there on time. Punctuality is the politeness of bosses."

I roused myself from the bed, confused and a little angry. "Wait a minute," I said, reaching around for the clothes I'd dropped (as instructed the previous night) on a pile of books.

"I'll leave with you," I said.

"No hurry," he said.

I was not at all pleased at the idea of being left alone in what was still a stranger's apartment. I felt what I was getting was a rather creative heave-ho. "Stay as long as you like," Noah said and took a little pause. "I want to see you again, of course, but I'm just not sure when I'll be able to. I'm very busy. I've got your phone number." He went to the front door, opened it, turned and smiled in a way that said he was only doing what he felt he probably should. "The front door will lock behind you automatically." He left. I'd been co-opted. I *had* given him my number the night before when we were discussing leaving the baths together but hadn't yet concluded we would. Now he'd said he'd call when he was free. What I heard implicitly – but clearly – was, don't call me first. Exasperated, one-upped, I looked around at the books, thought about the day in front of me, wondered whether I might as well just fix myself something to eat.

At the time I'm writing about I had only recently left a full-time job. A small inheritance had come to me unexpectedly when a favorite aunt died. Who would ever have guessed she'd saved so much money? My father would have been the one to know, and even he was surprised. As a matter of fact, how she amassed her impressive nest-egg had become a matter of much speculation in the family. Had there been a rich lover? A winning lottery ticket? Would an embezzlement charge be slapped on her posthumously? Dinner conversation with my parents and brothers when we got together once, twice a month had become each of us breaking the others up as we took turns spinning wilder and wilder tales of how Aunt Esther made her millions. (It wasn't millions; it was considerably less, but still enough to delight the nieces and nephews she'd smiled on from beyond the grave.)

So having given myself a year to write the novel I'd always said I'd write if only I had a year to write a novel, I was edging into a routine in fits and starts. Time on my hands: I'd never been good with it. With no reason, then, to race home that July morning I took Noah up on his offer, poured myself a bowl of bran flakes (bowl and flakes found where Noah said they would be) and another glass of orange juice, went onto his terrace (Noah lived sixteen floors above lower Manhattan with, I'd estimate, a 240-degree view) and sat down to think. I don't remember what I thought.

Truth to tell, up to that point in my still young-ish life I'd never been much of a thinker. More precisely, I knew my mother was right when she said, as she often did, "You've got a good head on your shoulders." It's just that I wasn't inclined to use it more than I absolutely had to. In situations where thinking might have served me well, I frequently did anything but. The notion, for instance, of taking mental inventory or putting options in perspective when an unread issue of *People* magazine was at hand carried no weight with me. I avoided thinking, brushed off anything that went beyond superficial considerations of who and where I was. So the chances are I avoided any kind of meaningful thought that morning on Noah's terrace. I paged through a handful of books I'd brought out to skim over breakfast, looked cursorily around at the sunlit panorama, maybe even counted water towers since I happen to love water towers and judge the quality of high-rise apartments by the number of water towers that can be seen from them.

I wouldn't want to be held to it, but my guess is that during this perfectly nice interval I decided I shouldn't expect much more from Noah, that the impassioned proclamations of the previous night were no more than standard heat-of-the-moment lies more cleverly phrased than most. I probably concluded that what was left me at that point were whatever luxurious minutes I could wring out of my sit on that metropolitan version of a front porch. I leafed through some books, read parts of them, perused the notes Noah had made in the margins. (He'd made many, in an angular, back-slanted hand. On one page of a dog-eared copy of Kant's *Prolegomena* he'd inscribed "Poppycock, Immie!") When an hour or so got idled away, I finished dressing, washed out the glass and bowl I'd used, thought about but didn't write a thank-you-for-the-use-of-the-hall note and left. The door did indeed lock behind me automatically.

ii.

Noah called me that afternoon somewhere between three or four. I was surprised but something told me – rightly? – not to let on. "What are you doing tonight?" he asked in an enthusiastic voice I not only recognized but to which I could already affix a facial expression. "I don't know. Tonight? Nothing." "We're going to Gage & Tollner. I'll come by at 6:15." "Sure. Okay. Sure. Fine." A silence: Gage & Tollner meant nothing to me. "Do you have my address?" "Yes." I didn't remember telling him. "Did I give it to you?" "No." "How'd you get it?"

(These were the days when my defenses shot up if I thought someone homosexual knew where I lived and might drop in on me without my wanting him to. Still somewhat homophobic, I had paranoid fears that I might put myself in a situation where the vice squad or, worse, gay-bashers wielding baseball bats would show up at my door in the middle of the night and drag me into the street while neighbors in bathrobes stood around astonished to learn that the nice-enough fellow downstairs was, would you believe it, nothing but a garden variety cocksucker.)

"*Calme-toi, amigo,*" he said. "You're in the phone book." Imagine my embarrassment. "I'll see you at 6:15." "Okay." "Aren't you going to ask me why 6:15, not 6 or 6:30?" "I will if you like." "In *The Prime of Jean Brodie* – the movie; I don't know about the book – the headmistress asks Jean Brodie to come to her office at 2:45, and Jean Brodie says to somebody or another, 'She thinks to intimidate me by the use of quarter hours.' Ever since I heard it, I think to intimidate people by the use of quarter hours." "I'm not intimidated." "I know. That's why I love you." There. He'd said it again. I realized I didn't mind hearing it.

Gage & Tollner is a well-known – though it wasn't to me – restaurant on Fulton Street in downtown Brooklyn. We went by subway. As we rode out, Noah told me how much he liked the place and that, though it was not exactly one of those off-the-beaten-track hash houses whose secret regulars guard tenaciously, he didn't go out of his way to introduce just anyone to it. How did he know it was the sort of venue where I'd feel completely comfortable, that the dark, carved wood was right up my esthetic alley, that the chandeliers with candles flickering in them and the four-square food made me want to jump up and click my heels in the air? The answer is: He didn't know. He suspected; he hoped; he put me to the test. He was saying without saying: This is the kind of thing I like; if you don't, so much for you. He was saying: I think we like the same things; I want to find out immediately, because if we're not on the same wavelength, there's no use wasting my time or yours.

I passed the test. I let Noah order – nothing fancy, sole *meunière*, potatoes, corn-on-the-cob, ginger ale. The food was fine, the dinner conversation had to do with his day and mine. Well, less with mine, since, as I say, I was trying to establish a routine and – I still used a typewriter then – was full of going through the time-honored motions of being a writer (gazing at half-typed pages, pulling them from the roller in big gestures, crumpling them, tossing them at the wastebasket). I'd finished the first drafts of several chapters of something I wasn't ready to call a novel. For reasons I'm about to explain, as dinner went on, I was even less inclined to say much about what I was doing. Noah, you see, was a publisher – no surprise, of course, what with all the books. But the night before he hadn't said a great deal about his work, and what he *had* said – during an obligatory and cursory exchange of autobiographical information as we reclined on his slightly damp bathhouse mattress – could have meant anything, could have meant he was an editor, a book designer, in sales, in marketing, in publicity, heaven spare us.

Over the perfectly-done sole he was explicit. He headed his own division at an established publishing house. It was a recent development in his life. For years he had been independent. He and his senior-year roommate had come out of Harvard with a conviction that what Bennett Cerf and Donald Klopfer had done before them with the Modern Library, they could do with something similar. The war was over; they'd saved a little money; they went to Europe to track down authors in France, Italy, The Netherlands, Austria, even some of the Balkan countries (the politics were sticky) who weren't yet being published in English because of "esoteric subject matter," "limited appeal." The two Charles River boys showed up on foreign stoops flashing high-wattage grins and working the *naïveté* Europeans so often expect from and patronize in Americans. They offered their prey small advances for exclusive publishing rights in the United

States; they promised solid translations and stylish production; they hedged on their plans for distribution – here language barriers were on their side. You, of course, have realized now why the name Noah Goodman sounds so familiar – if it does. He's one-half of Youngerman & Goodman. That's right, he is *the* Noah Goodman. He *is* the Noah Goodman who was the first to publish in this country so many household names and, in a couple of heady instances, Nobel Prize winners. His house and his reputation grew, and, as he reported it while slathering butter on corn, so did the headaches. Things between him and Stanton Youngerman – never all that copasetic – worsened over time until they both agreed it would be a relief to sell to a larger house and be subsumed into operations there; Goodman got *his* house, Youngerman *his*. So far, so *mezz-a-mezz* was his estimation of the split: he'd been his own boss for so long, it was not comfortable for him to be told by others what he could be doing to improve grosses.

Skipping names of the famous into our conversation like stones across water, Noah acted as if dealing with men and women whom I knew as syllabus requirements was, for him, all in a day's work. Needless to say, that's precisely what it was, but it sure took the wind out of my piddling sails. Before Noah had begun to fill in the outlines of his prominence and power in the publishing world, I had made a few tentative remarks about writing a novel. But the more he said about *him*self, the less inclined I was to offer more about *my*self." Why? Let's see. One, I suddenly felt that talking about my whatever-it-was-I-was-writing was somehow placing myself in competition with the major and minor classics he'd championed, a competition I wasn't ever likely to win. And two, I suspected there would be trouble if a potential second agenda become entangled in our whatever-it-was-we-were-doing. So by the time we got around to dessert I had backed away so gingerly from defining my project I had all but reduced it to a short comedy skit I was doodling with for my own amusement. I parried his tell-me-about-its with so many there's-nothing-to-tells that he finally stopped asking and said, "Whatever you do, you're going to be successful at it." I was so pleased at that – I hadn't fished for it – I felt as if a light had been turned on inside me, but, as was often my inclination, I was immediately skeptical. Noah, of course, had just presented impressive credentials for predicting achievement, but then again he had read nothing of mine, nor, I took note, did he go so far as to ask whether he could. "How do you know I'll succeed?" I begged gracelessly. "It's what I'm paid to know. It's the only talent I have. So shut up and let me exercise it."

Thus ended a subject I saw to it never came up again.

When dinner was over, Noah remarked that, though he'd admired my apartment when he'd come by to collect me and quite liked the way I'd decorated and lived in it, he'd prefer to go back to his. Said with the silky politeness of a man used to doing things his way: "If you're *absolutely sure* you don't mind..." I didn't. Those *books*. Back we went, where, on entering, Noah hustled to the stereo set and put a record on. "Do you know this?" he asked when the first strains of a piano piece I *didn't* know batted the air around. It was a piece which – no coincidence, of course – was cited by one of the grieving speakers at the memorial service. Noah must have played it for, or at least discussed it with, many of his friends: Beethoven's "Hammerklavier" Sonata. I'd never heard it before, or didn't remember having ever heard it. We settled – as near as anyone could settle – into two of Noah's reading chairs and listened in silence, Noah with his elbows on the uncomfortable wooden arms of the chair in which he was sitting. He rested his head against the fingers of his hands and rose only to turn the record over. Otherwise he remained immobile.

The sonata ended and, without bothering to speak or turn off the amplifier, he took my hand and led me to the bedroom. Again we had sex. "I love you," Noah said among many unintelligible guttural sounds. "I love you." I wondered whether I was expected to reciprocate; decided I wasn't. So I lay back and enjoyed myself as much as I could, which was a great deal. But not absolutely. The problem was mine (low-level but undeniable embarrassment over homosexual nookie) and his. I felt he still had no right to say what he insisted on saying: "I love you." We slept again, and again we woke. Again Noah dressed hurriedly – was he wearing the same clothes he'd worn the day before or were they merely identical? – and left me to use the apartment as I wanted. Again he rushed out saying he couldn't be sure when he would be able to see me again. The door locked automatically behind him.

I was less surprised when he called later that day and said he wanted to see the David Rabe play at Lincoln Center people were talking about, that he'd taken the liberty of reserving two tickets for that night. Could I meet him there at 7:45? "I'm still not intimidated by the use of quarter hours," I said. When Noah laughed, it was with all the joy of an audience watching the Marx Brothers in *A Night at the Opera*.

iii.

That's how it began, and that's the way it continued for the rest of the summer. Mornings, on leaving his apartment – rarely, indeed I think never, mine – Noah would peal off some version of his expecting to see me again but uncertain when. The inevitable follow-up phone call laying out the evening's plans came between three and four, and I was home or I wasn't. Usually I was, plugging away at the typewriter or staring vacantly over it. (I'd settled on a novel about a man who decides to die for love, literally.) Weekends we spent tooling around the city. What would have been a typical event? Well, there was the Saturday morning Noah called and said, "Drop everything – not your drawers, dummy! – we're going to the Met." He came by in a cab, ferried me uptown where we took the outside stairs of the Metropolitan Museum of Art two at a time, paid our suggested donations and made a beeline to the medieval hall. There he went up to the carving of a lady saint and said, "There she is!" 'She', according to the card on the plinth, was a Lindenwood reliquary bust of Saint Barbara, the patroness of firemen and architects. (She'd been incarcerated in a tower by her jealous father and then beheaded after she had added, to the two windows already in place in her tower, a third in honor of the Holy Trinity.) The unnamed sculptor – "School of Nicolaus Gerhaert von Leyden" – had given her a narrow, high-browed face framed by long, thick, fluid strawberry-blonde tresses. She wore a modest crown and a prim, purse-lipped expression. With her right hand she had her thumb and forefinger poised as if indicating a fraction-of-an-inch measure, and with her left hand she cradled a burnt-sienna model of the tower in which she'd been jailed by her vengeful parent. "What do you think?" Noah asked. I thought. "She's beautiful," I said, "but sour." "Ah-hah!" Noah snapped, "That's what I thought you'd say." He dropped to his haunches. "Now look." I dropped to *my* haunches and gazed up at the saint, who suddenly appeared not pinched but reassuringly serene, the kind of heavenly figure you might imagine would instill belief in frightened fifteenth-century souls. "You see," Noah said, "she was meant to be seen from below. Whoever the genius was who carved her knew what he was doing." We admired her some more on our haunches. "Remarkable, isn't it?" Noah asked.

Other times, not on our haunches, we attended plays, movies, concerts. We aired opinions about them from the minute the curtain descended (the last credit faded, the conductor lay down his baton) until long after we'd returned to Noah's apartment. Often when we got back, we'd be in the midst of some disagreement that needed settling. Before anything got done, a kettle put on the burner, a brandy poured, a mound of ice cream dished out, Noah would quick-step to a bookshelf to find corroborating proof of whatever argument he'd been making. Sometimes the substantiating book was where he expected it to be; sometimes it wasn't and he'd have to search through pile after pile, knocking them over, leaving the books exactly as they fell. Whether he found what he was looking for immediately or whether it took a half hour, his action when he finally put his hand on the sought book was the same. He'd smile – have I mentioned he had dimples in both cheeks? – with the vindictive triumph of someone who's just won a rancorous debate (the *arrogance*, I'd think lovingly) and say, as he'd said at Saint Barbara's side, "Ah-hah!" Was he always right? Was I always wrong? I don't remember. My best recollection is that he was right more often than me. Even though what we'd been contending then is lost to me now, I can still feel the ignominy of having been trumped.

Wait: I remember one battle. It had to do with a Shakespeare sonnet. Oh, which is it? Sonnet 73, the one beginning, "That time of year thou mayst in me behold..." For some reason it had come up in response to something we'd seen or heard earlier that night. We were quarreling over the second line. I insisted it went, "When yellow leaves, or few, or none, do hang..."; Noah said it went, "When yellow leaves, or none, or few, do hang..." (I didn't say these arguments weren't free of pedantry.) I maintained one of the reasons I remembered the line so precisely was that the progression of the number of yellow leaves from few to none lent an exquisite dying rhythm. Had Shakespeare put "none" before "few," the line would be choppy, unsatisfying, would lack its amazing grace. "Beamish boy," Noah said, "but that's Shakespeare. He's conversational when you expect him to be poetic. I'll rephrase that. Shakespeare finds the poetry in conversation. In discourse. He confounds expectation. Come to mention it, I can't think of a better definition of genius: the gift of confounding expectation." "You're wrong about this," I insisted. "You'll see I'm not," he countered. "Okay, wise guy," I said when we'd gotten to the apartment.

"Let me show you where you're wrong – I'm going to love this." I snatched *The Complete Works of Shakespeare*, which he had just ah-hahed over locating, and opened as quickly as I could to Sonnet 73: "That time of year thou mayst in me behold/When yellow leaves, or none, or few, do hang..." Foiled again.

Perhaps I remember this incident because there was a second lesson for me beneath the lesson in Shakespearean technique. The lesson was about me. I was the sort of person who too often expected the expected, was so used to adhering to what was expected that even when it wasn't there, I still saw or heard or smelled or tasted it. Whereas Noah, always on the lookout for genius, found it in the unexpected. He never pointed out this disparity between us to me, may never have even been inclined to. But the way I see things it accounts in some measure for what was to come.

Not that Noah's life was a string of uninterrupted small triumphs overshadowing my uninterrupted series of minor missteps. He had his downs. One bright morning when I was sitting outside drinking in the new day – and orange juice – I became aware that he was standing at the terrace door. I had the impression he'd been there for some time. Maybe not. I'd thought he was still in the bathroom, shaving. He continued standing there, not focusing on me – not looking directly at anything as near as I could tell. "I don't recognize my face," he said in uninflected tones. I was puzzled and probably would have appeared so had he focused on me. "I look in the mirror. I don't know myself anymore. I look at my face, and it's not the face I remember."

I realize I haven't given much, or any, physical description of Noah. Now, I think, is as good a time as any. That morning, in the door, wearing unpressed brown trousers, unshined cordovan shoes, a white t-shirt puckered with age, Noah, forty-eight, stood five feet ten, had thick, hairy, inordinately long arms that hung from his shoulders like parentheses, a thick chest, a medicine ball belly. His lined face was basically an inverted triangle. He had straight gray hair he parted on the left and kept long in the front so that it fell over his eyes. Sometimes, not often, he combed it back with his meaty fingers. His eyes were deep-set and dark under bushy salt-and-pepper eyebrows. They gave him a look that would have been grave had he not leavened it with those raucous laughs. I've said his smile was radiant. His teeth weren't, the bottom teeth discolored by coffee and tobacco.

I wasn't falling in love – hadn't fallen in love – with Noah for his looks, however. When I told friends about him, which I must have done, I'm sure I never described him as handsome. In truth, I thought he was plain, homely even. What I liked in him was something else entirely. And yet when said he didn't recognize himself, something in me shifted; I – who, of course, *did* recognize Noah's face as the face he'd had since I'd known him – instantly understood that he was handsome. No, that's not quite it. I understood he *had* been quite handsome, and if I looked closely, as he was trying to do with evident difficulty, I would be able to see through to the young man he'd been. I'd be able to see the fifteen-year-old Noah who – during the war – attracted, as he'd told me a number of times, soldiers to his side in Greenwich Village homosexual bars. Suddenly I could do what Noah couldn't; in the harsh morning light I could see him with the years stripped away. I thought, how awful to lose yourself, the self you knew; I thought, how far off is the morning when I will look in the mirror and see a stranger there? I said nothing to Noah. I didn't know what to say. He remained where he was for a few more seconds, then shrugged his simian-like shoulders and arms, turned and went back inside.

Another evening much later in the summer Noah, seated in the carved straight back chair he used for reading – well, he used anything for reading – got to talking about what he was looking for in a man with whom he could truly, deeply fall in love and with whom he could stay that way. Without saying so in that many words, he made it clear I wasn't the man. True, he had told me he loved me numerous times, but the frequency of his saying so was in indirect proportion to the length of time we spent together. On the surface little had changed. If anything, our romance was maturing into something approximating the comfort of devoted marrieds. The plays, movies, concerts we'd gone to nightly at the beginning of the affair now alternated with nights passed at home – his place or mine. We made love, experimented. I'd never liked being fucked but went along with it a few times. (Once after Noah'd fucked me, I went to take a piss and noticed blood in my urine. My stray thought was, I'd been deflowered; today, in the age of AIDS, it would be a scarier reaction.)

Noah rediscovered that he loved to cook. He hadn't cooked regularly for some time. He had no reason to. He disliked cooking for himself. But now he found he enjoyed paging through his mother's cookbooks for favorite recipes, got immense pleasure from rattling pots and pans, liked making roasts, loved fooling around with seasonings, was all but addicted to corn-on-the-cob. (In for the evening or out, we had corn every night; if out, we called ahead to make sure the restaurant we would be patronizing served fresh corn.) The nights we were at his house, was I allowed to pitch in? "No." "Go sit in the living-room out of harm's way." "Be surprised." "Your job is to gasp with delight when I remove the metal lid." He took great satisfaction in an appreciated meal, liked lolling around afterwards looking pleased with himself, ready on his full stomach to become expansive about anything that came to him or me.

What came up the evening I'm talking about was my trying yet again to pin him down on his attitude towards me. He gave me his answer by defining what he wanted in a dream man. "The man I'll fall in love with for all time," he said, cupping his hands to his left breast, "will fill me with such joy my heart will tip over." He leaned sideways in his chair to illustrate how this overflowing heart would cause him to list. I wanted to say, "And I don't fill your heart to overflowing?" But it was obvious; I didn't.

"I was on a beach once in Biarritz," Noah said, "when I saw a boy who gave me that feeling. He must have been eighteen or nineteen. He had a lean, smooth body. He looked as if he had never been touched, as if he had been delivered from the sea on a shell like Botticelli's Venus. His hair was black. His eyes were a very light blue. Or I imagined they were. He stood for the longest time looking at the horizon. He wasn't more than fifteen feet away from me, but I couldn't bring myself to speak to him. I know, I know. It was my Aschenbach moment, and I need to get over it."

I felt myself getting angry at being told about this unknown boy and also being told by implication that I didn't fit the bill. I thought Noah was being foolishly romantic, ludicrously unrealistic. I stewed, said nothing, smiled as if I were on his side, as if I could see that boy standing at the edge of the ocean, as if I shared in the appreciation of his beauty. But I knew something inside me had been chipped away, something irreparable had happened.

I'd even foreseen it somewhat – my undoing at Noah's hands – in a poem I'd written. And, like a dunce, had read to him. Like a bigger dunce, I'm going to quote it in full here. Not because I think it's very good (it's not, but it also isn't the worst thing I've ever read), but because I recently found it in an old notebook and have decided it gives a fair idea of my frame of mind during that singular summer:

"You see these two fingers," you said and held up the index and middle finger of your left hand. "If I press down on a certain spot, I can make your toes fall off."

I laughed as if I had never heard anything so silly – or witty. (Oh, I was so cocky and prone and pleased with you!)

"You don't believe me," you said and applied the fingers to points on my back. Damned if my toes didn't fall off! "See," you said. I looked at those pathetic toes, already hard as pebbles, at the foot of the bed.

"And if I press down here," you said and did before I even thought to stop you, "your feet will fall off." Presto! They swung loose and dropped free, exposing, on my ankles, hinges I'd never noticed before.

"And here and here," you said, your fingers moving rapidly, "your hands and arms." And now you turned cavalier.

"And if I press my mouth here" – I was powerless to stop you – "your legs and here your ears and nose and chin and here your head."

I was scattered about the room like birdseed.

"Next time..." you said, sweeping up the many pieces of me and sorting them into boxes containing the shriveled parts of anonymous others, "Next time you'll believe me when I tell you something."

"How can there be a next time?" I wanted to ask, but couldn't, of course, because my lips were where they had rolled, under the bed, cracked and drying out –

Orange rinds in the moonlight.

iv.

Noah began his open-ended trip around the world that December – after we'd been together, if that's what you want to call it, five months. Give or take a week. The official story on his extravagant departure was that he had finally gotten up the gumption to do something he'd talked about doing his entire adult life but kept putting off. The head of a prestigious publishing house, he explained, doesn't have time to troop the planet other than piecemeal, on weekend drop-ins to writers in need of wooing – "three days in Paris for talks over amiable meals and jocular wines, lucky if you get a free hour to breeze through the Louvre," that sort of thing.

But Noah no longer owned a publishing house. He'd sold, had he not? Nevertheless, a house, like Noah Goodman Books, within a larger house – where intramural competitions can stir ferocious acquiring tempests – provided even fewer opportunities for setting one's own pace. Dissatisfied with his new set-up practically from the first day that Youngerman & Goodman had been folded into Century and the Goodman imprimatur launched, Noah grew only progressively more hostile to what he'd gotten himself into and progressively more interested in finding a way out. He took a look at his bank account, huddled with his accountant, saw that his salary wasn't a necessity, that the income from his portfolio was enough to cradle him for the rest of his life. So – with a promise to be on call when absolutely needed no matter where he was – he wiped his hands of the mistaken enterprise and handed his authors to Youngerman, whose office at the other end of the floor was actually not much farther away than it had ever been.

While the sale was in progress, it wasn't confided to me. I was told when it was a *fait accompli* and in a manner not too far removed from, "By the way, did I happen to mention to you that..?" Actually worse. It came up during a cab ride home (Noah's home in that building hoity-toitily namely after a master painter) from some flashy European director's dismantling of *The Cherry Orchard*. Noah, whose genius extended to mimicry, segued directly from his send-up of the actress who'd just turned Madame Ranevsky into a Minsk fishwife to informing me that he'd put finishing touches on the itinerary for his upcoming trip – er-um – for the first leg of the trip. "What do you mean I didn't tell you I was going away?" "You never mentioned it." "Of course, I did. I must have. I've been telling everybody." "Not me." "The only thing I can think is that I've told so many people I assumed I must have told you." "You didn't." "I am. Going away. But not immediately, not for ten days."

It was all disingenuous and unworthy of him. Not to say transparent. And once he'd filled me in on the official story, I was able to piece together the *un*official story, which, I didn't bring up then, because I couldn't prove my theory and didn't want the humiliation of his scoffing at it. But which I bring up now. Though, with Noah dead, I have even less chance of proving it: Noah had chosen this particular moment in his life to circle the globe on a slow boat because it was the most graceful way he could think of to get away from me. He was framing something negative (throwing me over) as something positive (realizing a deferred dream).

An egocentric interpretation? Okay. I'll rephrase it. Our affair had reached the critical point at which you either go forward by acknowledging there is a couple here and it's time to start a life together with everything that implies – foremost: introductions all around to friends and possibly even family. *Or*, failing that, you go backward. Remaining in place is spinning wheels. It must have been as clear to him as it was to me. And Noah – used to life in a book-lined closet – was unprepared at his age and given his generation and everything to which he had accustomed himself to go forward. Except perhaps with the elusive fellow of heart-tipping capabilities – wherever that impossible dream was hiding out. Therefore it was obvious he had only one recourse: backing off. But colorfully. To Paris, Cairo, Bangkok, Johannesburg, Hong Kong. I, of course, wasn't the one making him pack his bags. I'm not that sold on myself. I'm convinced anyone who had gotten as close as I had would have forced the same action. I just happened to be the one standing in the wrong place.

Of Noah's departure here's what comes back to me. His extrication from Noah Goodman Books (a series of farewell lunches and parties to which I, of course, wasn't invited) and his preparations to leave (not knowing where he was going, he took shots for everything but bought no new clothes) left us little time to see each other. Or, more exactly, left us with a handy excuse to see little of each other. Meaningfully, we had no declared last dinner. He merely left town after a short phone call during which he promised to be in contact through the mail "or whatever."

And he was. Letters I threw into the drawer of my Mission desk after reading them arrived at sporadic intervals – the longer he was away, the more sporadic. The first was from London some time in March, 1975. The three, four months that had gone by with no word didn't seem too neglectful to me, considering. He *did* have to get his traveler's legs. The letter – typed on yellow foolscap – was what I was hoping for, funny and flattering;

Beamish Boy:-

Going to theater every night. Getting into trouble because I keep nudging the person next to me at crucial moments. Forget it's not you. Have been slapped by a Mayfair dowager and had my knee squeezed by an Earl's Court homosexual. That's pronounced ha-mah-sex-you-ehl, with an emphasis on the sex. As it should be. Pulled strings, and am now able to use the reading room at the British Museum. When the tourists come in every hour on the hour to look at the scholars, I'm one of the scholars they look at. I try to oblige by appearing important. But feel a sham. I'm not studying anything. Just testing the stacks. I keep dreaming up books I've always heard about and never seen. So I request them. They show up. I write racy Olde English epithets in the margins and send them back. But the staff is on to me. Tried to sneak the Magna Carta out the other day in a rolled umbrella but was stopped and told in a stern whisper and no uncertain terms by a female book warden, "It simply isn't done." The hotel has central heating but, like all things English, they're too polite to try to impress you with it. Are you writing? I hope so. No one else is. I've been reading some of the young novelists here, and am in a position to know.

Love,

Noah

Six months later from Paris:

Garçon Rayonnant:-

I have discovered the best food in Paris. The Jeu de Paume. I go every day and look at one painting. Just one. For as long as it takes. Sometimes it takes all day. Does the name Frédéric Bazille mean anything to you? It means something to me now. He's too early to really be an Impressionist, but he gives the impression. His masterwork is a painting of his family sitting on a terrace. They seem to be waiting to be introduced to each other. Bazille stands in the right corner, looking as if he already knew he would be killed in the Franco-Prussian War. I stared this one down for the better part of two days. The guards have evidently never seen anything or anyone like me. Not even Stendhal. You know about Stendhal, don't you? He patented the Stendhal Syndrome and then lived up to it. He would go anywhere to look at a painting and then swoon in front of it. I can't afford to do that. Not in my dirty underwear. I just look and look. For so long the guards are becoming my friends. The friendliest ones are called Claude and Daniel. I think they may be gai. They put me on to a small hotel near the museum, which makes my visits very convenient. Today I will be looking at a Picasso drawing. And while I'm at it, here's looking at you.

Love,

Noah

And some time later from Egypt. (He had been away much more than a year; I was thinking about him less and less frequently.) Again the letter was typed on yellow foolscap:

Greetings from the Nile, where up is down and down is up:-

Have visited the Sphinx. But she(?) couldn't answer my riddle, so I won't be seeing her(?) again. Have examined the pyramids and figured out what has baffled so many who've gone before. I know how they were built. Don't expect me to let you in on it. I can't tell just anybody. This is marketable information. There are many rich Americans who would kill to have their own pyramids. I've traveled among them and seen their eyes. I hear them thinking, what a way to go! I'm considering something like an Egyptian Forest Lawn. What do you think? Pyramids West? Boca East? I've started writing the brochure. "Who says you can't take it with you? Be interred with everything you hold dear. And everybody." Speaking of writing, I have been thinking of yours and for your sake have translated a hieroglyph inscribed on a fragment I unearthed in the sand near the ruins of Ozymandias's statue. "That habit, or necessity, of mind that raises a man far above the rank of journalist is the need to load solid matter into notices of ephemeral happenings; you have to develop a resourcefulness at pursuing a line of thought through pieces on miscellaneous and more or less fortuitous subjects; and you have to acquire a technique of slipping over on the routine of editors the deeper independent work which their over-anxious intentness on the fashion of the month or the week have conditioned them automatically to reject." Centuries later, Edmund Wilson would say more or less the same thing in exactly the same words. Odd. Would write more but have to get to Thebes. Rosetta Stone sends her love. In three languages.

And mine in one,

Noah

There were very few others; I venture to say that by 1977, maybe 1978, they stopped altogether. And had that been it, I probably would have considered Noah as someone receding gracefully into my romantic past. But the letters – clever, impersonally personal – *weren't* all.

There were visits. Yes, from time to time Noah returned to New York. He had to. He'd promised – if one of his authors put up enough of a fuss

– to edit their manuscripts or lend an ear to their worries about deals or book jackets or promotion tours. So he'd fly in from wherever he was, and I'd get a phone call in which he explained without my having asked that he was only in town for another day or so, had been here mired in meetings for a couple of days, would have given me some notice but had had very little himself. Was I free for lunch or brunch or dinner? Mostly, as fate would have it, I was. In some cut-off-nose-to-spite-face way I wished otherwise, but that's not how things fell out.

Our meetings were awkward, unsatisfying. Leastways, they were to me. Anyone eavesdropping on our conversations wouldn't have picked up anything more than a comfortable bonhomie, two pals catching each other up on what they'd been doing the last few months. Noah had the peppier stories, because he was reporting on the world. I was reporting on something much more parochial. I'd gotten my life on a well-paced track. I had finished my novel, decided I didn't like it and put it in a bedroom bureau underneath some pornographic magazines I'd masturbated to once each and never got around to throwing out. I'd had my year writing the book I always wanted to write if I had a year to write a book, and it hadn't been very fruitful. I took a reporting-editing position at a trade magazine in the music business, which had me going everywhere to meet everybody and gave great play to the gregarious side of my nature. I wasn't contributing much to society, but I was having fun. It sounded considerably less than that, however, compared to Noah's verbal slide-show.

Also, where I wasn't inclined to go into my involvements, Noah was happy to fill me in on his. There'd been a moody-eyed Istanbul boy who gave new meaning to the term "young Turk" and an Israeli built like a piece of military machinery. The one worth writing home about – although he hadn't – was Daniel, the Jeu de Paume guard. Apparently Noah's daily visits became dinner on Ile de la Cité once, twice, three times became nights together at Daniel's Pigalle apartment became a hot-as-a-crêpe-iron sexual thing. Daniel was not French, as it turned out (which explained his excessive friendliness) but an uneducated Corsican emigré. Noah fell in love with him "*because* he had no guile – no finishing – and *despite* his French being crude, his diction garbled, his idioms impenetrable." When together, they "barely spoke," and Noah gave me to believe this was more than okay by him. I took his word for it and was essentially unaffected, even though I thought the sketch being drawn for me was of someone who had a talent for tipping over homosexual hearts.

No, it wasn't hearing about Daniel that disturbed me on whichever stopover the story was spilled. Nor was it hearing any of the other stories that cropped up. What troubled me, what picked at scars I thought I'd forgotten, was what wasn't said. While Noah and I maintained we were overjoyed to see each other, what I detected in the air between us was something quite different: the sodden weight of obligation. I had the feeling that Noah felt he owed it to me to schedule these visits, when the truth – if "truth" is the correct word – was that time and distance had changed me, us. We were no longer lovers. Our time had come and gone. It happens. Why would he think I thought we were obliged to each other, that I expected full courtesies extended to ex-lovers? At first I didn't say anything about this, because I didn't know how to say it, how to bring it up without somehow embarrassing or insulting him. Too, I could have been wrong. Maybe he still had some stray romantic feelings towards me. I didn't want to put him in the position of denying the reason for his ministrations. I didn't want to put him in the position of fumbling to avoid hurting my feelings or exposing his own. I don't say I was *right* to sit through these clumsy encounters rooting around for topics of conversation, smiling as if nothing at all was bothering me. I'm just saying that's what I did.

Again, that's at first. Over the course of eight, maybe nine of these reunions, though, the reasons for buttoning my lip changed to repressed anger. Since I was more or less content to regard Noah as a friend I saw on the infrequent occasions when he was in the vicinity, I had no need to establish new rules. But *he*. He began to behave more and more as if he were trapped by something, an emotional debt. Flummoxed by it, he began to play – and draw me into – an odd game. It was a kind of conversational volleyball and went like this:

Noah (offhandedly): "I don't know if I'll be in New York again soon."
Me (casually): "Oh. Well. Call me when you get to town."
Noah (with deliberation): "It probably won't be before September."
Me (with calculated insouciance): "Okay. Call me in September."
Noah (with a nervous edge): "It might be as late as October."
Me (impatient but not showing it): "Okay, call me in October."
Noah (with a more pronounced nervous edge): "Or even November."
Me (more impatient but still not showing it): "Look. December, January. Call whenever."

Why couldn't he say what was on his mind? Or did I look that needy? Was my bare face hanging out that far? I didn't feel that needy. Perhaps it was merely stubbornness on my part, but I wasn't going to say it for him. He'd dropped me with a painful thud, but I'd gotten over it. Wasn't I behaving as if I had? It annoyed me that he didn't see it, or gave the impression he didn't. I felt as if Noah and I had had a meaningful fling and, men of the world, had moved on.

Then, without my having to say anything, he *did* move on.

v.

Eight or nine years later. London. Early December. The National Theatre. The press night for a bad play by a good playwright. I'm there with my friend Peter Grandau, who's reviewing for *The New Statesman* or

The New Society or one of those English periodicals I can't keep straight. We've got his reviewer's seats. Because I have the longer pair of legs, Peter insists I sit on the aisle. As we settle this negotiation, I notice someone six seats to the left in the row directly in front of us. Or maybe I think I recognize a hearty laugh. I look over and see the back of a grey head tilted to address a young woman with ginger hair cropped short, a witty nose and mouth. The man reminds of someone. It comes to me: Noah Goodman. Peter is making a point about something in the program, but I'm waiting for the grey head to swivel. Just as the lights start to dim and Peter says, "Here's hoping," the head turns. A familiar profile: a long face, a scalene triangle nose, an ironic turn of the lips. In my mind I do a double take and think, that man looks enough like Noah Goodman to *be* Noah Goodman, only that man, whoever he is, is much older.

I decide it's not Noah.

When the first act ends, it's sufficient for Peter and me to raise eyebrows at each other to establish that we're agreed on the low caliber of what we're seeing; further discussion isn't required. There isn't opportunity anyway, since an actress-friend of Peter's with the air of having an agenda races up to talk. Peter introduces her to me. She introduces me and him to her friend, a well-meaning short woman in awe of encountering a critic at an opening. The four of us make small talk. As we do, the Noah Goodman lookalike and his companion push past the people in the seats in front of us and start towards the lobby. The resemblance, I notice, is remarkable – too remarkable for it to be simply a resemblance. I decide this man, who hasn't noticed me, must be Noah. I excuse myself, saying I think I've spotted an old friend, and begin pursuit.

The lobby is crowded with people queuing for programs, ice cream, drinks, reconnoitering the bookstalls for written words that might shed light on the jumble we're watching. The Olivier Theatre lobby was designed with an eye to many conversation areas, and as I scan them, I don't see him – or her. Then I do. They're partially blocked from view by a large group of chattering people – a family, it appears. Noah and the young woman, however, are alone, consulting their programs as they talk. I go towards them, and the closer I get, the more I'm certain that this *is* Noah. The expressions, the way he holds his head at a forty-five degree angle as he throws himself into a guffaw. But it's Noah looking much older than what I knew to be his years. He's thinner. He fills out his clothes – that styleless wardrobe – less than he had.

When I'm maybe ten feet from them, Noah looks away from her – whoever she is – and directly at me. He's on the verge of saying something, I think. He looks past me. So when I stop in front of him, he has to focus on me. "Noah Goodman!" I say – reasonably sure I'm right but ready to be wrong. "Yes?" he says, expectantly. He's put on a generic smile, but there is, in his eyes, no sign of recognition. The young woman looks at me, amused. "You *are* Noah Goodman?" I say. "Yes?" he repeats, and then that marvelous, familiar smile crosses his thinner face. He points his right forefinger at me. "*Yes*!" He points at me twice more. "Yes! I *know* you!"

There is a stunning pause, during which – with only barely perceptible movement of some of his facial muscles – he conveys the information people convey when they're faced with someone they are convinced they should know but about whose identity they have only the vaguest clue. It's the look that says: 1) I know I know you; 2) I even have a hunch I know you well or once did or should know you well or at some time in the past have led you to believe I know you well; 3) I want to flatter you into feeling good about yourself by giving you as big a hello as I can summon; 4) I want you to think that in giving you this big hello I'm just as swell as I always was; and 5) I'm drowning here – please throw me a life preserver.

I let him dangle not so much out of cruelty but because I think there is the slimmest possibility that this is Noah's joke. Because in those few moments I'm not convinced he doesn't recognize me. Well, I don't want to be convinced. If he isn't kidding, if he isn't feigning this, I want who I am to come to him powerfully enough so that he's moved to smite his forehead as I'd seen him do so often in the old days. Why wouldn't I want that? The implications of his not knowing me are too much to cop to. Moreover, I know I haven't changed all that much. Certainly nowhere near as much as he has. But soon enough I have to admit to myself that Noah is *not* joking. He doesn't recognize me.

Or, perhaps, for some reason or another, it's important to him to be perceived as not recognizing me. But perceived by whom? By this young woman, who is now becoming even more visibly amused by the odd scene playing before her? For all she knows, according to the expression crossing her face, I'm someone who'd once been introduced to Noah at, oh, a cocktail party and now expect him to remember me out of the thousands of people he's met at cocktail parties over the years. It's probably what I would have thought had I been in her place, I think; and as I do, I also think, as she very well could be thinking, what kind of person puts someone else on the spot like this?

I realize it's getting to be long past my turn to speak. What I *want* to do is turn to the woman and say, Get this guy, we slept together the better part of the summer of 1974, and now he pretends he doesn't know me. What I do do is keep my gaze set on Noah and say, as if I were no more than one of those party pests from the past, "I'm Paul Engler."

"Of *course*, you are," Noah says.

I won't go into the particulars of the conversation that ensues. It follows the age-old formula for casual acquaintances – sincerely and with just the right amount of social distance – describing concisely the intervening *x* number of ____ (fill in: months, years, decades). While the young

woman remains generally silent according to the traditional third-person role in these colloquies, Noah informs me he's employed at the National Theatre and has been for almost exactly a year. He'd been brought on board because some thought had been given to starting an in-house publishing company – so many plays and playwrights getting exposure there, blah, blah. But what had sounded like an obvious idea to one and all the previous year was discovered to be, once Noah looked closely, impractical – playwrights contractually tied up elsewhere, blah, bloody blah. So the trial year for which he'd signed on is to end in just a few days. And – hold it! – he *expects* to be *back* in New York *before Christmas*. That's right:
Noah (with studied conviction): "I'll call you when I get to town."
Me (pleasantly noncommittal): "Do that."
Noah (with studied reflection): "Of course, I may not be back until after Christmas."
Me (pleasantly noncommittal): "Call after Christmas."
Noah (with more studied reflection): "Maybe even January."
Me (pleasantly noncommittal): "January it is."

A voice wafting through the lobby gently encourages us to take our seats for the second act.

So we obligingly part, and only when I turn away from him – from them – do I allow myself to think what has been the unthinkable: I'm forgettable. I will never be able to deny it; I'm the kind of person even former lovers forget. Or, if Noah hasn't forgotten and has put on the demonstration for some ulterior motive – this is not a possibility in which I'm inclined to put much credence – then *I'm* the sort of person who doesn't know enough to see through *his* sort of person.

Whichever it is, a brutal truth has come to light. I hate Noah for it – and, in some worse way, myself. And furthermore, in the awful circumstance "hate" seems such an inadequate word. It's quick, has a Teutonic snap, suggests a short temper, an *admirable* temper even. Where in the meager word is a suggestion of the other elements involved – deep hurt, frustration, bafflement, betrayal, embarrassment? A word that incorporates all those elements – "fury"? – would begin to convey something of what I mean when I remember those few aching minutes in the chilly, grey Olivier foyer and report simply: hate.

Anyway, December comes and goes, as does January. There's no call from Noah. Nor do I expect one. Nor, disliking him more articulately now than I ever have, do I love him any less. No, that's not right: Nor do I love the *memory* of him any less.

vi.

Which brings me up-to-date. The memorial service continued. Two demure Oriental women with melancholy expressions played Beethoven's "Spring" Sonata. An actress, who'd written a memoir published by Youngerman & Goodman, read Wallace Stevens's "Anecdote of the Jar." (Nicely, but she wasn't Noah reading it.) Speakers with and without notes came to the podium to mourn their lost friend, and as they did, I realized a pattern was emerging. With two exceptions, these were friends who were also and initially colleagues. Like Guillermo Tedesco, who said in his heavy-pile accent that without Noah's presence in his life as a "brilliant editor" and a special friend, "*un amico speziale*," he doubted his books would have amounted to a hill of beans. Wiping at his eyes with a large white handkerchief, he told stories, the cutest of them what Noah had said to Tedesco when he'd received a bad review on the front page of *The New York Times Book Review* – "Don't worry, Willie, nobody sees it anyway."

Tedesco was preceded and followed by others who didn't have National Book Award medallions in their dens but who similarly made vivid what Noah had been like as a public figure, as a revered publisher, how he'd inspired and astounded them over the years, how wherever he was in the office was its epicenter. One woman brought along television news footage she'd videotaped in which Noah was seen speaking at the 1989 PEN rally in Manhattan to support Salman Rushdie. (I'd been at the rally but had left early because the crowds were making me nervous. It amazed and dismayed me to learn that Noah had been there as well. I'd seen Susan Sontag; why hadn't I spotted Noah next to her? What's more, I'd read the press coverage. How had I missed his name?) A large television screen was turned on, and the videotape appeared on it. Noah spoke briefly – that is, only a brief excerpt from his remarks had been taped – and as he did, the winter wind whipped his hair around his face; he wore no overcoat, just a Burberry scarf that didn't go with anything else he had on. He spoke of "outrage" and said, as anyone who's seen the clips may remember, "Those who seek to silence Rushdie think by their actions they will silence his book as well. They seek in vain. All men die eventually, but words endure. They impregnate the air around us."

As he hurled the last sentence over the microphones, he raised his right arm, intending to grab a handful of space but grabbed instead a photocopy of *The Bill of Rights*. (Reams of them had been circulated, and the one Noah caught must have flown loose from someone's grip.) A cheer went up for the miracle that seemed to have happened – as well as for the victorious smile Noah aimed at his audience when he realized what had just occurred. The beauty of the moment galvanized those of us in the auditorium, too. I was crying (this was so much the Noah I knew) – and I wasn't alone.

When the tape flickered off, the women who'd brought it added, "I've read Noah's copy of *The Satanic Verses* with the edits he marked in the margins for his own amusement. I needn't tell you his is a much better version." We all laughed, and many of us nodded to indicate we were sure she was right.

But you see the trend, don't you? Eulogies about the public Noah, but very little about the private man, just hints that Noah might have had a private life at all, a life apart from work and the social circles into which his work took him. I found myself extracting clues from the odd paragraph, the occasional phrase. There were references to Noah's sudden travels; someone used the word "compulsive" to describe them. Another man talked of unexpectedly bumping into Noah and a male companion, a Dutch physicist, in the lobby of a Bombay hotel; this man and his wife subsequently had "one of those magic evenings you could always count on with Noah." The man paused for a moment and then said, reflectively, "Noah had so many good friends. I noticed he had a tendency to keep them in different pockets."

A younger man who cried as he spoke identified himself as someone who considered Noah an uncle – Noah was a good friend of his father's. He said when his sobs abated, "Noah treated me like an adult from the time I was twelve. He introduced me to the world." This man talked of family dinners, annual events Noah was regularly part of. But he reiterated that Noah arrived alone, left alone and "in a profound way kept himself *to* himself."

Only one woman, who patently came to the solemn party to be joyful, talked about the long personal friendship she had with Noah. She got the impression across that for some years theirs had been a *romantic* friendship. Ah, I thought, so *this* is the famous Sylvia Gomez whom Noah had several times mentioned to me as the one woman he'd gone to bed with – and adored there. Yes, I thought, I can see it – she's got spunk, she's got *élan*, she's got something of Noah about her. Hers was the only eulogy that gave any glimmer of Noah's life as a sexual being. Not that eulogies should, but you want to hear, hope to hear, there was romantic love in the life of someone you loved, that there was intimacy that went beyond smart words and guarded confidences at convivial dinners.

I knew there had been. I knew that Noah took great satisfaction from sex, from himself as a vital male. I knew he had led a secret life, had reveled in secret delights. On five continents. I don't by any means rule out the possibility that some or all of those who spoke – or the others who'd gathered to listen – knew as much as I did. Yet none of those commemorating the man mentioned it. They had apparently chosen, if they were privy to the information, not to bring it up, perhaps because they considered it inappropriate or trivial or sinful or perhaps because it was Noah's wish they keep mum about his being homosexual.

That was the information left out, but there was information sketched in that was new and provocative to me. It cropped up four or five times. References were made to "Noah's last illness," to how cheerful he remained "throughout his final illness," to the projects he was planning "right up until his illness overcame him," to his continuing to work "until his illness prevented him from coming to the office anymore, and even then he called in twenty times a day from his bed."

The illness was never named. Maybe it didn't have to be; maybe the speakers assumed we all knew Noah well and therefore had to have known about his last months. But I didn't know. I had my idea, but, no, had it been what I suspected, surely mention would have been made of it, certain kinds of jokes would have been told, certain reminiscences invoked, certain imprecations uttered. I discarded the hunch and waited.

The service ended after an hour or so with a renowned Manhattan cabaret singer who'd been asked to do a medley of George and Ira Gershwin songs that had been Noah's favorites. (I couldn't remember his ever playing Gershwin songs when I was around, but that didn't mean much. There must have been volumes of music we hadn't had time to get to.)

Finally Rosalind Paynter thanked us for coming and said refreshments would be served in the lobby.

People rose and left in groups, talking quietly. I looked around to see if there were any men exiting alone, as I was – other candidates for the category of former lover. Far as I could tell, there weren't. I'd practically gotten to the door leading from the auditorium to the lobby when I decided that what I wanted to do before I hit the road was remind Rosalind Paynter we'd met once and thank her for what she'd contributed to the service. (I wasn't inclined to stay to eat and put myself in the position of trying to explain, or refraining from explaining, who I was to people I'd never met.)

I saw her exchanging words with some of the other speakers on the floor by the podium. A small line of well-wishers waiting for her attention had already formed. It took a few minutes before I got a word. I said we'd met at a book publishing party a few years back. She remembered the party but not me, although she said, "Oh, yes," as if she did. Sensing those behind me impatient to have their turn, I came to the point. "What *did* Noah die of?" I asked with what I intended to sound as much as possible like genuine concern and as little as possible like idle curiosity. She leaned towards me and, it seemed, lowered her voice so only I would hear the reply; "Oh, it was AIDS – the bane of all our existences." Then she looked towards the next person.

By that time I had been to many AIDS memorials in Manhattan – so many, many too many. None of them had been like this one. AIDS had been mentioned at every one of them – even when disapproving family members were present. AIDS had been assailed, defied, confronted. Its ravages had been, if not itemized, referred to; humor, frequently black, had been resorted to. And yet at this memorial not a single person even wore a red ribbon – the decade's ubiquitous accessory.

Walking away from Rosalind Paynter, passing through that crowd –

all of them talking softly, some of them laughing – and then leaving the building, I realized that Noah's friends, certainly those close to him for "his final illness," had to have known what that illness was. Individually and/or collectively, however, they had chosen to remain silent about it, perhaps fulfilling a death-bed request. But in deference to what? In deference to the secret of a man who had devoted his entire public life – but evidently not his private one – to championing truth and honesty as the only imaginable way to protect civilization from every violent force threatening to rub it out.

As I walked slowly south through midtown Manhattan – tuning out the city's noise – I gradually became aware I was having very strong feelings. I was sad, I was angry. While I'd loved Noah and continued to love him – the strength that emotional pull exerted throughout the service amazed me – I was once again mad at him, as I had so often been mad at his repeatedly wounding me.

Intentionally or unintentionally, what difference did it make?

What's more, I had forced myself to pretend he wasn't slapping my psyche around. I'd kept it to myself, fearing, I suppose, that a confrontation would send him packing. (Funny, huh? Not confronting him had sent him packing anyway.) It's not that I held him accountable. Far from it: I held myself responsible for keeping quiet. Perhaps if I'd been able to bring myself to let loose, we could have locked horns like two homosexual stags, if there are such animals. Something might have been settled or, failing that, at least have been put on the table. But I hadn't. Yet, all the while accepting blame for my own timidity, I kept thinking that of the things he'd stood for in his life, there was one to which he had never – never! – owned up.

Okay, I understood why he'd spared himself – the times weren't hospitable to certain kinds of full disclosure. But at that life's premature close in an era, and during an epidemic, when every gesture counted: Silence! Noah? A man who understood the nuance of gesture as thoroughly as any man I've known? Now he'd lived and he'd died. And had been memorialized by the people who ostensibly knew him best without the reason for his death either abominated or honored, without the fullness of his life acknowledged or celebrated. In accordance with what? Some barely tenable nicety, some unfathomable discretion, some misplaced sense of shame.

I was angrier at him than I'd ever been. Swell time to get this angry, though, wasn't it? When there was nothing I could do. It was even too late for me to stand up in that memorial assembly and say, "Wait a minute here. There's something you all ought to know." Doing that had, of course, crossed my mind as certainly as I also knew it was not something I had anything approaching a right to do after so many years and in such an environment.

Sure, it's long been the fashion for people to tell you how crucial it is to get your anger out. That's all well and good. But there are times when you can only admit your anger is there, crouched like a tiger in a cage. Then you live with its remaining forever behind bars, pacing, pacing, pacing. So I walked home through the early afternoon traffic, amid the frenzy of the New York streets, trying to make peace with myself and with him, with the late Noah Goodman.

vii.

One evening – not too long after we'd met – Noah was outside on the terrace. It must have been somewhere around 8:30. The sun was setting. "Come here," he called in to me. I don't remember what I was doing. Reading? Listening to Bach or Beiderbecke, Monteverdi, Mahler, Monk? I don't recall. "Quick!" I roused myself and went to join him. He was bending over the railing with his arms folded on it. "Look over there," he said and pointed at a white high-rise that stood about ten blocks southeast of us. It was ablaze. Flames shot out of every window. For an instant I was astounded, and then it hit me. I looked at Noah. "Uh-huh," he said with great satisfaction. The building wasn't on fire. The setting sun, reflected in each of the windows, only made it look as if it were burning. All that intense red, orange, yellow licking at white. The illusion of fire became even more thrilling for its being an illusion. And for its being fleeting, one of those gorgeous, unexpected moments in life you want to go on forever while knowing each passing second could be the last. Aside from our murmuring "Wow!" or "Beautiful!" or "Amazing!" or who-knows-what-other insufficient expletive, we stood there silently.

I can only surmise that Noah had some of the same thoughts I had – glad to be sharing this reminder of the world's potential for mysterious beauty, wondering what it is in us that wishes for actual fire, what it is that takes pleasure in destruction viewed from a distance. This illusion of a burning building is symbolic, I thought. But of what, of what? I felt as if I did indeed know but couldn't put my finger on it for the moment. Just as well, I decided: pretentious notion anyway.

I do remember that while the fake flames still bolted out and up, Noah and I instinctively turned away at the same moment. We didn't want to see the spectacular lighting effect end. We wanted to take control. *We* abandoned *it*, not the other way around. So, of course, for us – for me – that fire never did end. As long as I can view it in my mind's eye, the (true? false?) fire rages.

CPSIA information can be obtained at www.ICGtesting.com
Printed in the USA
LVOW070051271111
256572LV00001B/216/P